To Live and Die
in the
Floating World

To Live and Die in the
Floating World

a novel

Stephen Holgate

Blank Slate Press | Saint Louis, MO 63116

Blank Slate Press
Saint Louis, MO 63116
Copyright © 2021 Stephen Holgate
All rights reserved.
Blank Slate Press is an imprint of Amphorae Publishing Group, LLC

For information, contact:
Blank Slate Press
4168 Hartford Street, Saint Louis, MO 63116
www.amphoraepublishing.com

Manufactured in the United States of America
Cover Design by Kristina Blank Makansi
Cover art: Shutterstock
Set in Adobe Caslon Pro
ISBN: 9781943075713

Dedicated to the crew of the MS *Wirreanda*
and the friendship we shared

1

Rory Gallagher And the *Ecu d'Or*

IT WAS NEARLY MIDNIGHT, and I was drunk and thinking of heading back to my dump at the *Ecu d'Or* when the Irishman Rory Gallagher came through the door of the smoky, flyblown bar on the pimply backside of Montmartre. I thought later how different things might have been if he'd chosen another bar or I'd been sober.

I'd met Gallagher three months earlier in a little town on the Loire where we'd each stumbled into short-term jobs at a campground. We'd both passed the previous few months kicking around Europe pretending to find ourselves. He couldn't have known I was working hard at not being found by anyone else.

In the way of such wanderers, we struck up a momentary friendship before parting bitterly over an Italian girl who decided to head to Paris with me instead of going with Gallagher to the south of France.

This checkered history flickered through my impaired mind as I saw him walk in searching for an open table. My first impulse was to keep my head down and hope he didn't see me. I should have followed it. Instead, under the influence of an alcohol-induced sense of brotherhood I raised my hand and gave him a welcoming nod—the nod making my head swim after several beers on an empty stomach because I couldn't afford both dinner and beer.

He cocked his head and squinted at me with one eye, trying to place me. When the other eye popped open I knew he'd made the connection. To my muddled surprise his frown morphed into a grin I should have recognized as the sort the big bad wolf would make running into one of the three little pigs in a dark alley.

"Kip Weston, y'old sod. What're you doin' drinkin' alone?"

I looked around for the two jolly Moroccans who'd been with me all evening, but found they'd drifted away at some point.

"And where's the lovely Giulietta?" he asked, memory sharpening the edge of his voice.

I essayed a "who knows?" gesture. "Heading to Brittany with some random Greek the last I saw her."

My confession about losing her took some of the menace off his smile.

"How was the south of France?" I asked him.

"Dunno. Never got there." He pulled out a chair and slumped into it with a theatrical sigh of weariness. "Needed to replenish my empty purse. Got work in Burgundy for a couple of months and didn't get any further south than Dijon."

"So, where you heading now?"

"Back to Dublin. I was promised a job startin' the end of September, and I've got to get back or lose it. How about yerself?"

I told him of my travels—with Giulietta and then without—and how I ended up in one of the smarmier quarters of Paris.

"Where ya stayin'?"

"Been at the *Ecu d'Or* the last couple of weeks."

"The *Ecu*? Migod, Weston, that's the sort of place where you wake up in the morning with stitches on your back and one of your kidneys missing."

"I'm broke."

"You were flush back in Beaugency. Made me wonder why you bothered with the job."

It had sounded pretentious even at the time to say that I'd taken the job because I wanted to spit the silver spoon out of my mouth, show my solidarity with the sort of people my father had dismissed as "the great unwashed."

For now, I only told him, "The money's gone."

"So, go home."

"Don't want to go home." The defiance I'd meant to project somehow came off as petulance.

"Ask yer old man fer some gelt. You told me he's swimmin' in the stuff. Has how many houses? And a yacht, as I recall."

At the mention of my father, I momentarily lost the power of speech. Gallagher couldn't have understood why, and I wasn't about to tell him.

I was suddenly very drunk and very tired, so I laid my head on the table and breathed into the pretzel crumbs.

The sound of a crow cawing made me think I'd drunk way too much, but it was only Gallagher laughing.

"And you were gettin' ready to take over yer father's business, yes?" He snickered. "Graduated from some toffee-nosed school in finance or management or something."

"No!" I barked into the table top, the word ricocheting back at me hard enough to make my eyes bounce. "I told you about that," I added more quietly.

"Ah, that's right. Comparative Lit-ra-chur!" I'd forgotten the irritating warble of his voice when he was full of himself. "Yeah, just to rub the old man's nose in it, right? Ya graduate *Magma Come Loudly* or some such Greek last spring. And now, in yer twenty-second year—"

"Twenty-third."

"—yer twenty-third year, yer going to write the great American novel about him and his kind, just to show you've got too much soul to take over the family business and make a real living." He snorted. "Rich kids."

In his mockery I recognized words I'd often spoken after a couple of drinks, and I recalled the sight of my father lying on the floor of his study, his eyes wide, blood seeping onto the floor under his head. I blinked and shook my head to make the image go away, a skill I had nearly mastered over the last few months.

"Enough about that, okay?" I muttered.

"Sure thing, Kipster. Meanwhile, why don't ya just give dad a call and get some money and take me out to dinner?"

"Someone stole my phone."

"Stole yer ...? Well, aren't you the pathetic case?" He reached into his pocket. "Here, use mine. We'll call him right—"

"I don't want to call my father!" Whatever my irritation with Gallagher, I didn't want to tell him that in fact I'd thrown the phone away, fearing someone could track me from it.

Gallagher leaned back in his chair and eyed me for a long moment. "I almost admire ya."

"But not quite."

"Not quite. Because yer a stubborn bugger and you don't know how to do yerself a favor."

While I contemplated this profundity, he ordered another beer for me and called up a whiskey for himself as if, being an Irishman, he had to keep up a certain image.

While I slurped the foam off the top of the bottle, Gallagher regarded me narrowly, like Ming the Merciless sizing up some poor sap for a bad end. I was about to tell him to knock it off when his expression bloomed into a smile.

"So, Weston, me auld friend, maybe ya could use a job." Gallagher had put on his accent thick as a brick, something he did when he wanted to sound charming. I half expected him to break into "When Irish Eyes Are Smiling." But that wasn't where he went with it. "Ya told me yer the nautical sort, done a lot of sailing. How about a job on a boat?"

Even while I wondered why he would be willing to help me—I mean, after the girl and all—I said, "A boat?"

"I knew that would wake ya up."

With a half-smile on his lips, Gallagher sipped at his whiskey and looked around the smoky room. When he didn't follow up on the boat thing I decided he'd been kidding.

After a bit Gallagher ordered another round. I'd almost forgotten about the boat when he asked again if I wanted work. He said he'd been working on a small tourist barge down in Burgundy, a *peniche d'hotel* he called it. "The *Celeste*. Owner's a Frenchwoman named Diane. She takes on a group of guests—six, that's all—and treats 'em like royalty for twenty-five thousand dollars per week. At the end of the week, she packs 'em off and takes on another group. Crew of three, plus Diane."

"What did you do?"

"Drove a car that accompanied the boat. An old London taxi, would ya believe? I ran errands, took the guests for excursions now and then. That kind of thing. Easy money, Weston, easy money." He hooked his thumbs into his belt and leaned back in his chair.

"So, why'd you leave?"

He gave me an if-only-you-knew smirk. "Like I say, I've got to get back to Dublin." He took a look into the depths of his drink. "Anyway, my departure leaves her a crew member short. Most of the guests are Americans, so she wants people who speak English. If you've got a driver's license, the job's yers—if ya have enough sense to get there first."

He shrugged his indifference. It was up to me. His Errol Flynn smile should have made me think twice but, like I said, I'd had a few and was having a hard enough time thinking once.

I needed the money and was tired of this part of Paris, the only part I could afford. Summer, with its endless possibilities, was nearly over and, with fall on the horizon, I felt like a grasshopper who should be thinking about turning into an ant.

So I said, "Sure. Why not?"

He bought me one more beer to seal the deal, and knocked back another whiskey. After a bit he mentioned that he'd just come in from Dijon on the late train, and the guys he hoped to stay with in Montmartre seemed to have moved on, and could he maybe flop at my place?

"You willing to risk a kidney?"

"Sure," he said, and we both laughed, though I didn't like the sound of his.

※

I woke in the morning feeling like my head had been popped off during the night and reattached without proper supervision. My head aching, my legs rubbery, I fumbled around the room looking for my notebook, a stained and dog-eared thing in which I'd scribbled a jumble of ill-turned paragraphs about my union-busting, corner-cutting, contract-shading father, who'd gotten fat and rich through ship-building, mostly for the government. He'd been twice investigated and thrice sued for outrages against the norms of honest business practices, but always came out cleared, and richer than he'd gone in, allowing my mother and my brother and me to soothe our collective conscience with the balm of luxury.

With my no-holds-barred exposé I was going to blow the lid off the whole thing, show that, whatever I'd done to him, he had it coming.

And there was a personal angle—there was Luz—but I didn't want to think about her or consider that what had happened with her had anything to do with my crusade against my father and his ilk. You can deny a whole bunch of stuff if you set your mind to it.

After a couple minutes of muddled searching, twice stepping over Gallagher sleeping on the floor wrapped in a spare blanket, I found the notebook. But, hungover and deflated, I could only plop myself onto the room's lone chair and stare into the void that was my life.

With sunlight pouring into the room, Gallagher eventually sat up, groaning and bleary-eyed, rubbed his face and looked around, trying to figure out where he was. When he saw me he jumped in surprise.

"What the hell are ya doin' here?" Then it came back to him. He staggered to his feet, still in his clothes, and offered to buy me breakfast. Together we lurched down to a cafe at the bottom of the hill.

※

We sagged on our elbows, leaning on the tiny table, neither of us saying much. My speech centers weren't working well, and Gallagher seemed preoccupied.

"Look, Kip, about that boat job. I'm thinkin' I shouldn't have mentioned it. Probably not something ya'd care for. Sorry I brought it up."

"S'all right. I gotta make some money."

"Sure, and anything's easier than calling yer father. Oh yeah, ya can't do that 'cause someone stole yer phone," he said with a snort. "I still don't get why you don't want to at least ask him for—"

"Enough about him."

I said it more sharply than I meant to and I could see his face set hard against me. I decided to make amends by taking his offer seriously. "Look. If I decide to follow up on this boat thing, should I tell the owner—"

"Diane."

"Diane, that you sent me?"

The mocking curl of his lip highlighted a smile that I should have read better. "Yeah, that's what ya want to do."

Overwhelmed with brotherly love, I said, "Rory, about the girl, I just wanted to say I'm—"

He waved a hand as he finished his coffee. "Forget about the girl. We're good now."

※

Out on the sidewalk we shook hands and said so long, Gallagher off to catch a train for London, me back to my fifth floor flop.

I hadn't got more than a few steps when he called, "Weston!"

"Yeah?"

"I almost forgot. Someone was looking for ya. An American in a gray suit. Maybe forty, forty-five. He came by the campground there in Beaugency about a week after you took off with whatshername. He wanted to know where you—"

I felt like I was in a nightmare production of *Hamlet*, but with me running from my father's ghost, not toward it.

"What's wrong?"

"I ... I'm fine," I stammered. "Why should anything be wrong?" I tried to laugh, but it came out as the sort of laugh they put you in a padded room for. "What about this guy?"

Gallagher squinted at me queerly. "He said he'd heard you were working there. Wanted to know where you'd gone. What's it all about? He a detective or something?"

I tried to breathe normally. "Detective? Why would a detective be looking for me?"

"If you don't know, I sure as hell don't," Gallagher snorted his skepticism. "He gave me his card. David something." He started to pull out his wallet. "Ya want it?"

"No!" I tried to collect myself. "So, what did you tell Dave?"

"'Dave,' is it? I thought ya didn't know him."

"What? No. That's just what you call someone named ... Look, you didn't tell him where I'd gone, did you?"

Gallagher cocked his head to one side. "If he's a stranger, like ya say, what do ya care?"

"I don't! I mean, I don't. It's just ..."

The Irishman looked at me as if I was foaming at the mouth. "I told this fella what ya told me, that ya were headin' to Paris." He shrugged, like it wasn't his fault he was still sore about the girl when this guy in the gray suit came by. "That a problem, Weston?"

"You told him I was heading for Paris? Why should that be a problem?"

"Yew tell me, then we'll both know." He could see through me like a window and had to know I was in some kind of bind. He rewarded me with his most irritating smirk. "All right. Have it yer way. So long, Weston."

"So long, Gallagher."

Still grinning, he headed down toward the Gare du Nord.

Me? I ran like hell back to my apartment pushed by a dread all too familiar. Though Gallagher couldn't have known it, I'd been running for months.

I threw my stuff into a backpack and made the midday train to Dijon, looking over my shoulder the whole way.

2

The *Celeste*

LULLED BY THE CLICKETY-CLACK of the train, and still feeling the effect of the previous night's excesses, I fell asleep before we'd got clear of the suburbs.

I woke a couple hours later, breathing easier with the passage of every mile between me and Paris. I sat up and watched the countryside rolling by. Beautiful country, Burgundy. Rolling hills, gentle slopes covered in vineyards, old villages, their stone houses gathered around an ancient church spire, wheat and corn and sunflowers ripening in the September sun.

Gallagher told me I'd find the *Celeste* somewhere between Montbard and Tonnerre on the Canal du Bourgogne. Only when I got to Dijon and looked at the map on the station wall did I realize Montbard and Tonnere were thirty miles apart, and good luck finding the boat.

Local trains don't run often and it was coming on dark by the time I shouldered my backpack and got off at a village station midway between the two towns. I asked the ticket clerk where I'd find the canal, and he pointed outside, where the street sloped down toward a stone bridge. I figured I'd head down to the canal and ask a lockkeeper if he'd seen the *Celeste* in the last couple of days. But the ticket clerk told me the locks had closed for the night. I pictured myself rolling out my sleeping bag under a bridge that night, miles from the boat and not sure which direction to go in the morning. No doubt, by the time I found the *Celeste* this Diane woman would have already hired someone else. I'd be out the money for the train and stuck in the French countryside, well and truly broke.

My foul mood deepened further when I walked out of the station and found it had started to rain. Cursing Rory Gallagher and myself, I pulled my baseball cap out of my backpack, yanked it low over my eyes, walked down to the bridge at the bottom of the street and looked up the canal.

And there she was, the *Celeste*, maybe fifty yards away, moored for the night, lights glowing warmly in the gathering dark. Parked beside it, next to the dirt towpath that ran along the canal, was the black and boxy London taxi Gallagher had mentioned.

She was a handsome boat, maybe a hundred feet long, the steel hull painted a dark green. A long, low-slung cabin, painted white, also of steel, ran most of the boat's length, from a few feet back of the bow all the way to a small well deck recessed below the railing. The long cabin had tall windows facing the bow and a series of portholes along the side, with several more big windows wrapped around the aft part of the cabin, framing a glass door. A scattering of canvas deck chairs lay along the top of the cabin.

Aft of this long cabin, beyond the well deck, rose a smaller stern cabin with two portholes. Its roof, too, formed a deck surrounded by a low wooden railing. On the forward part of this smaller deck stood the wheel, mounted high enough that the skipper could see clearly over the length of the boat.

I didn't see anyone on deck, so walked up the bit of duckboard that served as a plank and onto the well deck between the two cabins.

Through the tall windows of the larger cabin I saw half a dozen people seated around a dining table and a stocky young woman carrying a steaming platter of chicken coming out from behind a counter that separated the table, on one side, from the galley on the other. As she laid the platter on the table she saw me standing on deck and straightened up in surprise. Without taking her eyes off me, she said something to another woman—taller, fleshy, less young—who was circling the table pouring wine. She too looked surprised, and royally pissed off. She came out on deck and demanded in French, "Who do you think you are? Get off my boat." She hefted her wine bottle by the neck, evidently ready to throw it at my head.

The guests paused and looked at us curiously, then returned to their meal.

I answered in English. "I understand you're short a crew member."

Her eyes narrowed. She looked a little less angry and a lot more suspicious. Maybe thirty-five, she clearly had some hard years behind her, her face puffy, crow's feet around her bloodshot eyes. Yet there was something still attractive, even desirable, about her.

"What makes you think I'm looking for a crew member?"

"A friend said he'd been working for you but had to leave. He told me I should ask for a job."

"What friend is that?" she asked, but of course she already knew.

"Rory Gallagher."

If I'd thought invoking Gallagher's name would prove some sort of open sesame, it wasn't going to be that simple. The woman grunted as if she'd swallowed a bug and her eyes narrowed further, with a lot going on behind them.

I added, "He told me to ask for Diane."

"Did he now?" The woman lowered the bottle, no longer ready to throw it at me, but not exactly welcoming me either.

"And your name is what?"

"Kip Weston."

Her nose wrinkled in disbelief. "Kip? This is name—Kip?"

Before I could reply, I heard someone come out from the smaller cabin behind me.

"Diane, who is this person?"

I turned to find a solidly-built dark-skinned man—South Asian I guessed from his appearance and the lilting accent of his English. I took him for forty or so, a little older than the woman.

"He says he's a friend of Rory Gallagher's," she drawled in English.

"That sonofabitch," the man said, making it clear that knowing Gallagher was enough to get me thrown not only off the boat but into the canal.

"What do you think, Dilip, should we take him on?"

"A friend of that deserter? No."

Her tone ironic, flirtatious, Diane said, "You should learn to be more forgiving."

"That Irish bastard. He swaggers around here for a few weeks then runs off and leaves us short-handed as soon as he knew—"

"That's enough." Her honeyed tone didn't mask the warning in her eyes.

This Dilip guy continued his litany of Gallagher's offenses, though his voice gradually descended into a rumbling murmur that carried a lot of meaning I didn't catch.

Whatever words he might have swallowed, I could feel which way the wind was blowing and decided to blow with it.

"Yeah, Gallagher can be a real jerk that way."

Okay, pretty craven of me, but I needed the job.

Diane eyed me closely. "Did he tell you why he quit?"

"Said he had to get back to Dublin."

She "hmmmd" and cocked her head to one side, and I sensed that the story Gallagher told me wasn't even half the truth.

I should have turned around and walked off the boat right then, no matter how broke I was. But I didn't.

"Let me put this guy off the boat, Diane." Dilip's accent made the threat sound almost musical.

I sensed that his hostility toward Gallagher came from something deeper than the Irishman's jumping ship.

Diane gave Dilip a half smile, then eyed me in a speculative kind of way. "You're right, we're short a crew member. Do you know how to drive?"

"Sure."

Dilip made a low growl in the back of his throat. Diane gave him a look, and he waggled his head in that South Asian way, but said nothing.

"All right, Kip Weston, you're hired." Ignoring Dilip's exasperated expulsion of breath, she looked over her shoulder toward the dining room. "I have to get back to my guests. Dilip will show you where to put your things. We'll talk about pay later."

With an unhappy glance aimed first at Diane, then at me, Dilip led me forward along a narrow walkway, no more than a foot wide, both of us leaning in toward the long cabin to avoid falling into the water. When we got to the bow he pointed to one of the two small hatches recessed into the forward deck.

"You sleep here," he said, making it sound a lot like "Go to hell."

I raised the hatch, dropped my backpack and sleeping bag through the opening and climbed down a metal ladder.

The tiny berth—perhaps eight feet long and five wide, tapering toward the bow—had a bunk attached to the inside of the hull and, on the opposite bulkhead, a wooden shelf for my stuff. The bunk had sheets and a single woolen blanket. There was a head—a toilet—behind a door at the forward end, the space so tiny that I'd practically have to stand in the sink to take a piss.

Apart from a small lamp above the bunk, the only light came from the semi-transparent hatch, which doubled as a sort of skylight. But it wasn't bad. Snug. And I didn't have to pay for it.

I rolled out my sleeping bag on top of the blanket and called up to Dilip, "This'll be fine."

"It better be," he said, and kicked the hatch shut.

3

Unwelcome Aboard

AFTER THE LONG DAY OF TRAVEL I slept well—
no nightmares of my father—and woke at the first glimmer
of light through the hatch. I got dressed and climbed out
on deck to a cool September morning.

A low, dreamy fog hung over the canal, softening the
morning light. The line of poplars along the towpath cast
hazy shadows along the still water. Above the fog the pale,
open sky promised a warm day.

Across the canal, the village had begun to stir. The morning
sun, strong and clear away from the canal, cast sharp-edged
shadows on the stone houses and narrow lanes. A couple of
old men walked slowly toward a bar near the train station
for their fortified morning coffee. Behind the village rose
low brown hills with trees along their crowns.

I took a deep grateful breath. I'd landed a job and a place
to sleep and the air was good and the countryside beautiful
and I wondered how I could be so lucky.

The feeling didn't last long.

A faint snatch of voices pulled me toward the smaller
cabin at the stern. There I found the other two members of
the crew, Dilip and the young woman who had first seen

me come on board, standing in the dingy, pocket-sized crew's galley. Neither of them acknowledged my presence until Dilip, frowning at the need to speak to me, cocked his chin at a pot on the two-element electric burner. "There's coffee."

In a broad accent that said London to me, the young woman added, "And there's bread," nodding at a crumb-flecked cloth sack hanging from a hook.

I hadn't eaten since lunch the previous day, so tore a big hunk out of a day-old baguette left over from what the guests hadn't eaten the night before and smeared it an inch-thick with butter and jam.

The young woman looked to be a couple of years older than me, mid-twenties or so, stocky, with auburn hair and a face I wanted to believe friendly. She held a French coffee mug, big as a cereal bowl, in both hands and looked at me over its rim. "I hear you're a friend of Rory's."

It seemed no one needed to know anything more about me than that—and it wasn't gaining me traction with anyone.

"I know him. That's all."

She digested this without taking her eyes off me and decided to vouchsafe me her name. "I'm Molly." It took me a moment to translate her "Oym" to "I'm."

"Kip Weston."

She gave me a dubious grunt and looked toward the big cabin. "I've got to make breakfast for the guests. You need to go get bread."

Dilip took it from there. "Every morning you find the nearest bakery and get bread for the day. Molly will tell you what to buy. As soon as the guests come out for breakfast you clean up their rooms. After that, get in the car and run ahead of the boat to tell the lockkeepers we're coming and they should get the lock ready. You'll help them do it." He pulled a few euros from his pocket, but hesitated before handing them over. "You have a driver's license?"

"Yeah."

"Let me see it."

I tried to convey my irritation as I pulled my license out of my wallet.

Dilip looked it over like a counterfeit twenty. "You're from New York."

"Yeah."

"Rhinebeck?" he wrinkled his nose the same way Diane did at "Kip."

"That's what it says."

He handed me the money with a look that told me he'd caught my sarcasm and would remember it, then told me to get to work.

I started for the galley to ask how much bread to buy, but stopped and asked Dilip, "Where's Diane?"

His already stony features turned harder yet, and I understood that as far as Dilip was concerned I had no business asking any questions about the boat's owner.

"We need eight baguettes and six croissants. Get going."

Despite the icy start, the next couple of days passed well enough. The guests, three couples in their seventies, were all friends from upstate New York. I didn't see any need to tell them I came from that area too, and plenty of reason not to. They seemed like the kind who read newspapers.

During the day the guests sometimes liked to walk along the towpath from one lock to the next before coming back on board. Given the boat's slow pace—about four miles per hour—they didn't have to rush. One couple, more active than the others, occasionally took the two bikes we kept on top of the stern cabin and pedaled off for two or three miles, eventually waiting at one of the locks for the boat to catch up to them. Mostly, though, they seemed content to snooze in the deck chairs like aged house cats as the *Celeste* drifted south along the canal.

On my second afternoon with the boat I took four of them on a drive in the countryside, stopping at a nearby village to buy wine.

From their small talk, I gathered that the men had all made their stack with a brokerage firm in the city, one of the few that survived the crash in '08. My father had often invited men like them to our place on the Hudson, and I'd come to understand the nature of their profession as they laughed at tales of their own ruthlessness. Father enjoyed this kind of talk, but looked down on men who made their living by shoving digits around on a computer screen rather than making things. Still, my father, like these other men, had secured our prosperous life by stepping over the corpses of his competitors, so I figured it was pretty much the same thing.

I struggled to tell myself once more he had deserved whatever happened to him, though with the passing months I believed it less. Over time, I had developed a kind of mental discipline that allowed me to avoid thinking about it, but sleep seldom came easily.

The men on the boat had, in their retirement, turned garrulous and charming, even childlike in their way, going all puffy and round-faced with booze and good food until,

I suppose, they would eventually look like newborns. It made me wonder if innocence was something that could be reacquired. More likely, their behavior could be attributed to diminished testosterone levels.

As Gallagher had promised, my duties proved easy enough. At least he got that part right. I enjoyed buying the bread, the warmth of the bakeries welcome on the chilly September mornings, the air rich with the aroma of newly-baked bread, the baguettes and croissants warm in my arms as I walked back to the car. Cleaning the rooms before we got underway could be a little frantic, but the guests were a tidy bunch and I managed to take care of the housekeeping while they lingered over breakfast.

For the rest of the day I drove along the canal, staying a lock or two ahead of the *Celeste*, giving the lockkeepers a heads-up of its approach, helping them close the downstream lock gates, crank open the sluices to fill the lock, then push on the long iron handle that opened one of the upstream gates while the lockkeeper took care of the other. It didn't seem like much, but by having things ready when the *Celeste* came I saved them maybe five minutes a lock, which, especially on a day when there might be twenty or more locks to negotiate, really added up.

Given the boat's leisurely pace, and with some of the reaches of water between locks a kilometer or more long, I often waited quite a while for the *Celeste* to catch up. Then I'd sit in the car reading or scribbling in my notebook, sketching out the excesses of my father and his cronies, dreaming of how I would one day turn this dross into the gold of a literary sensation, justify what I'd done.

When I had worked myself into a sufficient emotional lather for the day, I would put the notebook away and work on my French with the lockkeepers. I'd had several years of it back in school and, having kicked around in France for the previous few months, I was becoming pretty fluent.

The lockkeepers were mostly women of a certain age, as the French say, who, while their husbands farmed or worked in the nearby villages, tended vegetable plots around the pocket-sized cottages given to them in exchange for working the locks.

Over the course of those first few days some of the frost came off Molly's manners as she realized, whatever my as-yet-undiscovered shortcomings, I wasn't Rory Gallagher. It made me wonder how he had landed so firmly in everyone's shit house. It had to be something more than leaving them short a crew member.

Even Dilip needed to work harder to keep up his ice man routine. It helped that we had to work together at every lock. After the lock had filled and the lockkeeper and I had opened the gates—we were descending a long stretch of the canal working our way south toward Dijon—he eased the *Celeste* into the lock and threw me a line, which I looped around a bollard, then pulled hard to help slow the boat as he threw the propeller into reverse. He'd give me a thumbs up when he'd stopped the boat, and I would pull on the rope again to keep the boat from banging around inside the lock as the lockkeeper closed the upstream gates and opened the downstream sluices and the level of the water in the lock fell. Then I'd throw the line down to him at the bottom of the lock before helping to open the downstream gates, and the *Celeste* got underway again.

In the evening the guests dined around the wooden table next to the galley, talking and laughing while Molly served up meals worthy of the finest restaurants around. Diane kept their wineglasses filled and beguiled them with smiles and small talk. It was funny, her English was good, but she put her French accent on thick when she spoke to the guests. They loved it.

Afterwards, tipsy and overfed, the couples staggered down the narrow passageway toward their rooms or wandered up to the saloon, a sort of combination ship's library and lounge near the bow, for a nightcap and a quiet read.

※

Though Molly and Dilip continued to maintain a certain distance from me, it was Diane who proved hardest to know. She seldom appeared on deck until late in the morning, long after I'd finished cleaning the rooms and driven off in the taxi. Once the boat was underway, I spent no more than a few minutes on board until we moored for the night, so had no chance to talk with her during the day. In the evenings she played hostess with the guests, retired when they did and generally kept to her cabin the rest of the evening. I often heard sad French saloon songs playing faintly long after she had turned out her lights.

I think it was during my second or third day with the boat that I came on board at one of the locks to get a sandwich from Molly. She handed me a grocery list, telling me she didn't have any money on her and to get it from Diane. As I headed toward her cabin, Dilip jumped down from the wheel to block my way. When I told him I needed money for groceries he pulled a wad of euros out of his pocket and slapped them into my hand.

"You don't bother Diane in her cabin. From here on out you get the money from Molly. I'll see she has enough. You understand?"

I said I did.

The incident with Dilip somehow summed up the peculiar and oppressive atmosphere on the boat. Despite the friendly manner the crew put on for the guests, they betrayed a deep uneasiness in the way their smiles faded the moment the guests turned away, in the tension of their movements as they went about their work, in the dark signifying looks shared among them, in the words spoken just outside my hearing. At first, I thought it had to do with me and my connection to Gallagher, but came to realize something larger lay behind it, deeper and obscured from view.

Given my own evasions, I should have felt right at home. Yet, for now, the rest of the crew kept me at a distance, unassimilated—not unlike the guests themselves.

When the others weren't watching, Diane would sometimes lock onto me, her eyes searching mine, as if trying to fathom whether I had knowledge of something I wasn't admitting to. For the life of me I couldn't figure out what it was she thought I knew.

4

Marius Carbonne

THE CRUISE WITH THE NEW YORKERS ended on a Saturday morning, five days after I'd started working on the boat. I shoehorned the six of them and their luggage into the London taxi—it had jump seats facing back, and they didn't seem to mind holding some of their luggage in their laps—and headed for Tonnerre, where they would catch a train back to Paris.

After a week on the boat the guests were surprised to find they weren't far from where they'd started. That was our life, traveling, over the span of several weeks and numerous parties of guests, along the canal in a long orbit that stretched from Dijon to Fontainebleau and back, giving our paying customers—and ourselves—the illusion we were heading somewhere when we were really only going round in circles.

This bunch had enjoyed having a fellow American as part of the crew and, as I drove them into town, treated me like an old friend, saying "Kip" this and "Kip" that and telling me what a good time they'd had. I'd always figured that calling someone by their first name was a mark of acknowledged equality, even of comradeship. Yet, as they pretended to a certain rough egalitarianism, something about the way they batted my name around—they likely used the same tone when talking to their dogs—made it clear they didn't see me as being of their own social class, and their cordial tone carried a whiff of condescension. With a flush of embarrassment, I wondered how often I'd done the same thing.

One of the guests, a tall heavy-set fellow named Harry, who seemed to consider himself the senior partner of this group, called up from the back, "Say, Kip, why didn't you mention you were from our part of the country?"

I gripped the steering wheel tight enough to make my knuckles go white. "Sorry?"

"Diane says you're from Rhinebeck."

She must have got it from Dilip.

"Rhinebeck? No. Never heard of it."

Harry's wife, Elizabeth, who also seemed to consider him senior partner, frowned. "But I was sure Diane said—"

"I'm from Aspen."

That seemed safe. Wrong.

"Oh, Aspen!" she said. "We go to Aspen every winter. You must know the Sheckleys. He's the mayor, or something like that."

"We moved from there to Spokane when I was young."

That took care of it.

"Oh," she said, a little disappointed. "It's funny, because we were saying just last night that you looked like a young fellow who lives near us. Very prominent family. His picture was in the paper."

My hands started to sweat.

"Something about his father," she continued. "Beat him up something awful. His own father! And he was supposed to have taken a lot of money too."

Over the pounding in my ears I barely heard her husband say, "Now, Elizabeth, we don't really know anything about it. Hardly more than gossip. And I'm sure this boy had nothing to do with it. Does he look like the sort who would strike his own father?"

His wife giggled into her hand. "Oh, I know. It's ridiculous, isn't it?"

I was shaking by the time we got to the station.

I managed to pull myself back together, at least outwardly, by the time I got back to the *Celeste*.

I'd understood from Molly that we would have a couple days off between parties of guests, and I'd said something about taking a train into Dijon, spend the day looking around. She must have mentioned it to Diane because when I came back from dropping off the guests Diane told me I wasn't going anywhere.

I searched for a look in her eye, some difference in her manner, that would tell me the guests had spoken to her about the crimes of the young man from Rhinebeck. If they had, she gave no sign, though, in truth, I could never tell what thoughts lay behind those eyes.

I took another tack, saying, "I thought the new group didn't come until tomorrow evening. I'll be back by then."

Diane raised her chin, but for some reason couldn't quite bring herself to look at me. "No, there's been a change of plan. They're arriving in a few hours."

"These are the people from New Mexico?"

"No. I canceled that party." Her tone said that this was all I'd get out of her.

"Okay. You'll want me to pick up the new guests at the train station?"

"No!" She snapped, then trying to appear composed, added more quietly, "They're coming later today, on their own. And you have work to do before they arrive."

We spent the afternoon polishing brass, mopping decks, cleaning windows and making the wooden railings shine. I cleaned the guest rooms and toted the dirty sheets back to the washer and dryer that were crammed into a corner of the crew galley. Dilip and Molly worked silently, their heads down except now and then to look up the towpath. The mood on deck, already edgy, ratcheted up like the charge in the air before lightning strikes. Every half hour or so Diane came out on deck, barked a few orders, then retreated to her cabin.

※

About five o'clock that afternoon a big Mercedes with smoked windows appeared on the stone bridge over the canal, turned down the towpath and drove slowly toward the *Celeste*. Dilip and Molly stopped their work and regarded the silently approaching limousine.

Diane came out on deck, her arms wrapped around herself so tightly I wondered how she could breathe. With unsteady steps, she walked to a spot at the top of the plank and pasted a dazzling smile on her face.

Dilip threw me a warning look. "Don't speak to him unless he speaks to you first. You don't ask about his business affairs. And you call him Monsieur Carbonne."

The long, dark car rolled to a stop on the grass verge on the far side of the towpath, next to the London taxi.

For several long seconds nothing happened. Then, almost simultaneously, the front doors opened and two men stepped out. The one coming out from behind the wheel was tall and olive-skinned with dark curly hair. By his appearance a few years older than me, he wore blue jeans and a short-sleeved lavender shirt. The other, square-headed and fifty-ish, had a short, squat body like a weightlifter and close-cropped gray hair. In contrast to the younger guy, he dressed in sharply creased slacks, a white shirt and a sport coat.

The two of them took a moment to look around, glancing toward the trees, down the towpath, at the boat. The older one lifted his chin toward the younger and they opened the car's rear doors.

From the side nearest the boat stepped a tall powerful-looking man of about sixty, with long white hair swept back in a casual way that only the best hairdressers can do. The expensive suit, the shirt open to his chest, the crocodile shoes, the designer shades, all of it spoke of the sort of businessman my father considered vulgar, the kind who needed you to know he had lots of money. The bulge of his belly testified to the quality of his table.

The curly-haired driver stood on the far side of the car and held the door open for someone who seemed to be having second thoughts about getting out. With an impatient click of his tongue, he opened the door a little wider.

From inside, a long thin hand spangled with rings reached toward the top of the door, then dropped back. It gave the disturbing impression of a swimmer who has gone too far from shore and is about to go under.

The driver frowned and snapped his chin up—an order to get out.

At this, a tall slim girl, maybe twenty, with long dark hair emerged from the car like Venus emerging from the sea—a sort of depraved-looking Venus, with dark, deep-set eyes and a pallid complexion, her face too thin, but one you couldn't take your eyes off of. Her tight skirt and high heels forced her to take mincing steps as she made her way toward the boat. Gold chains glinted from her neck and wrists.

Though she walked only a few feet behind the big man, Carbonne—who could this be but the man Dilip mentioned?—took no notice of her, but opened his arms theatrically and cried, "Diane, *ma petite fleur!*" My little flower.

Diane's smile spiked an extra hundred watts. "Marius, *mon amour!*"

He came up the plank like a king, granting Diane a broad smile as if it were the greatest boon he could bestow or that anyone might wish to receive. As he stepped onto the deck he clapped his hands on Diane's shoulders. They exchanged kisses on the cheeks punctuated with loud "ahhs" and "mmms," held hands and looked at each other while making further smiles and exclamations. Yet everything passed at arm's length, their cries of affection like lines from an under-rehearsed stage play.

Diane brushed her cheek with her hand—to treasure Carbonne's kiss, or to wipe it off?—then turned and held out her arms to present us, her crew, gathered on the well deck between the two cabins.

Carbonne exclaimed, "Ah, Molly!" took her hands in his and bussed her cheeks while she reddened under his attention.

A funny thing when he came to Dilip. Carbonne gave him only a clap on the shoulder and for a moment dropped his act. "My old friend, *le moine.*" The monk.

The Monk?

I almost missed Dilip's reaction, it passed so quickly, his mouth twisting in distaste, his eyes narrowing. He replied simply, "Monsieur," and looked Carbonne in the eye, not defiantly, but as one old acquaintance to another. They exchanged a few words that I was surprised I didn't understand, as my French is pretty good. It took a moment for me to realize they were speaking some sort of patois unfamiliar to me. Carbonne gave Dilip an ironic half smile that struck me as the first genuine gesture he'd made before he again clapped Dilip on the shoulder, this time as a gesture of dismissal, and turned away.

When he spotted me, the smile on Carbonne's face disappeared. Keeping his eyes on me, he inclined his head toward Diane and raised his eyebrows.

She introduced me as a new crew member, saying something to the effect that she had known me for a couple of years, and I was trustworthy. She said it so convincingly that I almost believed it myself.

Carbonne regarded me steadily for several uncomfortable seconds, then nodded and said, "*Bon*."

While this had been going on, the other two men came on board, standing behind Carbonne, hands clasped loosely in front of them. I wondered why Diane wrinkled her nose until I caught a whiff of the overpowering cologne coming off the younger one, like he'd recently fallen into a vat of Old Spice, speaking, I was sure, to some kind of insecurity.

The young woman came up the plank last. The two men, like Carbonne, appeared to ignore her, though I sensed they were in fact watching her closely. Carbonne murmured something to the older of the two men who, in turn, nodded to the other guy, and they both headed back to the car to get the luggage. As they went down the plank, Diane with unconvincing enthusiasm clasped her hands together and said, "Let me show you to your room." At last, Carbonne looked at the girl, giving her a curt thrust of his chin, indicating she should follow him.

After they had disappeared toward their room, Dilip retreated to the deck above the smaller cabin, where he settled into a canvas deck chair aft of the wheel, his feet propped on the wooden railing, facing down the canal. It struck me that, while everyone else hovered close to Carbonne, he wanted to get further away.

Carbonne's men came back on board, each carrying a couple of bags. As he stepped off the plank, the younger man dropped one of the suitcases. When he bent down to pick it up I nearly choked from the fumes of his cheap cologne. Yet it was what I saw, more than what I smelled, that caught my attention. As he reached down to grab the suitcase his untucked shirt rode up his back, revealing a swath of olive skin—and a gun tucked into his waistband.

Kidnap victims being all but a form of legal tender in some countries, I'd heard of European businessmen going around with bodyguards. Still, it surprised me.

Out of the corner of my eye I saw Diane glaring at me from the dining area. She understood what I'd seen and waved her hand in the direction of my berth. She didn't have to say, "Get lost."

Making my way along the narrow walkway toward the bow, I couldn't help thinking of what lay behind her irritation. It was the same thing I'd seen in her eyes as she beamed her greeting to Marius Carbonne.

Fear.

※

I kept to my cabin the rest of the afternoon, waiting until well after dark before making my way aft to scrounge for leftovers in the crew galley. Molly always made a little extra of what she served the guests, which we rounded out with pasta or whatever else we found at hand.

As I crossed the deck toward the aft cabin, I glanced through the windows toward the dining table. Carbonne, his suit coat draped over the back of his chair, a glass of red wine in his hand, sat laughing with Diane, patting her shoulder, patting her thigh. The younger woman, expressionless, sat a couple feet back, as if she were there and, at the same time, not there at all. Outside the door stood the older of the two bodyguards. His eyes shifted toward me, made their assessment, shifted away.

While I put together some dinner, I stood in the shadows at the back of the crew galley and watched Carbonne rise from the table. With an expansive gesture and a lupine leer he whispered something in Diane's ear. She turned away laughing, though I caught the look in her eye and saw no humor there. Carbonne laughed with her, but his expression turned dark and he said something more, this time thrusting his hand toward her, no longer urging but waiting. Her laugh died and she rose to her feet.

Throughout this, the girl had remained seated, distant and unsmiling. Carbonne raised his hand, telling her to get up. She turned her head away. He repeated the gesture, a dangerous look in his eye. She turned and said something to Diane.

I don't know what she said, and I never asked, but Carbonne's slap came as fast as the flick of a snake's tongue, catching her on the side of the head, knocking her to the floor. Diane recoiled, breaking Carbonne's hold around her waist. He glared at Diane, a warning in his eyes, then turned back to the girl on the floor.

The older bodyguard heard the commotion and quickly went inside. Carbonne waved him away. The guard saw the girl lying on the floor and looked toward his boss for an explanation. Panting, his face like a clenched fist, Carbonne jerked his thumb toward the doors, making clear he should go back to his post. The gray-haired guard didn't leave but continued to stare at his boss. For the first time it struck me that, while the guard worked for Carbonne, he had not surrendered his judgements to him. The big man must have seen it too and shouted at him, "Get out!" With a last glance at the girl, the bodyguard turned slowly and retreated outside.

The girl got to her feet and didn't cry, refusing Carbonne that satisfaction. When she didn't rise quickly enough, he grabbed her by the arm and jerked her to her feet. She refused to look at him, but when he put his arms around the waists of both women they headed with him down the passageway toward his room.

5

The Sun King Departs, the *Celeste* As Prison

STILL SHAKEN by what I'd seen the previous night, I got up early the next morning and went aft to the main galley to get money from Molly for the croissants and bread.

Molly looked up from making eggs and sausage and reached into her pocket for a few euros. As she handed me the money for bread, she saw I was wondering about our new guests. The look on her face said, "Don't ask."

I took the coins and headed for the car.

By the time I bought bread and returned to the boat, Diane was setting the table for breakfast, her face pale, her movements listless. She cast her dull eyes in my direction as I handed the bread to Molly.

From the passageway Carbonne called, "Brigitte! *Allons-y!*" Let's go! Not an invitation but an order. Disheveled and blinking, he wobbled into the galley in his bathrobe, looking both diminished and more sinister without his patina of style.

He ran his fingers through his hair and grunted unhappily when he saw me in the galley. This time I didn't need any stink eye from Diane to know I should make myself scarce.

As I crossed the well deck toward the crew galley to find some breakfast, I saw an expensive late model Citroen approaching along the towpath, trailing a cloud of dust. It stopped on the grass near the Mercedes. No one got out.

Dilip came into the galley with me and took half a baguette from the cloth sack. I got the feeling he wanted to talk but couldn't bring himself to speak to someone he still associated with the faithless Rory Gallagher. While we drank our coffee in silence, the younger bodyguard came out of the main cabin carrying a single suitcase, which he put in the trunk of the Mercedes. The older one came out on deck and took his post by the door.

A moment later the girl appeared from the passageway and without a word sat down at the table. The mark from Carbonne's blow to her face glowed a dull red and her sullen expression of the previous night had taken on a bitter note of humiliation.

With everyone up, I started toward the main cabin to clean the rooms.

Dilip gripped my arm. "No. Wait."

I'd fled my family's fortune for a lot of reasons, only one of them the immediate result of what I'd done. I'd wanted to show I could live life on my own, just a regular guy, treated like anyone else. All very noble, but I still bridled at someone giving me orders and had to swallow the impulse to yank my arm from Dilip's grasp and push him into the clothes dryer. Instead, I took a deep breath, poured another cup of coffee, and resigned myself to hanging around in the cramped galley with him.

It was odd. In the main galley Molly was washing up with her back to Carbonne and Brigitte, ignoring them both. Diane made herself busy polishing the wood we had already polished the day before, treating the two people at her table as if they weren't there—or, more, as if she weren't.

After his coffee, Carbonne began carrying on much as he had the evening before, arms outspread, taking everything in his embrace, ignoring the lingering reverberations from the night before. Diane manufactured a smile and managed a coquettish toss of her head that probably took a year off her life.

When he finished breakfast, he rose and kissed Diane on the cheek, then made a brusque snap of his head toward the girl. Reluctant to appear subservient, the girl—Brigitte, Carbonne had called her—took her time until I wondered if she was deliberately courting another blow. Finally, she rose from her chair, light as smoke rising from a fire, her natural grace a declaration of her independence, however much Carbonne might think he owned her.

Dilip punched me in the arm. "Get your eyes off her. She's Carbonne's," he said, as if she were an item of personal property. "You don't look at her. You don't talk to her. You don't think about her."

His warning only made her more attractive, and my view of her more sympathetic.

As soon as the two guests left the dining room, Molly turned away from the sink—she had washed the last dish some minutes before, but had continued to stand with her back to Carbonne—and Diane gave up her polishing.

A few minutes later Carbonne reappeared, wearing the suit in which he'd arrived, and reassumed his monarchical pose.

I'd thought the four of them—Carbonne, the girl, the two bodyguards—were our guests for the rest of the week, but now it seemed he was leaving.

Diane knew enough to take his arm and come out on deck with him, smiling and cooing. Brigitte wandered out behind them, the younger bodyguard trailing behind her.

Diane kissed Carbonne on the cheek and they held each other's hands. After returning her kiss Carbonne spoke with the older bodyguard, nodding toward the girl and then toward the rooms down the passageway. The guard said something and the two men shared a laugh—though the bodyguard had waited until he saw his boss laugh first. The previous night's tensions, the slap to Brigitte, apparently forgotten, Carbonne clapped him on the shoulder as he had Dilip the day before. The curly-haired younger guard stood in the cabin doorway looking hurt that the boss had not graced him with the same show of familiarity.

With a push to my back, Dilip said to me, "Now. Go. Get out on deck."

We stepped out of the crew galley together, but Carbonne looked only at Dilip, raising his chin and winking.

Again, Dilip said only, "Monsieur."

Carbonne beckoned the girl with a gesture, laid his hand against her cheek and gave it a pat, less a gesture of affection than a reminder that he could strike her at will.

With that, he raised his hand toward the rest of us, opening and closing it a couple of times like a child saying goodbye, and walked off the boat without looking back.

As he reached the foot of the plank a short dark-haired man with a thin mustache, got out from the passenger seat of the Citroen, walked over to the Mercedes, opened the rear door for Carbonne and got behind the wheel. A moment later both cars drove off along the towpath, crossed the stone bridge over the canal and turned up the road, dust from the towpath rising into the air until it too disappeared.

I swear I heard everyone on board exhale.

For some time Diane stood on deck, looking down the empty towpath as if watching something of herself disappear with Carbonne, some part of her he held hostage, and she was wondering if she would ever get it back. Eventually, she headed for her cabin, but not before casting a long, resentful look at Brigitte.

Puzzled by her behavior, unfamiliar with these people, this scene, I'd taken it all in like a spectator watching a movie. Unlike most moviegoers, though, I was on the run and happy for now to hide in the dark of this most peculiar theater.

At the slam of Diane's cabin door, the two guards looked at the girl to see what she made of the older woman's hostility. She glared back at them, and with a toss of her head retreated toward her room. The guards shrugged at each other, then followed her inside to get some breakfast.

I headed off to clean up the rooms.

The passageway led along the port side of the long cabin, with all three guest rooms opening onto it from the right. The girl had the middle of the three guest rooms, with the bodyguards in the rooms to each side of hers. As usual, I started on the room closest to the bow.

A suitcase lay open in the middle of the floor with cheap knock-offs of stylish clothes strewn around the bed and the dresser. The odor of cheap cologne hung in the air like poison gas. I walked through to the bathroom, but had hardly started cleaning before the younger guard charged in, looking madder than hell.

"What do you think you're doing?"

I held up the cloth and brush in my hands and let him figure it out for himself.

All my life, house staff had taken care of this kind of stuff for me. Since I'd come to Europe, I'd taken a couple of pretty menial jobs, mostly because I needed the money, but also, like I said, because I pictured myself becoming some kind of working class hero. What the experience had taught me was that I didn't much care for working. So it was hard enough cleaning up after someone else without having to take any grief over it from this asshole.

"Get out! Stay out of my room!" He pointed toward the door and said, "Out!"

That was fine with me.

As I slammed the door behind me, the older guy came up the passageway to see what the shouting was about. He gave me a kind of sour smile and a weary shake of his head, not exactly apologizing for the other guy's attitude, but letting me know he didn't share it.

"Go ahead and take care of my room," he said and went back to the table.

He was a tidy kind of guy, his clothes neatly hung up, his shaving kit put away, and it only took a couple of minutes to make the bed and clean the bathroom.

At Brigitte's door I stopped, uneasy with the idea of walking into the bedroom of a rich man's girlfriend. I can't say my hesitation came from any premonition of what might happen. But everything that came later started from the moment I knocked on her door.

Her voice layered with hostility, she asked, "*Qui est-ce?*" Who is it?

"Kip. I've come to clean your room."

With a suddenly lighter tone, she called, "*Oui!*" and I went in.

She stood in the middle of the room in her underwear, though that word can't describe the diaphanous bits of lace that somehow revealed more of her than if she'd worn nothing at all.

I recalled Dilip's warning that she was Carbonne's property and I was not to talk to her, look at her, or think of her. But, right then, the only way I could have stopped thinking about her was to be pithed like a biology class frog.

We played a game. She pretended she always walked around half-naked in front of strangers, and I pretended not to notice. Still, I caught her sidelong glances in my direction, assessing my reaction to her. Neither of us acknowledged the mark on her face from the night before.

The guest rooms are small, and as she stood near the foot of the bed she had to know it was difficult to get past without brushing up against her, especially when she wouldn't move. In truth, the idea of brushing against her had its appeal, but I managed to get by with, okay, minimal contact—which made her laugh in a way that irritated me, but also made me want to do it again.

It was all deeply strange after what had happened the previous night. She couldn't have known I saw Carbonne strike her, so she had no need to put on a charade, pretending everything was okay. Instead, I got the feeling she was trying to raise her own spirits by vamping around for my benefit, convincing herself that nothing could disturb her equilibrium.

Her bathroom, cluttered with jars of this and tubes of that, took a while to clean, giving her plenty of time to get dressed and leave. No such luck. She had at least put on a robe, though it barely reached her thighs.

We couldn't have been more aware of each other's presence, but neither of us said a word as the room got smaller and warmer with each moment I stayed.

Her enjoyment of my discomfort started to annoy me. Finally I left, though, in my own act of defiance, not before stopping and making a point of looking her up and down.

She laughed as I closed the door behind me.

A moment later, the *Celeste*'s big diesel rumbled to life, and I knew we'd be underway in a couple of minutes.

Molly handed me a grocery list and some money and gave me a look that told me she'd heard the young guard's shouting.

I asked her, "What are these guys doing here? What's going on?"

She looked like she wanted to explain, but shot a meaningful glance toward the passageway to warn me someone might be listening and said nothing.

※

It was a bad start to the morning and to this peculiar cruise, making me wonder what kind of bizarro world I'd entered.

The rest of the day passed routinely, giving the knot in my chest a chance to unravel. Driving into a nearby village to buy groceries, I had fun watching in the rearview mirror as people came out of the shops and onto the curb at the sight of a London taxi rambling down their main street.

After delivering the groceries to Molly, I drove along the towpath, staying ahead of the boat and working the locks, chatting with the lockkeepers as I went. Long reaches of water, sometimes three or four kilometers, separated the locks in this part of the canal, and I was soon a good forty-five minutes ahead of the *Celeste*. While the woman who looked after the lock sat on a stool in the sun and snapped beans from her garden, I pulled an apple from her tree—she sniffed to let me know she'd seen me—leaned the driver's seat back and read a Simenon mystery I'd found in the boat's saloon.

The pleasant September sun stood lower in the sky than it had been only a couple of weeks earlier. The leaves were turning yellow on the trees that lined the canal, the ripe wheatfields lying just beyond glowing a deep gold under the cloudless sky. The day looked like a Monet painting.

※

After Marius Carbonne's departure we soon fell back into our daily routines. The worst of the tension on board dissipated, though an air of unease persisted, like a quiet strain of music barely heard.

Wishing to avoid both the irritation and the temptation of our first meeting, I made a point of waiting until Brigitte went to breakfast before cleaning her room. For the most part she kept to herself, spending her time in her room or sunning herself on a chaise longue above the saloon, wearing a bikini that didn't cover much more than her sunglasses did. Around her slim waist she wore a delicate gold chain, which struck me as incredibly sexy.

Whatever her occasional provocations—she seemed to enjoy slowly turning over whenever I passed—she gave an impression of solitude, an impression made stronger by the earbuds she wore whenever on deck, playing who-knew-what music, insulating her from everything and everyone around her.

She probably understood better than anyone that her apparent isolation was an illusion. Always, one or the other of the guards sat a few feet away, not really looking at her but positioned where she couldn't move without him noticing. Otherwise, they ignored her, and I began to understand her need to get some sort of reaction out of me when I'd come to her room, affirming she still existed.

If Brigitte's nature came clearer each day, so did that of her bodyguards. At first, I'd thought they were there to protect her—from what, I had no idea. Over those first days, though, I came to understand they were in fact keeping her a prisoner, our boat a floating jail.

The thought shook me and I wondered what I'd gotten myself into with this job. A second realization came on the heels of the first and plumbed its own depths of foreboding—Gallagher got out because he knew what was coming. Diane must have said something to him about Carbonne and the girl and the guards and whatever lay behind their presence, and he'd decided he didn't want any part of it. That's why he'd left, and why he'd been happy to hand the job over to me. His words that morning in Paris before we parted ways, "We're good now," came back to me wearing a new and sinister shade. Now I understood why Diane had given me those searching looks. She wanted to know if Gallagher had warned me about Carbonne. She should have realized that if I'd known, I wouldn't have taken the job.

I wondered what else Gallagher had known that still remained obscure to me.

⁂

On the second evening after Carbonne left, I put on a sweater and went up on the steel deck above the saloon looking for Molly, who usually settled into one of the deck chairs after dinner and had a smoke.

At first, as I climbed onto the upper deck, all I saw was the red coal of her cigarette in the dark, which glowed more brightly as she took a drag and watched me settle into the canvas chair across from her. We sat like that for a while, each of us waiting for the other to speak first.

She won.

"How long have you been working for Diane?" I asked.

She waited before answering, inspecting the question for hidden bombs. "This is my fifth year," she said in her broad accent, her personal pronoun coming out as "moy."

"The cruises go all year long?"

"No." She took another drag and decided maybe she owed me more than that. "The season ends a few weeks from now. Mid-October. It picks up again in May."

"What do you do in between?"

Talking about work seemed to relax her.

"I graduated from a cooking school in Paris." The flicker of a smile crossed her face, the first I'd seen from her. "Always wanted to be a chef."

"Even as a girl in England?"

As if a switch had been thrown, her smile morphed into a scowl and she said with real heat, "Australia. I'm no facking Brit."

I'd heard that Australians had only one adjective, and that was it. Her patriotic point made, she blew a long stream of smoke into the night air. "At the end of the season I get a job in one restaurant or another in Paris until spring." She made a point of adding, "I've got a boyfriend in Paris."

I patted my pockets as if searching for pen and paper. "Hold on. Let me write that down somewhere."

She rationed out one more smile, this one more enjoyable because she tried to repress it.

"So, when the season's over Dilip finds a job too?"

Her sidelong glance told me I was asking a lot of questions on a boat where inquisitiveness wasn't welcome.

"He stays on the boat in Paris with Diane during the winter. He's been with her ever since she got the *Celeste*. Eleven years."

I'd noticed that while Molly had a room in the stern cabin and I had mine forward, Dilip had no room of his own, and I'd figured he slept with Diane. Molly's renewed silence told me something more.

"Ah. But then Rory came on board," I said, "and he's a charming guy, and Diane liked him. And one thing led to another and he was in bed with her and Dilip was out."

Molly leaned forward until her face was inches from mine. "Two things, boyo. One, you have no idea what you're talking about. Two, you'd be smart to keep your mouth shut about anything to do with Rory Gallagher."

We let that settle for a moment.

"Diane and Dilip go way back?"

Again she paused. "Yeh."

"Before the boat?"

Every word she spoke now bubbled up through a thick layer of reluctance. "They knew each other in Marseille."

"They're from Marseille?"

"Yes. No. I mean she's from Marseille. He's from Sri Lanka."

"Sri Lanka? What was he doing in Marseille?"

When she didn't reply I decided to skip down to the question I'd been wondering about all day. "So, you know these guys, the ones with Brigitte. They've come to the boat before, with Carbonne?"

A long pause before another flat, "Yeh."

"The younger one's a hothead."

She sighed at feeling compelled to answer my question.

"His name's Paul," she said in a low voice, as if he might be skulking within earshot. "He may be stupid, but at least he's vicious. Watch out for him. He's trouble."

"And the other guy, the gray-haired one?"

"Serge. He's okay, I guess. Everyone calls him *le Pecheur*, the Fisherman."

"And you know her too, Brigitte I mean."

Molly made a sort of neutral grunt. "Her or girls like her." She blew out a long trail of smoke. "You're mighty free with the questions. What about you? Don't think I don't see you looking around at the locks sometimes like you think someone's after you."

In the dark she couldn't see me flush red.

"Why would anyone be after me?" I was getting better at dissembling since Gallagher first surprised me with his mention of the man in the suit.

She kept her eyes on me for a long time before saying, "I'm getting cold."

She rose and flicked her cigarette into the canal, its brief hiss like the full stop at the end of a sentence. "And you're better off not asking more questions," she said before heading back toward her room.

6

I Get My Chops Busted and Make New Friends

ABOUT TWO O'CLOCK the next afternoon we stopped a couple of kilometers north of Dijon and moored for the night. It struck me as odd, stopping so early, though everything about this tour was proving odd. We might have made Dijon easily, but we didn't budge until the next morning, then went through the city quickly. It seemed that Serge and Paul didn't want to moor any place where Brigitte might find it easy to jump ship and blend into a crowd, which only deepened the mystery of what she had done to cause her business tycoon boyfriend to keep her on the *Celeste* under guard.

We'd been heading south ever since I'd come on board. But over the course of the next couple of days the canal made a long sweeping turn that brought us around north. The countryside sloped sharply downward through this stretch, and I spent most of my day jumping from lock to lock, barely staying ahead of the boat until we stopped for the night near a village called Chateauneuf, perched on a hilltop about a half-mile from the canal, its stone turrets and surrounding stone walls a reminder that many of these villages had once been local fortresses.

I helped Dilip moor the boat just beyond an old stone bridge, pounding in the metal stakes then cinching the lines around them. The canal has no current to speak of, so we only had to tie up well enough to keep the boat from drifting in the wind.

The canals weren't as old as the villages, only a couple centuries, which is like yesterday in creaky old Europe. Idle docks, empty moorages and abandoned warehouses dot its banks, especially near the small towns, testifying to the fact that the canals had once been the highways of commerce, back when life spooled out more slowly and horses pulled the barges along the towpath. Railroads and highways and big trucks had pretty much put an end to freight barges except along the bigger rivers. The canals became literal backwaters, the villages half-dead, no more than a quaint background for the few boats that passed, making our journey peaceful, picturesque and exquisitely dull. This appealed to the sedentary old couples who were the boat's usual cargo, giving them the sensation of going places without causing undue excitement.

This made our current batch all the more puzzling. What were they doing here? And why did no one—Diane, Dilip, Molly—want to talk about them?

Occasionally, as I waited by a lock, with the *Celeste* approaching, I'd see that Diane had come out on board to sit on the aft deck with Dilip, casting baleful looks at whichever of the two bodyguards was on Brigitte duty. As usual, Brigitte herself lay on the deck above the long cabin, sunning herself, earbuds in, her head being sonically cleaned by the music she played. Sometimes, if it was Serge on watch, Diane dropped her hostility for a few minutes and talked with him amicably enough, always in the same argot she'd spoken with Carbonne. Seeing them like that was like wandering backstage at a play to find the two actors who were playing deadly enemies chatting happily about where they might go for dinner after the performance. It gave me the impression they had known each other a long time. Mostly, though, Diane kept to her cabin.

Molly, too, had fallen into a sour mood. She took pride in her meals and enjoyed watching her guests take pleasure in them. But Brigitte and her two keepers didn't want to spend any more time together than necessary, and generally ate dinner in their rooms. The dining room, with its polished wooden table and warm lighting, stood as abandoned as the old docks we passed. Denied the pleasure of watching her guests enjoying her dinners, Molly compensated by making more than usual for the rest of us.

Dilip and I could have taken the dining table as our own, which would have made Molly happy. His sense of propriety, though, kept the two of us in the cramped crew galley, our knees practically touching as we ate, our conversation limited to a few words about the day's travels and what lay ahead tomorrow. At least we were talking.

Generally, Diane skipped dinner and stayed in her room all evening. On the rare occasions she joined us the mood lifted and, especially if Molly, too, drifted into the crew galley, they told stories of past cruises and departed guests, happy to have me as a new audience for old tales.

Even in my few days with the bunch from New York, I'd found that the crew gave nicknames to their guests that reflected the amiable disdain they held for their paying customers. In the camaraderie of the tiny galley, they laughed at the memory of *Monsieur l'Amiral*, a guy from Tulsa who liked to parade around the boat wearing the 18th century naval officer's hat he'd bought in Paris. Dilip snickered at his remembrance of Mr. Chin-Chucker, a 75 year-old codger who had fallen in love with Diane like a schoolboy, expressing his fondness by giving soft taps under her chin whenever she passed. Diane protested Dilip's mockery of the old guy. "He was very sweet," she said. And there was the story of the night some oily rags caught fire under the deck and how, after Dilip had extinguished the blaze, Diane ordered the crew and the guests as well out onto the towpath, forming an arc around the boat to protect it from the local fire department, whose truck soon came speeding down the towpath, its fey French siren boop-a-dooping as it approached, the firemen wielding axes, eyes glowing with fiendish glee at the prospect of saving the boat by chopping its woodwork into kindling.

On one of these enjoyable evenings, as Molly cleaned up in the main galley, Diane stood in the doorway of our little galley and sang a French song about lying in bed smoking after making love. She blinked a lot as she sang and needed to steady herself against the doorframe. At one point Dilip had to grab her arm to keep her from falling. He shot me a look that told me I hadn't noticed anything, confirming my growing realization that she spent a lot of those solitary hours in her cabin listening to her sad songs and drinking. I wondered what had happened in her life to give it such melancholy.

When she finished her song, I rose and offered her my seat. She waved me down, but I could see it pleased her. Behind her, Dilip motioned me to insist.

"*Tres gentil,*" she said. Very kind. She lifted her empty wine bottle. "Someone go ask Molly for a bottle of the Cote du Rhone."

I was nearest the door, so volunteered.

As I came into the galley I saw that Molly wasn't alone. Paul, the younger bodyguard, had come around the counter that marked the border separating Molly's galley from the dining area, and put his arm around her waist. When she tried to bat him away he pulled her around roughly and grabbed her arm.

"Get yer facking hands off me!" she said, her face red with anger and not a little bit of fear.

He made a nasty sort of laugh.

"Leave her alone."

I said it in English, but Paul didn't need a translation. He pushed her aside, knocking her against the stove, and turned on me.

In French, he replied, "Shut up and mind your own business."

Fueled by a couple of drinks and the memory of him chewing me out about his room, I entered the galley in a reckless mood.

"I said leave her alone."

A more cautious part of me asked what the hell I thought I was doing.

Paul leered at Molly over his shoulder. "I know her type. She's been wanting me to do this since I came on board."

"Loyk bliddy 'ell!" Molly shouted.

This was all said in a mix of French and English and Australian, but we understood each other perfectly.

Paul scowled at Molly, maybe for refusing him, or maybe for me being there to see it. Embarrassed now as well as angry, he came at me from behind the counter.

At my father's insistence, I'd taken some martial arts classes as a kid, but I'm not much of a fighter. Still, I stood my ground, taking heart in my righteousness—and, like any dopey guy, unwilling to back down with a girl watching.

Man, was he fast. I saw his right start to come up and the next thing I knew I was on the floor.

Pushed by adrenaline and quick reflexes, I jumped up before I'd felt the full impact of the blow.

He came at me again, and might have really beaten the shit out of me, but before he could throw another punch Diane burst into the cabin, letting loose a stream of curses that straightened him up better than any champ's uppercut. Dilip came in behind her and jumped between Paul and me, letting Paul know he'd be happy to take him on.

That's when Serge came out of his room to see what the commotion was. We all froze in place like misbehaving children when Dad walks into the room. He looked at each of us in turn. When he'd sized things up he shot Paul a dead-eyed glare and cocked his chin toward the passageway behind him.

Paul tried to maintain his tough guy thing, raising his head and sticking out his chin as he walked out, but he wasn't fooling anyone.

Serge gave us all a look that said if things needed to be set right he'd do the setting, then followed Paul out. An instant later we heard the sound of someone stumbling up the passage after being shoved in the back, followed by the slam of two doors.

As the two of them disappeared, the punch that had knocked me down truly hit home. The deck under my feet suddenly felt oddly uneven and I leaned against the counter to steady myself.

Molly was rubbing her arm where Paul had grabbed her. In the emotional hangover of the brief fight I thought she might cry, but she held herself together. She didn't trust her voice to speak, but she gave me a look that let me know she appreciated what I'd done.

Dilip winced at the swelling on my face, "You'd better put some ice on that."

I let out a shaky breath and thanked him for having my back.

"Don't think I was trying to protect you. I just thought that if there was a line forming to take a swing at that sonofabitch, I wanted to be at the head of it." But he said it with the first real smile he'd given me and I knew that, though it had cost me getting my chops busted, he and I were going to be all right now.

Dilip took Diane's arm and started leading her back to her cabin. Before he got her out the door she stopped, looked over her shoulder at me and called out in English, "Stout fellow!"

She said it in the way you might say "good boy" to a dog, but I felt as pleased as if she had pinned a medal to me.

On her way out she gave a toss of her head in the direction of the guest rooms and muttered, "Bastards," meaning, I thought, all of them, the two bodyguards and Brigitte and, especially, Carbonne for turning her boat over to them.

It made me wonder again what hold Carbonne had on her, and what these three—Paul, Serge and Brigitte—were doing here.

A pleasure cruise without pleasure is a peculiar thing.

※

Like a seeker setting off to consult the Oracle, I went looking for Molly up on deck later that evening and, as I'd hoped, found her having her evening smoke. The light from the little *epicerie* next to the canal—a sort of *maman et papa* grocery store—lent us its faint glow.

Molly screwed up her face at the sight of the ice bag I pressed to my face, then rose from her chair and started to leave. I didn't detect any hostility in it, only embarrassment about what had happened earlier.

"Thanks for helping me out," she said as she walked away.

"That's not good enough."

She stopped and asked, "What do you want from me?"

"I want to know what's going on."

"Ask Diane."

"That's like telling me to ask the moon. Who's Brigitte? And why does she need two guards?"

Molly expelled a weary breath at my ignorance, but didn't give me an answer.

"And what kind of businessman is Carbonne?" I asked. "If I'm wandering into trouble on this boat I deserve to know what kind of trouble it is."

She took a drag from her cigarette and thought about it a moment. "Okay. I'll tell you something important." She waited, wanting a response, my buy-in to whatever she said next.

"What?"

"You're better off not knowing, that's what."

As she spoke, the light went off in the store next to the bridge, pitching us into darkness and making Molly no more than a silhouette against the bit of light spilling from the stern cabin.

I couldn't let it go at that.

"So." I dabbed at my face with the ice bag. "Are you happy working on the boat?"

"Sure, why not?"

"I mean, is this what you want to do with your life?"

That put her back up. "A lot more than you want to spend your life cleaning up people's toilets." She let it go at that for a moment, then relented. "We all want things we don't have."

"That's a fact." I thought of home and the likelihood I would never dare go back.

Molly released a long sigh and looked up into the night sky as if the answer lay there. "I'd like my own restaurant. Not in Paris or anything. Just a good restaurant in a town where the people who live there can feel at home and know they'll eat well. And when I close up for the night, I'll climb the back stairs to my place with a couple of friends who like to come with me because it's homey there, a good place to have a drink at the end of the day."

Her words came quietly, spoken more to herself than to me. She must have pictured it a hundred times—the restaurant, the friends, the apartment—all the things she didn't have as she drifted aimlessly along the canal, cooking for tourists on someone else's boat.

Aware she'd revealed more than she'd meant to, she went quiet. Or maybe she'd heard herself singing an elegy to her dreams, and didn't like the sound of it.

"I'm not dead yet. It could still happen." She must have caught how off-key her note of optimism sounded for she quickly wrapped her arms around herself. "It's getting cold," she said and once more headed toward her room.

This time I didn't try to stop her.

7

The Floating World, and Revelations Over Drinks

BY MORNING, MY HEAD throbbed like someone was inside it with a sledge hammer, trying to get out. A look in the mirror revealed my swollen cheek turning color.

I stumbled up the ladder from my tiny berth and came out on deck, the sky barely lighted by the as-yet-unrisen sun. Molly handed me a few euros and, though she said nothing about the previous night, she was good enough to wince at the sight of the bruise on my face.

I drove up the hill to Chateauneuf, where I found a bakery just opening its doors, the air warm and close and smelling like heaven if heaven is a freshly-baked baguette, which maybe it is.

After buying bread and croissants for the day, I walked around the still-sleeping village, feeling oddly content for a guy who'd had his face bashed in the previous evening.

As I made a round of the narrow hilltop I found a pocket-sized viewpoint, nothing more than a small graveled plot and a wooden bench perched on an outcrop overlooking the countryside below. No one had set up this spot for tourists—of which the village probably had none—but simply for the pleasure of the villagers, who could stop for a moment and remind themselves of the beauty around them.

The early morning sun, just coming up, cast its light on the rolling hills, the patches of woods, the land glowing green and gold and blue. Nearly a mile away, the canal traced a meandering silver line through the countryside, hatched by the shadows of the trees along its banks. A cool wind blew from the west.

For an unsettling moment I felt the temptation to get in the London taxi, leave the *Celeste* behind and drive away— to Normandy, to Brittany, anywhere far from this boat and these people. But no. Diane would report the car stolen and I'd spend the next couple of years as a guest of the French Republic.

The bread was getting cold. With a last glance at the country around me, I drove back down to the boat feeling like a condemned man reporting to prison.

※

When I'd delivered the bread and went up the passageway to clean the rooms, I ran into Paul heading for breakfast. We reflexively backed away from each other in the narrow passage, though he favored me with a nasty curl of his lip at the sight of his evening's handiwork stenciled on my face. But there was something subdued in his satisfaction, and he glanced uneasily over his shoulder toward Serge's room and left me alone.

When I knocked on Brigitte's door she mumbled something about "not now," so I went the few steps down to Serge's room. He stood at his bureau, dressed in gray slacks and, as always, a fresh white shirt. A small caliber automatic peeked out from a holster tucked into the back of his belt.

"I noticed Paul tucks his gun in his waistband."

I thought I was pretty bold, commenting on the firearms they carried. Serge, though, took my remark with the equanimity of a handyman asked about his work belt. "One day Paul is going to blow his own ass off."

He gave me the hint of a smile. I think he liked that I'd stood up to his younger colleague, and I remembered his wordless challenge to Carbonne when the big man had knocked Brigitte out of her chair.

"You're from Marseille?" I asked him.

He paused as he put a handkerchief in his back pocket—people still used those things?—and I wondered if I'd asked one question too many. But he looked at himself in the mirror with a tired frown and said, "Yes. And I'll be happy when this is over, and I can get back to my family."

I'd never thought of bodyguards having families. My surprise must have shown. He laughed and said, "I've got a son your age. I need to spend more time with him." He looked around his small cabin and sighed. "I'm getting tired of this. Very tired, *mon vieux*." Old friend.

Whistling a minor-key tune, he slouched off to breakfast, leaving me to clean up the room.

I'd barely finished when I felt the deck vibrating under my feet as the diesel engine cranked up. I went out on deck and pulled up the plank, then leaped onto the bank, yanked the mooring stakes out and threw the stakes and the lines to Dilip. He returned to his post at the wheel atop the stern cabin and waved to me in a friendly way—a first. I waved back. Dilip smiled and engaged the propeller, and the boat got underway. I needed to get punched in the face more often.

※

Over the course of the previous few days, Diane had scolded me a couple of times for returning from my shopping trips with the wrong kind of lettuce, weary carrots, or *pates* of uncertain provenance. I thought of telling her I'd done pretty well for someone who'd hardly set foot in a grocery store his entire life. But that would open me to questions I didn't wish to answer.

After lunch she told me I needed a course in remedial shopping. She got into the back seat of the car and directed me to a local *épicerie* she knew from her years on the canal.

The sixtyish woman behind the counter greeted her warmly, calling her "*cherie*." Even as she squinted at Diane's puffy face and bloodshot eyes, she told her how good she looked. Diane frowned at the sort of diminished compliment usually reserved for the ailing and elderly. Turning to me, the woman said, "*Elle etait la fille la plus belle sur le canal.*" She was once the prettiest girl on the canal.

Diane took a wire shopping basket from a stack near the counter and passed it to me as we walked down the aisles of the little grocery. Murmuring to herself, as if speaking of someone she had known long ago, she said, "Yes, wasn't she once so pretty?"

At the meat counter she took up her role, coyly turning back the wink and flirtatious smile of the gray-haired butcher who complimented her choices. He directed his words at me rather than at Diane to give his flattery full weight. As she took up her purchases he patted her hand and gave her a parting smile.

In the produce aisle Diane gave me a short course on how to tell good vegetables from the merely acceptable, then took me through checkout where the woman again made an affectionate fuss.

"Yes, such a pretty girl," Diane whispered as we headed back to the car.

It had been a tough visit for Diane. The warmth of the greeting she had received only underlined how far she had declined in their eyes, and hers.

When we got to the car, I opened the door for her, knowing the storekeepers would see my deference, which would, I hoped, make her happy.

Driving back to the boat, she told me I'd get a thousand dollars a month, pro-rated to my short tenure, plus tips plus meals, paid at the end of the season in October.

"That's fair," she said with a little upward inflection, allowing me to take it as a question or statement, as I wished.

"Sure."

I didn't want to tell her that, barring a couple of recent jobs, one of them at the campground where I'd met Gallagher, I'd never worked a day in my life and had no idea whether it was fair or not. And, for myself, I wanted to practice my untapped gift for self-reliance, make clear I didn't need a rich family behind me to make my way in the world.

Anyway, whatever she thought fair was a lot better than nothing, which was all I had after fleeing the family wealth.

Thoughts of family brought back the image of the last time I'd seen my father, lying on the floor. I'd become adept at pushing the image aside, though I feared that each time I did I paid a cost, advanced the gradual corrosion of my soul. One day I could, no doubt, erase all those memories. But what would be left of me then?

Thinking that getting bashed by Paul had given me enough cred to ask a question, I said, "Diane, who are these people? What are they doing on the boat?"

She kept her eyes on the road and said nothing.

When her silence began to make me wonder if I only imagined I'd said anything, she said without looking at me, "Just do your job. You're safer that way."

That sent a shiver coursing down my back. Safer from what, I wanted to ask, but knew I had heard everything she had to say on the subject.

She must have sensed my unease because she allowed her mask to slip long enough to give me a brief sad smile and tap me gently on the hand where it rested on the stick shift, letting me know that, as much as these questions might bother me, they were eating her alive.

※

The rest of the day played out in eventful uneventfulness. With the countryside sloping uphill, we climbed a lot of locks and I spent much of the afternoon dashing from one to the next, cranking the sluices open and leaning hard against the iron bars that opened the gates.

By evening I was dead tired and wanted nothing more than to get away from the boat for a while. After grabbing some dinner I took a walk along the towpath, my shoes scritching agreeably on its gritty surface. As my eyes adjusted to the gathering dark, I sensed the deeper shadows of the trees along the canal and could smell the surrounding farmland. Frogs croaked moodily along the banks of the creek that fed the canal. The clouds I'd seen on the horizon that morning had blown in, closing off the sky, extinguishing the stars, squeezing the world into the narrow bounds of the canal.

We live in the floating world. So the Japanese have said. The image appeals to me. Nothing fixed, all in flux. We simply float along. And we on the *Celeste* inhabited our own particular province of that floating world defined by the banks of the canal and the reaches of water between the locks. Nothing else existed. We floated aimlessly by the hamlets, the farms, and the old stone houses with their wooden shutters, all of it like a painted backdrop, maintaining the illusion we were going somewhere. Even the few words I exchanged during the day with the lockkeepers, bakers and clerks were all fleeting connections, leaving no more trace than the wake of our boat. None of these momentary acquaintances knew we carried a bacillus, introduced onto the boat by Marius Carbonne, who then walked away, a bacillus that might yet prove benign, or was poised to mutate into a plague that threatened us all.

No one had yet offered an explanation for the presence of our guests, and our cruise seemed without purpose. Each evening we stopped earlier, and each morning got underway later. Our trio of passengers paid no attention to the passing scenery, asked no questions, took no walks, requested no drives into the country. They remained static figures in a silent landscape, their passivity sapping the life from all of us. As much as Brigitte fascinated me, I yearned for the end of the week and their departure.

Walking in the dark, straining to catch a clean breath against a tightening band of tension, I thought again of following Gallagher's example and taking off, but was forced to contemplate the irony that, after a lifetime of taking money for granted, I was now paralyzed by the lack of it. Except for the few dollars in tips from the previous guests I was broke.

Over the previous few days, traffic on the canal had nearly vanished. Where we had earlier passed a few boats rented by French families on holiday and even the rare commercial barge, we now had the canal pretty much to ourselves. So the sight of another boat moored a couple hundred yards up from the *Celeste* took me by surprise. Rarer yet, it wasn't a barge or a rental boat but a sailboat of about thirty feet, its mast stepped down, evidently motoring along the canal during the day on its auxiliary engine.

Light spilled onto the water from a hooded working light clamped to the railing, aimed toward the open engine hatch. The large script on the boat's stern, visible in the spill from the light, indicated it was the *Canute* from Bosham, England.

A tall man with curly hair crouched next to the open hatch, a wrench in his hand. His ruddy features, tanned a deep brown and furrowed by long exposure to the sun, made him appear anywhere between fifty and seventy years of age. He looked up as I stepped into the circle of light from his boat.

"Good evening," I said in English.

"Good evening, yourself." He looked down at the engine and back to me. "Do you have a spare hand?"

"Sure."

"Right, then. Come on board and see if you can't help me out."

"I'm not much of a mechanic," I warned him as I side-stepped up his narrow plank.

"No need." The man narrowed his eyes at the sight of my bruised face but said nothing. He handed me a small wrench and we got on our hands and knees over the engine hatch. "Put this spanner over that nut there—no, that one. Now hold it tight. That's it. Now here, on this one."

When he'd finished tightening the bolts he crossed the deck and pushed the starter button near the wheel. The engine rumbled to life. He stood with his head down, listening. Apparently satisfied, he cut the motor, closed the hatch and turned off the work light, casting us into darkness until our eyes adjusted to the bit of light coming from the cabin below.

The man offered his hand. "Many thanks. Dick Armistead."

"Kip Weston."

"Would you care to join me for a drink, Mr. Weston?"

A new voice, a woman's, thin and weary, called from below. "Are you talking to someone out there, Richard?"

With one side of his face faintly illumined by the cabin lights, the other in darkness, his attempt at a smile came off as a twitch, bending only one corner of his mouth.

"Yes, I am, Elizabeth," he said, his voice guarded. "Perhaps you'd care to join us."

An unhappy mumbling drifted up from the cabin, ending in a sigh. "And you have no doubt offered him a drink."

Again, that twitch of the mouth and an edge behind the over-polite voice. "Yes, I have, Elizabeth. Would you like to bring up the port?"

To the sound of glasses tinkling on a tray, a tall, thin woman came up the steps from the cabin. The lights from below cast her in silhouette, her long shadow thrown across the aft deck. She set the tray with the port, glasses and a bowl of nuts on a small wooden table and shifted a couple of deck chairs closer before turning to me, her face lined and fiftyish, her eyes both sad and kind.

"I'm Elizabeth. Please, come, sit down. It's nice to have a visitor."

Dick poured two glasses and poised the bottle over the third with an enquiring look toward his wife, who frowned and shook her head, leaving the impression that she had brought up the third glass only so she could refuse him.

I pretended to ignore this byplay and sipped at the port, sweet and strong, awakening a sleeping memory from years earlier.

My father was partial to port. After dinner parties at the house, while the women settled into the living room, he would lead the men into the clubby atmosphere of his den, like characters from a Scott Fitzgerald novel. What century did he think they lived in?

Mother would smile to the other wives and say, "We'll let the boys sneak away to their clubhouse," adding in a stage whisper, "No girls allowed." Father fumed, but knew that causing a scene would make him look weak in front of the men.

At the age of fourteen I was, for the first time, invited to join their company. My older brother, Elliot, had been admitted to these after-dinner gatherings and I was keen to join him. I took a seat and Father handed me my own small glass of the after-dinner wine which, in my ignorance, I gulped like a soda. The expression on my face as the stuff went down, and immediately wanted to come back up, set my father to laughing. His face red, he waved an arm to encourage his friends to join in his laughter at me as I sat there trying not to vomit. After sharing an uncomfortable chuckle, the others turned to my father with pitying looks until he grudgingly dismissed me to my room, where my stomach repented of the port, and dinner as well. It was a long time before I was again invited to sit with the men.

A petty incident, but it might have been then that I started to think of getting back at him someday, though, as a boy, the thought made me tremble, as if I were plotting against God.

Odd how a sweet wine could bring back such bitter memories.

Dick Armistead took a few nuts from the bowl and asked, "So, what brings a young man from America out walking along the Canal de Bourgogne on a fine evening in September?"

I described my work with the *Celeste* and let them know it was moored a short distance down the canal.

"Ah, yes, the *Celeste*," Dick said. "We've seen it once or twice over the years. Owned by a Frenchwoman as I recall."

"You must have spent a lot of time on the canals."

Even the fondest nostalgia carried a quantum of regret, and both emotions played across his face in equal measure as he said, "Indeed, we have," and explained that he and his wife were headed toward "the Med," where they hoped to find berths as caretakers on a private yacht for the winter.

"We used to spend the entire year on the sea, sailing out of Marseille, Cannes, St. Tropez, Nice. But we're older now and pass most of the year on our own boat, wandering about—here in France, back home in England, Belgium, the Netherlands. We work only part-time now."

At this, Elizabeth blew out a sharp breath and meaningfully eyed the bottle of port on the table. "Tell him the real reason we can't find regular employment anymore."

Dick made a tight smile. "I thought I would leave that to you, Elizabeth. You enjoy it so."

It occurred to me that they liked to have guests on board in order to give voice to a lifetime of grievances and shared sorrows. Trying to steer away from these shoals, I asked, "You've spent a lot of time around Marseille?"

"Oh, yes," Dick answered. "Sailed out of there many a time." Elizabeth crossed her arms and turned away. Dick ignored her. "An exciting city. Seedy and vibrant and fascinating and dangerous."

"I met a man from Marseille the other day," I said. "Ever heard of Marius Carbonne?"

I expected a reaction, but nothing like what I got.

While Elizabeth looked at me open-mouthed, the tall Englishman set his glass on the table and turned his head to the side until he looked at me with only one eye, as if what I'd said was too much for him to contemplate with both.

"You met Marius Carbonne?" he asked.

I backed and filled. "No," I lied. "Like I said, I met someone from Marseille. He mentioned the name. I guess this Carbonne guy's a big-time businessman down there."

It took a moment for Dick to form a reply. "I suppose you could call him that, if you consider a criminal mob to be a business enterprise." He saw the surprise on my face, though he couldn't have seen my heart contracting at the realization of what I'd got myself into. "Yes, he's the biggest Mafia *capo* in France, maybe on the whole Mediterranean, outside Sicily."

I don't like to think of myself as naive, but how else to explain having missed what now appeared obvious. While I'd often dismissed my father and his cronies as a bunch of gangsters, even as I accepted the privileges his wealth brought me, I had never seen him bring fear to anyone's eyes as Carbonne brought to Diane's, nor did my father need the presence of armed men around him to project his authority. I had vaguely wondered if Carbonne's business lay on the shadier side of the law, but the scale of criminality suggested by Dick and Elizabeth Armistead made my stomach drop as my life flew into a patch of unexpected turbulence.

Working to keep my voice even, I said, "So he's famous?"

Dick let out a mirthless chuckle. "Infamous might be a better term, wouldn't you say, Elizabeth?"

"Infamous? Yes. There's a story going round about him even this week. Something about his girlfriend—as far as I can make out from the French newspapers," she said with that perverse pride I'd seen in other Brits as they disdained any knowledge of French.

"Girlfriend?" I managed to ask.

"Or mistress, as they call it if you have money," she said.

Dick leaned back in his chair. "Something about her disappearing. Probably dead already and buried in a shallow grave somewhere. Or, as I understand how these things are done, dropped out of a helicopter into the ocean."

I wanted to tell them that, no, they could find her only a couple hundred yards away, in hiding on the *Celeste*. But I managed to keep my mouth shut behind conflicting waves of fear and surprise—and acute uncertainty about whether I would have squared off with Paul if I'd known he was a gangster.

No wonder the others were impressed by my boldness that night.

Once this couple got off the subject of their own lives, the tensions between them eased. Elizabeth even took Dick's hand as she spoke of the dangers young girls can face when rich older men take a fancy to them. Was I hearing something of their own lives, a daughter gone astray?

We spoke a little longer of life on the canal and the fine September weather, though I was no longer really there, my mind running toward new and more urgent concerns, my legs twitching with an impulse to run off into the night, though I was unsure whether I wanted to run away from the *Celeste* or back toward it.

In reality, I had only one choice. I was broke. Everything I could claim as mine was in my berth on the boat. Unlike Gallagher when he deserted, I had no home, no job I could run back to. Besides, as foolish as it sounds, in my couple of weeks on the *Celeste* I'd developed a certain loyalty to the boat, to Diane and Dilip and Molly, and I didn't want them thinking of me as they did of Rory Gallagher. So I soon made my goodbyes and walked back along the canal.

※

When the *Celeste* came into view, I felt I was seeing it for the first time, not clearly yet, but its lines becoming sharper, filling me with disquiet. At the same time—and how crazy can a person get?—I felt a thrill of excitement. After a life of dull privilege, where even my transgressions lacked weight, I confronted a real challenge, something of consequence, the stuff of real life—danger and evil, loyalty and steadfastness. I told myself I was ready.

Did I say I don't like to think of myself as naive?

The lights of the *Celeste* glowed warmly in the night, though that light seemed now to carry a sinister tone. Notwithstanding the blackness of the water and the shadowed woods around me, I understood now. The real darkness dwelt onboard.

8

A Spiritual Person Goes for a Swim

THE NEXT MORNING, on the way to buy bread, I drove along the towpath toward the spot where I had visited the *Canute* the previous night. With a rising sense of hope, I thought I might stop and talk once more to my new-made friends, tell them of Brigitte and Carbonne and the bodyguards, ask them to call the police, though I'd insist they had to leave my name out of it.

But when I came around the bend leading to their mooring spot I found it empty. The Armisteads had somehow slipped by us, probably underway as soon as the locks opened that morning. However unfairly, I felt abandoned, as if they had deserted me, condemning me to the dark micro-verse of the *Celeste* and its unhappy inmates

※

Late that morning the wind shifted from a cool northerly, carrying its promise of fall, to a surprising Mediterranean wind coming up from the south, pushing back the bank of clouds and letting the sun shine strongly, like a parting gift from Dick and Elizabeth Armistead as they motored away toward warmer waters.

The unexpected boon of a warm day this late in September made the lockkeepers chatty, happy for the sun. The clear skies also brought Brigitte back out on deck, as if she were one of those little windmills in a bulb, powered by sunlight.

About midday, as I stood in the shade of a lockkeeper's apple tree watching the *Celeste* approach, I saw that Serge too had come out on deck, taking a chair on the stern next to Dilip, the two of them talking as if they'd known each other for years. As the boat entered the lock it was Serge who threw me the line to loop over the bollard. While the rope went taut and I pulled hard to slow the boat, I wondered if I would ever figure out the far more tangled lines connecting Dilip and Diane with these gangsters.

A few minutes later the boat motored out of the lock and onto the canal, Brigitte took out her earbuds, got up from where she had been lying on a towel above the main cabin and walked to the edge of the deck. For a breathless moment she stood motionless, gazing into the sky like an acolyte of the sun, then clasped her hands together, raised them over her head and arced into the canal.

At the sound of the splash, Paul leaped up from where he'd been sitting in the well deck, doing Brigitte duty, and ran to the rail just in time to see her swimming away like a mink.

Serge too jumped up from his chair next to Dilip and raced down the ladder. He slapped Paul on the head and pointed toward the escaping Brigitte while shouting something that no doubt included the French word for "dumbshit." When Paul did nothing, Serge, still shouting, swept his hand toward Brigitte, clearly telling Paul to jump in the canal and chase after her. Paul looked back at him with a faceful of dread and I realized that this ruthless gun-toting mobster was afraid of the water.

Serge hit him again and Paul, cringing, scrambled up onto the railing, where he teetered unsteadily, trying to work up the nerve to jump in. Finally, Serge worked it up for him by shoving him overboard. With a howl like a mashed cat, he fell into the canal, spluttering and gurgling and flailing his arms while Serge doubled over laughing.

Behind me, the lockkeeper, a sixtyish woman in an old housedress, cried "oh-la-la" making as if she were scandalized, but I could see her smiling behind the hand over her mouth.

Smiling with her, I put the car in gear and motored along the towpath, catching up to Brigitte as she reached the edge of the canal.

A concrete abutment supported the bank here and Brigitte was having trouble grabbing the top of it to boost herself out of the water. I got out of the car, reached down and pulled her up, her form so close to mine I could feel her warmth. My reward was a smile that would melt stone, much less my heart. While I tried to go back to breathing normally, she turned and giggled like a schoolgirl to see Paul half-swimming, half-drowning, his face a picture of terror. I suppose I could have called to him that the canal was only about five feet deep and he couldn't possibly drown, but where was the fun in that?

I got back in the car, reached over my seat to open the passenger door and told Brigitte, "Hop in."

Looking incredibly sexy, all wet like that, she slid into the back seat, still laughing. Yet, after she pulled the door shut she leaned over my seat, her mouth so close to my ear that it gave me goosebumps and she whispered, "Kip, I am a spiritual being."

What the hell was that about? And why did I let it throw me so far off-center? I had no idea what she meant or why she found it important to make such a confession to me at that particular moment. But it made me ask myself if she was more interesting than I'd thought, or only crazier.

With these thoughts chasing each other around in my mind, I drove the few hundred yards to the next lock, dropped Brigitte off where Serge had put out the plank, and watched her stride on deck with the aplomb of a model on a runway.

As she stepped onto the boat she gave Serge a cool gaze and a toss of her head. "What? Did you think I was going to run away dressed like this?" she told him, throwing a hip in his direction that needed only a rimshot from a snare drum to make her burlesque complete.

Diane, too, had come out on deck and didn't look happy about any of this. She gave Brigitte a look that I thought spoke to the disgust she still felt for having been forced to share Carbonne's bed with her, and maybe to a lingering contempt for herself.

"Go put some clothes on," she snapped at Brigitte.

Trailing a smile designed to throw Diane's disdain back in her face, Brigitte headed down the passageway to her room.

Paul caught up with us before we finished locking through, one shoe gone, the dirty canal water streaming from his clothes. His face red with rage and humiliation, he stumped unsteadily up the plank and splatted onto the deck, heading for his room and some dry clothes. As he passed Serge, the older bodyguard bopped him on the back of the head, like Moe bopping Curly, before telling him,

"At least you don't smell like you fell into a cologne bottle anymore."

Paul's face went from red to purple. I figured that if I was Brigitte, and Paul didn't bust a blood vessel, I'd be very careful around him in the future.

Shaking her head at this farce, Diane barked a harsh sort of laugh, set her hands on her hips and said, "I don't mind if Brigitte is a bitch. As long as it's understood—I'm head bitch."

Like her nemesis, she headed back to her room, the two of them like boxers going to their corners at the sound of the bell, waiting for the next round to begin.

After I helped Dilip moor for the night, I remembered that Brigitte had left her music on the deck chair above the long cabin when she dove into the water, and decided to go fetch it for her—as good an excuse as any to satisfy my urge to see her.

I had often wondered what music she listened to. I was surprised to see that she hadn't been streaming from her phone, but listening to an MP3 player. When I picked it up, I put one of the buds in my ear—somehow putting both of them in would have seemed too intimate an intrusion—and turned it on. I expected rock and roll or that insipid pop the French love. Instead, I got a soft, soothing voice speaking of tranquility and transcendence. With a jolt of surprise I realized she'd been listening to a meditation program.

"A spiritual being" she'd said. Confronted with the possibility that she was a much different person than I had imagined, I suddenly didn't know what I would say to her if I knocked on her door.

Made shy in the face of a nature more complex than I had imagined, I left the player on the dining table for her to find later.

※

Dilip and I continued to share dinner in the crew galley. We didn't say a lot, though Dilip's hostility had long since mellowed into a sort of amiable resignation to my presence. We talked about the work day and what to expect the next morning, how many locks lay in front of us, the best grocery stores in the villages along the way. Occasionally, he told me stories of other cruises and I would talk a very little about home, both of us dancing around anything of importance. I knew why I didn't want to talk about my background or why I had left the States. And I could understand why he didn't want to talk about Marseille or his connection with a gangster like Carbonne. But I sensed a second screen lay behind the one he presented, and he did not wish to pull either of them back.

After a while, and especially if we started laughing, Diane would pound on the wall to shut us up. Dilip's look would turn inward then. With an embarrassed shrug he would head back to her room, where I could hear them arguing, though I could never tell about what. Given the presence of our discontented guests, and with Carbonne's shadow looming over all of it, they had plenty of fuel for their bickering.

9

Brigitte Is Taken Away, the *Flics* Stonewalled

BY SATURDAY MORNING my spirits had lifted at the thought of our guests' imminent departure. I longed to see them gone. My ambivalence toward Brigitte made the prospect both easier and harder. Since I'd pulled her out of the canal she had dropped her former taunting disregard, even giving me an occasional smile, a small tentative thing that seemed fresh and real. When she lay on the deck she would watch me closely as I worked the lock, making me wonder if her spirituality, or whatever it was, allowed her to sense my secret, that I was a fugitive.

With the boat usually stationary, I could wait half the day for her to come out of her room. One morning I finally got impatient, knocked and went in. At least she was dressed this time. But she lay on the bed in a languorous pose, her earbuds in, giving me a maddening smirk.

It pissed me off, knowing that, despite whatever connection I imagined between us, she had gone back to jerking me around.

When I'd finished cleaning her bathroom, I came back into her room to find she hadn't moved. I tried to ignore her, but felt her eyes on me as I tidied up. Of course she hadn't begun to pack yet and her clothes were scattered around the room. When I picked some of her underwear from the floor so I could sweep—I was sure she'd left it out on purpose—she snickered at me.

Before I could think, I threw it at her.

She made a show of outrage, then cocked her chin at me and demanded, "Why don't you make my bed?"

"Get out of it and maybe I will."

She lay back and shut her eyes. "I'll bet you could do it without even waking me."

I stuck to sweeping the floor.

When I ignored her—or acted like I was ignoring her, because who can ignore a beautiful woman flirting with you from her bed?—she gave me a sad-eyed look and said, "If I make people angry, it's only so they have to admit I exist."

A form of apology, I suppose, but my lingering sense of distrust made it difficult to accept. "You exist all right."

Her manner changed. She seemed to regret, at least a little bit, tormenting me, making me wonder which of her personas was real and which a pose.

"Thank you, Kip, for rescuing me the other day."

"You didn't need much rescuing."

"You made sure Paul didn't get me." She laughed again at the memory of him thrashing around in the canal. "And I was grateful I didn't have to walk back to the boat barefoot."

I had my back to her, but I could hear the smile in her voice. Damned if I didn't smile with her.

She saw it and laughed. "I knew you liked me, Kip."

Her words said so much about her need for friendship that I decided I couldn't let her down. Even if she was only here until the end of the day, she would know I'd been her friend. If, somewhere deep inside, I wanted to be more than that, it was a secret I kept, even from myself.

Things get mixed up and by the time I'd finished the room I was ready to make the bed with her lying there, just to see what came of it.

Maybe Brigitte could see what was going through my head because she laughed, but not in a mocking way this time. And I was ready to prove that I for sure knew she existed.

That's when Serge walked into the room.

"Get out of bed," he snapped at Brigitte.

His abrupt appearance wiped the smile off Brigitte's face.

"Why should I?" She wanted to sound defiant, but her wobbling voice robbed the words of conviction.

Serge turned to me. "You have the keys to the car?"

When I pulled them out of my pocket I expected him to tell me to cut my cleaning short and get all three of them— Brigitte, Paul and himself—to the nearest train station toot sweet. Instead, he snatched them from my hand and turned to Brigitte.

"Get out to the car," he told her.

Brigitte's face turned pale beneath her tan. "Why? Where am I going?"

"Never mind about that."

Without taking her eyes off Serge, Brigitte rolled out of bed and started to pull her suitcase from the closet.

"Leave it." He nodded toward the passageway. "Go."

I thought of Dick Armistead's remark that Carbonne's girlfriend was probably lying somewhere in a shallow grave. At the time, I'd thought how wrong he was. Now I feared he'd only spoken too soon.

Eyes wide, legs unsteady, Brigitte crossed the room. I thought of the smile she'd given me only a moment ago.

I stepped between them. "Look, Serge—"

"Shut up." He reached around me, grabbed Brigitte's arm and pulled her toward the door. "Come on."

"What's going on?" I asked.

The look in his eyes made me take a step back.

Her face stiff with fear, Brigitte said, "Serge, don't do this."

"Be quiet." He pushed Brigitte into the passageway. "Get going," he said, his voice flat, deadly, betraying no trace of the more amiable man I had come to like.

I took a deep breath to recover my nerve and followed them out on deck, uncertain what was happening, but seized by an urge to stop it.

Paul was leaning against the car, his phone to his ear, saying something I couldn't catch. Dilip, Diane all looked on and did nothing. Searching for help, I looked to each of them and got nothing but averted eyes.

"What's going on?" I asked no one in particular—or all of them at once. "Leave her alone."

Serge turned on me, his eyes cold as a lizard's. "Stay out of it, or you'll be sorry."

At the top of the plank, Brigitte turned to Diane and said something to her in that argot I couldn't understand, trying to claim a connection, make a last appeal as a sister *Marseillaise*.

However cold the set of her face, Diane had to be thinking that she had once occupied Brigitte's place in Carbonne's universe, that this might have been herself. At that moment she couldn't have looked at Brigitte any more than she could have looked at herself in a mirror. Instead, she lowered her eyes and nodded wordlessly toward the car.

Serge poked at Brigitte like a pirate prodding a prisoner to walk the plank. When she still didn't move, he gestured for Paul to come get her.

Still talking on the phone, Paul ambled over. Serge tossed him the keys and barked at Brigitte, "Go!" It was the first time I'd ever heard him raise his voice.

Paul ended his call and grabbed Brigitte by the arm. "Come on," he told her and pulled her toward the car. He tossed her into the back seat and got behind the wheel. Serge followed, getting into the back seat with Brigitte. The taxi drove slowly down the towpath and out of sight.

The silence on the boat spoke of foreboding and bad faith. Molly turned back to her work, Diane to her cabin. Dilip retreated to his chair, turned it around and stared off the stern as if he couldn't bear to look at any of us.

I fought against a sense of shame for my inability to do anything, telling myself that without anyone to join with me in saying no I couldn't very well beat up two professional bodyguards then grab a hawser and swing through the air like Captain Blood with a girl under my arm.

Sick to the depths of my gut, I went up on the deck above the long cabin, fell into one of the chairs and looked out over the bow, a bookend to Dilip gazing off the stern.

✻

That's how, half an hour later, I was the first to see the police car driving down the towpath toward the boat. It came slowly, no siren, flashers off.

As the car pulled up next to the boat Dilip saw it too and got up from his chair, leaned over the railing and quietly called, "Diane."

She came out on deck, hands on her hips, her fingers tapping nervously.

The car parked in the middle of the towpath and two policemen got out, plainclothes men, one older, one younger, who walked up the plank, looking around the boat as if they were thinking of buying it.

A thought flashed through my mind that they'd already found Brigitte's body and had come to ask who killed her. A ridiculous idea. There'd been no time for that. Besides, Serge and Paul would do whatever was needed to make sure no one found her anytime soon.

I rose and walked to the end of the long cabin, overlooking the well deck below. Dilip stood near the wheel on the aft deck. Molly came to the door near her galley, standing directly below me, making the three of us an audience for whatever bit of theater came to pass between Diane and the *flics*.

The older one was tall, perhaps fifty, nearly bald, the younger one shorter, dark-haired, a little unsure of himself in the company of his senior colleague. Though I expected the older one to do the talking, he jerked his chin at his partner to take the lead while he rolled his head as if he had a stiff neck.

The younger cop introduced himself, saying he and his partner had come from Dijon to ask some questions.

In full Joan of Arc mode, Diane crossed her arms and raised her chin. "Do you have any identification to prove you're who you say you are?"

With these two men having arrived in a standard blue-and-white that said Police on the door, it was a question meant more to provoke than to clarify. The younger man sighed and fished a small wallet from his pocket.

Diane inspected his ID as if proofreading it, shrugged and looked at his partner.

"And your friend? He looks like a criminal to me."

The taller detective twisted his mouth in displeasure but also produced his ID.

"All right," Diane said grudgingly, "what do you want?"

The older cop looked around at the rest of us. I could tell he didn't want to be there, didn't want to have anything to do with this. "I'm sure you'd prefer to speak in the privacy of your cabin," he said.

"I certainly would not. I have nothing to hide. Anything you want to say to me you can say in front of my crew."

The French have developed the shrug to an art form, perfectly balancing resignation with worldly cynicism. The senior detective's, honed over years of seeing the worst in people, was an entire existential essay.

"As you wish," he said. He took a deep breath and let it out slowly, demonstrating his self-control, then flicked his hand at his partner, telling him to take over.

With an uncertain glance at the senior detective, the other said, "We understand you're a friend of a man named Marius Carbonne."

"What of it?"

That didn't seem to be the kind of answer he expected, and it took him a moment to add, "You were one of his girls down in Marseille."

"I don't know what you're talking about."

He looked at his partner, who snorted impatiently for him to get on with it. The younger one cleared his throat. "Were you not arrested for prostitution in August of 2008 while in his employ?"

Diane narrowed her eyes and dropped her chin. I thought for a moment she might head butt him. "Trumped up charges simply to harass Marius. I was out of jail by that afternoon."

The younger guy was starting to get irritated. "Yes, Mr. Carbonne's lawyers were very aggressive about freeing you."

"And why is that anyone's concern? If you've bothered to look that up, you also know the charges were dismissed."

"Because you had a powerful friend."

"I resent your insinuation. Anyway, I haven't seen him in years."

Once more, he looked at the older policeman, like an actor looking at the prompter to tell him his line. He got nothing but an impatient glare, and continued as best he could. "Yet you were his special girl at one time, no? And you haven't gone back to Marseille in all these years, haven't looked up your old friend?"

"Didn't I just tell you I haven't seen him?"

At first, I'd thought she wanted to talk to the police in front of us simply to put them off-stride. Now it hit me that she needed witnesses who could attest that she had said nothing to compromise Carbonne.

"And he has never visited you on this boat?"

"Are you deaf?"

The shorter detective chewed at his lip, wondering where to take the conversation.

"We're looking for another friend of his, Brigitte Del Ray."

Diane wrinkled her nose as if the *flic* was putting off a bad smell. "Who?"

"We believe she has information regarding a criminal inquiry involving Monsieur Carbonne—an investigation into the murder of a government prosecutor in Toulon. And we understand that she is somewhat alienated from Monsieur Carbonne. This makes her someone we want to talk to, someone who's life may be in danger because of what she knows."

"Why would her life—?" Diane cut herself off, not wanting to hear the answer to her question. "Never heard of her."

"She hasn't been on this boat?"

"Why in the world would she be on this boat?"

The younger *flic* shifted his feet and regarded the rest of us on board before turning back to Diane. "Can we look around?"

"Do you have a search warrant?"

The taller cop snickered, as if saying to his partner, "You see the sort of thing I've had to put up with all these years?"

The younger one drew himself up straight and said to Diane. "No, I do not. I thought, as a matter of courtesy and, as you have nothing to hide ..."

"You march onto my boat without my permission and ask me a bunch of ridiculous and insulting questions about matters that do not concern me. Then you want me to let you poke around my boat looking for god-knows-what, all as a matter of courtesy. No, you can't. And now I want you off. Go away," she said with a flick of her hands as if shooing off a dog.

Diane never lacked for style.

The young detective pulled at his chin while he searched for a suitable reply. His partner gave him a twitch of the head, telling him to wrap things up.

Huffing in frustration, the younger one said, "Thank you, madam, for your patience. Perhaps we will speak again."

"And perhaps the world will end," Diane scoffed. "You can guess which will come first."

The taller detective squinted at his partner and nodded toward the plank. The two of them retreated to their car, sauntering leisurely to cover their bruised dignity.

The younger one opened the driver's door and started to get in. Halfway into the car, though, he stopped and looked toward the grassy area where the London taxi had been parked. He gestured to the older detective, who came around to where his partner, kneeling in the grass, ran his hands over the marks the taxi's tires had left and glanced up at his partner. The taller man turned and looked toward the boat, making the connection. The younger one rose, slowly following the tire tracks out to the dirt towpath and along it for maybe twenty yards. He stopped and looked off in the direction the taxi had gone. The older cop came over to him and they spoke for a moment, the younger policeman gesturing in the direction of the tire tracks.

I wanted to shout, "That's it! Catch up to them before they do anything to her."

Diane and Dilip must both have sensed what I wanted to do and gave me a look that said I'd better keep my mouth shut. No doubt they would each say to the police that I was making up stories, wanting to draw attention to myself. Or they would invent some grudge I held against them and claim I only wanted to see them in trouble. Molly would remain silent. The senior cop, I felt certain, would refuse to follow up. Whatever I did, it would go nowhere. I'd never felt more helpless.

The older one glared at Diane. She glared back, daring him to do something. Clearly, though, he had no interest in any of this. It struck me like a blow. He had come with the younger detective to make sure nothing happened, to see that the younger man didn't do anything rash, like actually making an effort to find Brigitte. In the end, he only shrugged once more and walked back to the car.

His partner momentarily refused to move, but when he saw it would get him nowhere he, like me, gave up. After a last glance at Diane and the boat, he got into the car and they drove away.

Unmoving, she watched them leave. When they had gone out of sight, her knees buckled and she gripped the doorframe to keep from falling. Dilip saw it and came down from the deck to help her. But she waved him away and returned to her room, shutting the door after her.

It had been a strange interrogation and a stranger departure. The two policemen knew something was up, but the older one had kept his partner from pursuing it. In the end, they had bobbed and feinted but pulled their punches, unwilling to press their questioning, as if they were the ones under suspicion. Had the more experienced of the two felt they were sailing too close to a menacing wind, the shadow of Carbonne hanging over them as it did us? In any case, they'd accomplished nothing and left.

10

I Discover a Shrine, A Friend Gets Cold Feet

AN HOUR LATER THE London taxi returned, driving up the towpath from the direction it had disappeared and stopping on the grass verge. My stomach twisted under opposing torques of fear and hope.

After two minutes that seemed like twenty, Serge got out of the back seat, talking on his phone, laughing, relaxed now, the murderous edge gone. He ended the call, came up the plank and glanced back at the car.

After getting out from behind the wheel of the taxi, Paul stood in the grass, lit a cigarette, and took a long drag. Only when my chest began to ache did I realize I was holding my breath. He dropped the cigarette in the grass and crushed it under his heel. When I was sure he too would walk onto the boat, he opened the door to the back seat.

Brigitte got out of the car trying to look defiant, but she walked toward the boat the way she had left it, pale and shaken. As she approached, she saw me standing on the deck above the long cabin and gave me a look that I can still see in my mind, maybe because I'll never read it clearly, a storm of expressions suggesting relief, terror and anger—and something else as she walked by me, a plea for my help.

Now I understood. The others had known the police were coming. Paul's phone call while he waited for Brigitte had likely been to Carbonne, telling him that they would drive her away in time. And they knew, too, when the police had returned to Dijon, making it safe to bring her back. Diane's edginess had been less about Brigitte's fate than about the possibility of the police arriving before they could get her off the boat—and, no doubt, about her disgust with herself that Carbonne could still command her to do as he wished.

When Brigitte came to the foot of the plank she hesitated, though she knew she had little choice but to walk back into the high-toned jail that was the *Celeste*. With a sigh that might have turned into a sob, she lurched unsteadily onto the boat. Paul laughed as she stumbled on the narrow plank. Serge gave him a look that shut him up and held out a hand to steady her as she stepped onto the deck.

Diane had come out of her room when the taxi returned. As Brigitte walked past her I saw, behind Diane's habitual resentment of the younger woman, something that surprised me, something that looked like pity.

Both sides of her regard made sense. If, as the younger detective said, Diane had been Carbonne's "special girl," she could hardly help but take out on Brigitte her humiliation at being replaced, if not by her, then by someone much like her, younger and fresher. But she also knew the perils of being the mistress of a mafioso, perpetually at risk of harm for knowing more than she should. Diane knew, the price of having lived on the arm of a gangster was that neither she nor Brigitte would ever again be entirely safe from Marius Carbonne.

※

With a shout that must have echoed from one end of the boat to the other, I bolted upright, nearly falling from my narrow bunk in the dark. I'd been dreaming of my father, lying on the floor, bleeding, pleading for my help. In my dream, I did nothing, but stood there and watched him die. As I turned my back on him, I heard a noise and found that he had risen to his feet, holding out his arms, beseeching me to come back and save him.

Groggy and terrified, I staggered to the head and threw up. It's easy to be tough during the day, repress everything, act like it never happened. At night, when the sentry over my mind falls asleep, it all comes roaring back.

After rinsing out my mouth and running my toothbrush over my teeth I went back to bed, trying to shake off the echoes of the harrowing day. In the end, no one had packed to leave that day, even after the police left, and Diane made no arrangement for me to pick up a new party of guests. Things would stay as they were. Serge and Paul, on Carbonne's orders, had full control of the boat. We now served them, not Diane. No longer was Brigitte the only prisoner on board. We all were.

I lay uneasy in my bunk. Every time I dozed off, I woke with a gasp from a dream of Brigitte in terrible danger, Paul about to stab her, Serge ready to shoot her, Carbonne strangling her. Afraid to go back to sleep, I had lain awake for a long time when I heard a light footstep on the deck above, followed by a tapping at my hatch.

My heart nearly burst through my chest in joy. Pushed by my shame at having done nothing to protect her that afternoon, I was certain my thoughts had drawn Brigitte to my berth, seeking safety and comfort, and granting me absolution for my cravenness. Climbing the ladder in my bare feet, I pushed open the hatch—and found Molly peering anxiously down at me.

"Kip!" Panic pushed her whisper to a high-pitched hiss. "They're arguing in her room, and I—"

"Brigitte's room?"

"What? No! Diane and Dilip. I've never heard them like this. You've got to do something."

For an instant I marveled at my transformation over the previous few days from pariah to savior. "Like what, find them a marriage counselor?"

"Be serious! Go back there. Stop them before someone gets hurt."

I knew I didn't have much choice unless I wanted to slide back into pariahville. "Okay, let me get my pants on."

"Hurry!" she whispered and scuttled aft.

I could hear them shouting as soon as I came up on deck, though I couldn't make out what they were saying. Diane's voice suddenly rose to a shriek—loud, anguished, drunk—while Dilip's voice played under hers, deeper, quieter, then abruptly louder and urgent.

Leaning against the cabin to keep from tipping into the canal, I ran aft along the narrow walkway, crossed the deck and knocked on Diane's door. They couldn't hear me over their shouting. I opened the door and went in.

They were caught up in what looked like some kind of macabre dance, struggling in the middle of the room, Dilip with an arm clasped around Diane's waist as she tried to twist away. At the same time he reached up as if to hold her hand, which she'd raised over her head. That's when I saw that their dance had a darker edge. He was trying to take something from her hand as she waved her arm wildly to keep it away from him.

"No, Dilip! Dilip, leave me alone. Let me go! If you love me, let me go."

When Dilip again grasped at her hand I finally saw what it held—a small caliber automatic pistol.

"Please! I can't bear it anymore. I thought I was rid of him, but I'll never be rid of him. I can't go on with him in my life."

As she tried to free herself from Dilip's grip she caught sight of me standing in the doorway and stopped, staring at me open-mouthed.

With a move both quick and gentle, Dilip snatched the gun from her hand. She didn't seem to notice.

Still staring at me, she said quietly—to Dilip? to me?—"I thought I was rid of him but I can't get away. I can't ..." She waved her hand as if trying to brush something from her face, a gesture that for a moment made her look like the little girl she must once have been.

Again, as they had earlier that day after her confrontation with the police, her legs went out from under her.

His arm still around her waist, Dilip caught her and sat her on the edge of the bed, her chin on her chest, old and worn out.

He set the gun down on the nightstand and looked up at me. "She's all right now. Go back to bed." He spoke quietly, as if afraid to wake Diane, who sat dazed, seeing nothing.

It couldn't have been easy for him, but he said to me, "Thank you for coming."

It was the first time I'd been in their cabin. On the nightstand, next to the gun, stood the old CD player that played Diane's music, saloon songs by French singers of an earlier era. On the floor lay a vodka bottle, nearly empty. In a cheap frame above the bed hung a picture of Diane smiling on the quay of some small Mediterranean port, young, beautiful, happy. But these weren't what caught my attention.

Against the wall, a small niche allowed just enough space for a chest of drawers. On top of it, surrounded by withered flower petals and flanked by a pair of smoldering censers from which rose thin clouds of incense, was a small bronze figure of the Buddha, cross-legged, his eyes half-closed, his graceful posture reflecting the immeasurable serenity of the Enlightened One. In front of the figure, a small yellow candle flickered in the faint breeze coming through the door. A small time-darkened mirror in a brass frame backed the pocket-sized shrine, amplifying the candlelight, giving an illusion of depth.

After the violence of their struggle, I felt the balm of the sudden silence, breathed the incense, its strange pungent scent whispering "peace, peace" into the currents of despair swirling through the room.

Dilip appeared content that I had seen his shrine, witnessed this side of him, and that I had also witnessed the deep and troubling emotions of the woman he loved and tried to protect. Holding Diane close, he nodded toward the open door, letting me know I should go now.

I shut the door behind me and went back to my berth at the other end of the boat, but sleep eluded me.

※

Well past midnight, I again heard a knocking against the hatch.

I wanted to tell Molly that Dilip was far better suited to tame Diane's demons than I was, but satisfied myself with a groan of complaint that I hoped carried up on deck. Once more I rose from bed and opened the hatch—and nearly fell back down the ladder at the sight of Brigitte looking down at me.

She saw my jaw drop open and, naturally supposing I was about to speak, put her hand over my mouth. In fact, under the effect of her presence I could no more have formed words than I could have flapped my arms and flown to the moon—though her face above me and the touch of her hand on my mouth made me feel I was already halfway there.

With a glance toward the main cabin, she shooed me back down the ladder, then followed me into my small berth.

When I turned on the lamp above my bed we reflexively looked up, realizing the light would show on deck through the translucent hatch. I threw a t-shirt over the lamp, dimming the light to the softest of glows.

To the degree that I'd thought about it at all, I'd imagined that Brigitte slept in her barely-there lingerie. But in the dim light I saw her standing in an ankle-length flannel nightgown, barefoot and modest as a nun.

She whispered, "I can't sleep."

I wanted to tell her she didn't need to make excuses to come see me. But when I finally regained my power of speech, the only words I could find were, "It's all right."

"I shouldn't be bothering you. But today was ..." Her voice wavered with the fear still vibrating in her.

"You're not bothering me. Really."

Something in my tone must have given me away because she laughed softly. But when she spoke her tone grew serious. "This morning, when I left the boat, I didn't expect to come back. I thought they would ..." She forced out a sharp breath, trying to expel the lingering terror.

"But you came back. You're safe."

"Am I?" She looked toward the hatch as if afraid Serge or Paul might at any moment come clambering down and take her away. "Marius says he would never kill a woman. It's a code of honor among them he says." She scoffed at the thought. "Honor. Him."

While she spoke I noticed she was shifting her weight from one foot to the other on the metal deck.

"You're cold."

She laughed apologetically. "I'm freezing. Can I get into bed with you?"

What's a gentleman to say?

"Sure."

My bed barely held even my narrow frame and after a bit of fumbling, we realized the only way to keep one of us from falling out was to lie with our arms around each other, a bit like two boats in the same small lock.

Her breath was sweet and she smelled of flowered soap. My god, what a wonderful thing a woman is. I didn't want to let on what a pleasure it gave me, lying with her like that, but the response of my body betrayed me. Brigitte was gracious enough to pretend not to notice.

I'd have been content to pass the night like that, with her in my arms and not a word said. But I had to ask. "What happens now? To you."

"Whatever Marius wants. He'll keep me here until he decides what he wants to do with me." Her voice became very small. "Eventually, he'll decide to kill me."

For a moment I was too astonished to speak. "But why?"

"I saw too much. Heard too much."

"About ...?"

"He never wanted me near when he conducted business. He didn't want me to know anything. And I didn't want to know. But one morning, when we were on his boat and he thought I was still sleeping, I came up to the galley to make some coffee. Marius had a meeting room next to the galley and I could hear him and some of his men talking, complaining about a new prosecutor in Toulon, a man named Bleriot, who had told the press he was going to bring Marius down. I heard Marius say he needed to be stopped—just like a real businessman might talk of putting up a new building or buying a factory." I felt her shift in my arms. "You know that's what he's always wanted to be. A real businessman. It embarrasses him to be a criminal. It makes him second-rate. Sometimes, when he's feeling weak or anxious, he'll say that being a criminal in Marseille is like raising dairy cows in Normandy. He thinks anyone can do that. He says it takes real skill to succeed playing by the rules. People admire you then. That's what he really wants, to be admired. He's—how do you say it?—insecure. Deep down, he's an insecure little boy."

"And you heard him say he was going to kill this prosecutor?"

"He never says anything that clearly. They speak in a code. One they all understand. He said he needed to stop this Bleriot. I heard that much. What I didn't hear was one of his men—they call him the Razor—come into the gallery behind me. When he saw me he started shouting to Marius that I was spying on them. He pulled a gun and put it to my head and shoved me into the meeting room. I thought he was going to kill me right there. But Marius laughed and held up his hand to stop him. He thought it was funny, seeing me so frightened. Besides, no one gets to kill his girlfriend. And no one does anything violent in front of him. He makes sure he's never around when his men commit the crimes he's ordered. That way, no one can say they saw him there. His men will go to prison for years, even take the guillotine, rather than say a word. No, when there's bloody work to be done he disappears."

"Smart," I said.

"Smart? Maybe. But I think it also means he's weak. It's when we—the women he keeps—finally figure out he's a weak man, that's when he casts us off." She paused, understanding she had passed sentence on herself. "Anyway, while the Razor held a gun to my head, Marius asked me what I'd heard. I told him I hadn't heard anything, that I'd just got there when he found me. Marius didn't believe me, but he thought I was just a stupid girl and wouldn't have understood anything. He told the Razor to let me go, and told me to go back to bed like a good girl. I heard them all laughing after I left. But now, with this investigation, he can't afford to be so sure I didn't hear them plotting."

Something about the incident she described plucked at the memory of my father banishing me from the company of the elders after I had guzzled his port. My heart grew to embrace hers and I held her tightly, the closeness I felt not simply physical.

"How did you come to know a guy like Carbonne?"

She lay still for a long time. "Chance. My own foolishness. I was in Marseille with my boyfriend, Andre. He was from a rich family and got invited to a party down there. I was eighteen, just graduated from *lycee*. Marius was at the party. In Marseille some of the rich love to mix with the top gangsters, love to pretend they don't know who they are. But they do. They envy how the gangsters seem to do what they please, seem so tough. And the gangsters love to impress the rich.

"Marius looked so imposing in his expensive suit—rich and vulgar and fascinating. He laughed loudly, accepted everyone's attention like a Roman emperor. After a while I saw him looking at me, following me with his eyes. I wanted to say, 'Can I put them back on now?' Andre had told me who he was and, like a fool, I felt flattered that he'd paid any attention to me. I'd never been around anyone dangerous. It seemed glamorous and sexy. He probably saw right through me, because one of his men came up and told me that Monsieur Carbonne had his eye on me—as if I didn't know. It excited me to be approached like this. This man told me I could have anything I wanted—clothes and jewelry and sea cruises. All I had to do was go home with Marius that night." Brigitte tried to laugh at her folly, but couldn't do it. "I'd gone to a convent school for years, which makes you either want to become a nun or do something truly wicked. And I didn't want to become a nun. So Marius was right. I was just a stupid girl. And I found out that while he may be an emperor, I wasn't the empress. Just a '*putain*,' a whore, who only has one customer."

"Don't talk like that. Remember, you're a spiritual person." I said it lightly, a joke between the two of us, and she smiled. "You're still with him?" I asked. "With Carbonne?"

"With him? Even after all that, I stayed in the same bedroom for a while, but ..." She raised her head in defiance. "He knows I'm disgusted with him, with myself. We all reach that point. From the moment he thought I'd heard him in his meeting, he started thinking of getting rid of me. Pretty soon he'll find another girl as foolish as me. Maybe he already has. But that doesn't mean I'll be free. He thinks he owns me now, like a car or a horse. That's the part you don't see coming. That's why he picks stupid girls like me. He'll never let me be with another man. He'll put me in one of his bordellos. I might as well be dead."

We were both thinking the same thing.

"Yes," she said. "Diane was the exception. Diane, Diane, Diane. He talks about her all the time. How smart she was, how beautiful before she started drinking too much, how funny, how great she was in bed, how she understood him. A man like him, you'd think that was the last thing he wanted."

"She was drinking hard even back then?"

"Yes. That was part of why he got rid of her. Men can drink all they want. Need to show they can hold their liquor. But he sees it as vulgar in a woman."

"Does he love her?"

"No. He loves only Marius Carbonne. No one else. But when he tried to send her away she refused to go off with nothing. He respected her for that. He respects no one else. Not even himself."

"That's why he gave her this boat?"

"For standing up to him? Maybe. It's also a way of guaranteeing her silence, and his way of keeping track of her. She's trapped on a boat on the canal, easy to find. And she knows he can take it all away whenever he wants."

"But why are you here?"

She expelled a bitter laugh. "I'm waiting to be killed or to go to a brothel. I'm here because the Razor went to the office of this prosecutor, Bleriot, to bribe him into leaving Marius alone. That's much simpler than killing him. But people like Marius and the Razor don't understand honest men. When Bleriot refused to take the money, the Razor thought he simply hadn't offered him enough. He doubled his offer. Bleriot laughed. You can't do that. Gangsters are like children. They can't stand to be laughed at. So he threatened Bleriot. Bleriot slapped him. That was too much. The Razor lost his temper and shot him. They arrested him before he could even make it out of the office. That's another problem with being a mafioso. Most of the people who work for you are idiots or they'd be doing something else.

"When he heard about what the Razor had done and that he'd been arrested, Marius got terribly upset, enough that he and his men talked about it in front of me. You can't imagine how much I wish I hadn't been in that room when they did. The police questioned Marius. Of course he said he didn't know anything about it. But word had gotten around about me, how he'd kept me close but was about to throw me away. Marius knew the Razor would go to prison rather than talk, but he wasn't sure about me. If I'd been a man he would have killed me weeks ago. Instead, for now, he's put me on this boat where he thinks no one can find me. Now the police have come. Maybe they won't come back. Maybe they will. So I'm dangerous, and eventually he'll decide he has to kill me. Every code has its exceptions."

"Would you talk to the police if they came again?"

She thought about it for a long time, or maybe she was only trying to decide if she should tell me.

"I want to live. And for now, I'm here and alive. I don't think ahead. It's too frightening."

I held her tight. "I'll do anything I can to keep you from going back."

It was a rash and foolish promise. But I've never regretted making it.

She sighed and pressed hard against me and I turned off the light and kissed her on the mouth. And, oh, did she kiss me back. She slipped off her nightgown. Around her waist she still wore that delicate gold chain and it was still incredibly sexy.

We made love on my narrow bunk, awkwardly at first, then not so awkwardly, slowly and gently, then quietly and hard and it didn't feel like I was making love to a jaded courtesan, but to a girl who liked me. And I think she did it also for herself, an affirmation that she was alive.

Afterwards, we lay in each other's' arms with no need to say anything we hadn't just said. After a while she kissed me on the nose—I don't know how she found it in the dark—left my bunk and climbed up the ladder.

She'd hardly lifted the hatch before she gasped and lowered it again and scampered back to bed.

"Paul's out on deck," she whispered. "He's having a cigarette right above us. He almost saw me." I glanced up toward the deck, waiting for Paul to open the hatch and shoot us dead. But Brigitte's fear gave way to a bizarre giddiness. She asked in mock alarm. "Now what will we do?"

With a killer standing right above us, we made love again, very quietly and more relaxed, more just for fun—and not so innocent this time. If one of us made any noise, the other would point up toward Paul and say "Ssh!" then we'd smother our laughter in the other's shoulder, which only made us laugh more. Don't ask me why living on the edge of getting shot should seem so funny. Maybe, for Brigitte, risking her life meant she still had one.

Finally, we heard him walk back toward the main cabin. Brigitte got out of bed and picked her nightgown from the floor.

"Kip?"

"Yes?"

"Thank you."

"For what?"

"For being sweet to me."

I took her hand and pulled her to me. "I think you're pretty wonderful."

She put her hand over her mouth, but her smile gave off more light than my lamp ever could.

I kissed her once more and let her go.

11

An Invitation to Brazil, the Monk Confesses

I ROSE LATE the next morning and went about my work, rummy with lack of sleep and dreamy with a bliss hangover from holding Brigitte in my arms. Honestly, that was the best of it, just holding her in my arms and not thinking about anything.

A cool breeze had come up, ruffling the water, breaking the reflection of the boat into shards of shifting color. It seemed like the perfect image for the fractured lives of those on board.

Trying not to make it obvious, I wandered around the boat, hoping to steal a moment with Brigitte, to put my arms around her and ... Yeah.

Eventually I figured out she had kept to her room that morning. I went up the passageway and knocked on her door, as if I only wanted to clean up.

She told me, "Go away," adding a conciliatory, "Please, Kip," that didn't make me feel much better. Chagrined and heart-bruised, I walked away.

※

When we'd moored the previous night I'd seen a bakery a few hundred yards away. As I sometimes did, I grabbed the bread bag from the crew galley, took one of the bikes and rode off to buy the baguettes and croissants, trying to understand why Brigitte had sent me away that morning. The more I thought about it, the more I realized the trouble we'd put ourselves in.

※

The bakery had already been open a couple of hours and offered barely a hint of the usual warmth and aromas, like a faint memory of better times.

Pedaling back to the boat, I saw dark clouds blowing in from the north, smelling of rain, carrying the first true taste of autumn.

As I pushed the bike up the plank I heard the sounds of an argument. Or, more accurately, I could hear Brigitte's voice raised high, though I couldn't catch the words. I went into the main cabin to give Molly the bread and found Brigitte, her face red with anger, standing next to Serge, who was sitting at the dining table drinking his coffee.

Seeing her huffing and puffing like that, caught up in a passion, tripped a deep, primal reaction that transported me back to the night before.

She didn't need to be a mind-reader to understand the expression on my face. She went silent in mid-*cri*, and I sensed her mind running along the same lines as mine.

Whatever her thoughts, she had the presence of mind to resume waving her arms and shouting at Serge while he drank his coffee and tried to ignore her. He looked up and gave me a wink, as if he and I were commiserating over a common burden, and motioned for one of the baguettes I'd bought, broke off a large piece, split it with a table knife and buttered it while Brigitte shouted.

"And why not?" she demanded. "Yesterday you packed me into the car and drove me all over the countryside without a word of explanation. But when I want to go for a ride you tell me I can't leave the boat. I'm sick of this boat, sick of my room, sick of doing nothing all day, sick of everything!"

Serge shrugged, letting her know how little hie cared what she was sick of. With a hint of a smile, he looked at me and asked, "What do you think, *mon vieux*? You want to take this girl off my hands for a couple of hours so I can get some peace?"

Maybe he and Paul were only playing good thug-bad thug with us, but over the past week I thought I'd detected in Serge a sort of gruff friendliness. And I was raw enough to enjoy the validation of a tough guy's goodwill.

"Sure, why not?" I told him.

Startled by his willingness to give in, Brigitte looked first at me, then at Serge.

Serge buttered his bread and cocked his head toward Brigitte without looking at her. "All right? Now leave me alone." He flicked his hand to dismiss her and went back to his breakfast.

※

We agreed that I'd drive her up to a nearby village, famous for its wines, and be back in a couple of hours. Of course it wouldn't be that simple. Paul would accompany us. When Brigitte protested, Serge gave her a look that warned her not to push it.

Paul didn't want to come with us any more than Brigitte and I wanted him along, but Serge wasn't going to let her go anywhere without one of them keeping an eye on her. "And I'm still finishing my coffee. Besides," and here he turned toward me, "you'll be safer that way."

Carrying in my mind the ambiguity of that message—safer from what?—so similar to Diane's, we drove off.

The village Brigitte wanted to visit sat at the top of a bluff above a meandering river, about fifteen minutes away. It was a pleasant drive through fields and pastures, then past vineyards planted along the lower slopes of the bluff. The threatening skies shaded everything a deep green.

If the beauty of the countryside brought me a measure of peace, it didn't do much for Brigitte and Paul, who hugged opposite sides of the back seat, pouting like two teenagers going on a date arranged by their mothers.

When we got to the village I parked in the main square. I figured Paul would tell me to stay with the car, but Brigitte said, "Come on, Kip. Come with us."

All morning she had been acting as if the previous night had never happened. Did she regret having come to my bed? Or had the evening simply been part of an advanced course in jerking me around again? But the smile she gave told me she remembered it all, and happily, and I realized she needed to protect us both from discovery. She was looking after me a bit.

I said yes and returned her smile, savoring the unspoken warmth.

Giddy with sudden delight, we both laughed before we could think to be careful in front of Paul. Fortunately, he was about as perceptive as a drawerful of doorknobs and only grunted at our silliness.

With Paul trailing a few steps behind us, we strolled through the village, stopping in a few shops. When we ducked into a shop for a wine tasting Paul didn't follow, but hung around in the doorway looking like he was trying to use mind control to sour our drink. But his power source was too weak for the job, and Brigitte and I made a point of showing how much fun we were having.

When we came out, Brigitte told him to buy a couple of bottles. He stuck his chin out and made a face. But she was still, at least in theory, his boss's girlfriend, and he did as she told him. After he paid, he held out the bottles for me to carry. I shook my head and told him, "I'm driving." My excuse didn't make a lot of sense, but that didn't occur to him. With a truculent scowl worthy of a four year-old, he tucked the bottles under his arm, mumbling to himself.

As much as Brigitte and I were enjoying ourselves, it was a small village and we soon exhausted its possibilities. We were drifting toward the car, ready to head back, when Brigitte stopped and cried, "Oh, isn't it beautiful?"

It took a moment to understand she was talking about the village church, a small, plain structure sitting on a rise in the middle of the village.

"I haven't been to church in so long," she said, a statement I wouldn't normally have expected from a gangster's mistress.

Paul grunted in a negative kind of way and said we had to get back to the boat.

If he hadn't said we needed to leave we wouldn't have insisted we needed to stay. So, we walked up toward the church, Paul shuffling behind us, grousing in that *Marseillaise* dialect.

It's funny how a village church can look like nothing special and at the same time feel deeply sacred. Centuries old, the church seemed less an extension of the village than the village an extension of the church, nestled around its protective embrace.

We went in through a narrow entrance to the side of the broad double doors, which I supposed were opened only on the most solemn occasions. The damp cold air exuded a sense of chilled holiness, sanctified by countless generations of villagers who had sat in the church's hard pews seeking salvation and hope for a better world than the one they lived in.

I couldn't help thinking of our starched white Episcopal church back home, a shrine to collective complacency, where we basked in the assurance that our wealth reflected God's pleasure at stacking the deck in our favor. You know the old joke. How many Episcopalians does it take to change a light bulb? Two, one to mix the martinis, the other to call the electrician. My parents wouldn't have recognized it as a joke. Before I'd been become a fugitive, I wouldn't have either.

It's funny how, when you travel, the country you most truly discover is your own.

Brigitte dipped her fingers in a font of holy water and crossed herself. To my surprise, Paul did the same. But when she genuflected toward the cross above the altar, he shifted awkwardly from one foot to the other and went back outside.

Brigitte rose with a smile. "I knew that would get rid of him."

She walked slowly down the aisle of the old stone church, breathing its silent, heavy air. "Oh, Kip, the windows. Aren't they wonderful!"

In fact, with the sky dimmed by the gathering clouds,

their muted colors barely registered, but she found in them something I did not.

"You *are* a spiritual being," I said.

"Yes."

Perhaps it embarrassed her, talking seriously. In any case, she laughed and gave me a come-hither tilt of the head. Side by side, we walked toward the altar, a modest block of carved stone with an embroidered cloth thrown over it, topped by a small wooden cross. We found that we were holding hands. I started to let go, but she held on tightly, and we stood before the ancient altar, hands clasped. She gave me an enigmatic smile then, to my surprise, kissed me briefly on the lips and held my eyes with hers, giving me a penetrating look I hesitated to understand for fear of being wrong.

Suddenly shy, she looked away.

Against the wall stood a table holding a rack of votive candles, two or three of them already lighted, testifying to the fact that we weren't the only ones to visit the church that day.

Brigitte's smile faded into something more solemn as she led me over to the table, put a coin in a metal box, picked up a candle and lighted it from one of those already burning. She stood for some time, her lips moving in what could only be prayer. After a bit, she stepped back, bowing her head once more.

Before I could think whether to say something, or ask something, or just give into my yearning to kiss her, she grabbed my arm and said, "Look, the door to the crypt! Let's go down."

She led me toward a low arched doorway behind the altar, where a circle of stone steps led down into the darkness.

"Really?" I didn't want to tell her that the idea creeped me out. Besides, I didn't know how to say "creeps me out" in French.

"Yes. Come on!"

We descended the steps, hand in hand.

A narrow window at one end of the crypt allowed just enough light to cast a glow over the darkness. As our eyes adjusted we found, amid the slabs of stone etched with the names of long dead notables, a sepulcher topped by reclining effigies carved in stone; a knight in armor, dozing easily in eternity, hands clasped over his chest in prayer. Beside him lay his lady, her hair modestly covered, frozen forever in a similar prayerful pose. The clammy air gave off an oppressive smell of dust and mildew and the accumulation of years.

I wanted to get out of this place and run back upstairs, but when I turned to Brigitte I found her eyes glowing, an ecstatic smile on her face. Before I could ask what it was about this place that could possibly make her so happy, she whispered, her eyes radiant. "I'm glad we made love last night."

I didn't want to belabor the obvious by saying I'd enjoyed it too. And I understood she meant something more than the simple act of sex.

"Kip, you can't know how beautiful everything is until you think you're seeing it for the last time. Yesterday I thought I was living my last hours on this earth. Everything looked so wonderful, and I can't tell you the pain I felt for leaving it. I had never realized what a miracle the sky is, how blue and endless. And I was leaving it behind. I looked down at myself and thought, 'These are the clothes I shall die in.' I looked up at the sun and thought, 'It's going to be warm later today, and I will never feel it.' But here I am, with you, and everything is beautiful. And, you're beautiful too." She laughed and ducked her head, then slowly raised it again, her face calm and serious. "I wanted to come here and give thanks, to light a candle and celebrate."

She kissed me lightly on the mouth. Before I could respond, she broke off and, laughing with pleasure, twirled like a ballerina.

The sound of footsteps in the sanctuary above us killed the moment. We looked at each other, both of us thinking the same thing: Paul had returned to fetch us back to the boat.

Brigitte's eyes searched the dark crypt. "There's a door," The smile returned to her face, this one more wicked than grateful. "Let's run away!"

It took both of us to pull open the ancient wooden door. A rush of fresh air stirred the old crypt like life itself and we ran outside like two kids playing hooky.

After the darkness of the church, the clouded skies shone like midsummer, and we shaded our eyes as we ran down the street laughing.

Brigitte cried, "Let's run away and fly to Brazil!"

"Brazil?"

"All right, Alaska. Zaire. Mongolia."

We both nearly fell over laughing, but I felt something serious behind her suggestion and I considered the appeal of getting away from the boat and restarting life somewhere else with her. Whatever the flickering dream we shared, our imagination failed us. In the end, we ran only as far as the car.

We both skidded to a stop and slapped the fender, like a couple of kids claiming to win a race. Panting, our faces red, we stood, grinning at each other, trying to catch our breath.

"Kip, while we ... were standing at ... the altar ..." Brigitte's smile wavered like one of the candles in the church. "I thought ..."

Too much had happened between us too quickly. It felt both baffling and blissfully transporting. I wanted to say something in return, but didn't yet know what, and was almost grateful for Paul's angry voice as he came up on us, steam coming out of his ears.

"You two think you're funny? I should kill both of you right here."

We all knew he didn't dare, and his rage only underlined his impotence. I don't know how we kept from laughing at him. It was probably the fear of getting shot.

Our disdain must have shown because he lunged angrily at Brigitte. She skipped backwards, out of his reach and I stepped between them.

Okay, I'm making myself sound like some kind of two-fisted savior of young women, what with Molly and now Brigitte. The truth is I didn't want Brigitte thinking I was chicken. Guys will do almost anything to impress a pretty girl, even if she's nothing but trouble. Maybe especially if.

Before either Paul or I could work up the resolve to throw a punch, it started to rain, a sudden shower that soaked us in seconds. Paul looked up, maybe trying to figure out where it was coming from. He told us to get in the car, as if the only reason he didn't flatten me was that he didn't want to get any wetter. We both knew that if he decked me again, I'd have a new set of bruises he'd have to explain to Serge, and Serge would find out Brigitte had given Paul the slip once more. As much as he wanted to slug me, double that and that's how much he didn't want Serge knowing we'd made a fool of him again.

We were all playing a dangerous game, and we knew it.

※

It was a long, silent drive back to the boat in a hard rain, with Paul's impotent fury coming off him like steam. Brigitte and I worked hard not to laugh. We needed to keep in mind that he had a gun and no sense of humor.

I'd thought the boat would stay put that day. After all, we were no longer making any pretense of conducting a real cruise. But when I got us back to the place where we'd moored, the *Celeste* was gone.

Paul swore under his breath. "And now you've lost the boat, you *con*."

"It's a canal, Paul. It's not like they can sneak away."

That was language too close to what Brigitte and I had done to him at the village, and he swore again. But what was he going to do, shoot us? Well, yes, maybe.

Driving slowly down the muddy towpath, we caught up with the *Celeste* locking through about five miles from where we'd left it. Dilip had put up the tall canvas awning that protected him from the rain. No one else was on deck.

As I pulled to a stop beside the lock, I saw Serge in a rain slicker helping the lockkeeper close the gate.

While Paul pulled Brigitte out of the car, I ran over to Serge and tried to get him to let me take care of the lock. He thumbed up the hood of the slicker and looked at me in an odd, searching way. Before I could ask what that was about, he gave me a gruff smile and waved me away, saying,

"No, I think I like your job better than mine." He nodded toward Paul and Brigitte going up the plank. "I'll do this, and you can spend your time keeping an eye on that *salop* of a girl, and that idiot with her." His smile looked weary. "You don't know how tired I get of this job and the people I have to deal with."

I had little doubt his sentiments extended to his boss, Marius Carbonne.

Serge finished with the lock, got back on the boat, pulled the plank in after him and tossed the slicker to me as the boat got underway. "I changed my mind," he called. "You can have your job back. I'm too old to work outside in the rain."

I caught the slicker, but as he went back onto the boat he stood for a moment at the rail, still looking at me as if I were suddenly more interesting than before. While I tried to figure out what this was about, Dilip throttled out of the lock. He too looked over his shoulder at me with an expression I couldn't decipher.

This working class stuff is no joke. I spent the rest of the afternoon working through the locks in the rain, fondly imagining the drawing room back home with a nice blaze in the fireplace and the staff bringing me a warm brandy.

I was wet and tired and cranky by the time I pounded in the mooring stakes that evening and Dilip threw me the lines, still regarding me in a curious way.

So, I was puzzled but not surprised when he followed me into the crew galley that evening as we scratched around for some dinner.

"A man was asking after you today," he said. "An American."

I tried to say something, but had suddenly lost my voice.

"He said he'd been looking for you. Needed to talk to you. Someone had told him you were working for the *Celeste* and he tracked us down."

"Gallagher." I said his name like I was invoking Beelzebub. "What did you tell him? The American."

"I said I'd never heard of any Kip Weston."

"A guy in a gray suit?"

"A suit, anyway."

When Gallagher had offered me the suit's card, I'd turned it down because I already knew who it was, Dave McElroy, a private detective who worked for my father, taking on a variety of dubious assignments, which would include bringing me back to face charges. After passing my first week with the *Celeste* expecting him to be waiting for me at every lock or hiding behind an apple tree to jump out and nab me, I had allowed myself to believe I'd given him the slip.

"Did Diane see him?"

Dilip put a hand on his hip to imitate Diane at her most imperious. "Kip? I would never hire anyone with such an absurd name."

We both laughed, and I exhaled in relief.

More serious now, he told me, "He said maybe you'd taken another name and described you."

My mouth had gone dry and I had to lick my lips before asking, "And you ...?"

"We told him we hadn't seen anyone like that."

"Did he believe you?"

"I didn't think I should ask."

"But he went away."

"He went away." When I didn't say anything, Dilip asked, "What's this about?"

He waited a long time for me to say something. When I couldn't, he let it go with a shrug that said it was my business, not his.

※

The next morning I felt everyone's eyes on me as I went about my work. I braced for hostility, or at least suspicion, but found that on a boat full of knaves, rogues and fugitives, having a stranger on my tail made me a figure of some consequence.

Only Brigitte, forced to adjust her notion of who I was, looked at me uncertainly. I wanted to explain, but couldn't without the others hearing me and knowing more than I wanted them to. She finished her breakfast and went back to her room, telling me not to bother cleaning it up that morning, casting a cloud over my heart.

At lunchtime I came on board to get a sandwich while the boat locked through. Diane, coming back from the saloon with a book in her hand, stopped and made a show of looking me up and down.

"Well, if it isn't Kip Weston, man of mystery," she drawled. "Now you're a full member of this Ship of Fools."

For months I'd kicked aimlessly around the Old World, trying to put my home and everything about it behind me while, at the same time, needing to conceal why I had run. I'd nearly succeeded, but now I almost wished I'd been around when the guy in the gray suit had come by, so I could say to him, "I beat up my father pretty bad," just to see the reaction I'd get from the others. And to acknowledge my regret.

※

That afternoon Dilip moored the boat early and raised the hatch in the well deck to work on the engine, which had been coughing and sputtering the last couple of days. After an hour or so, he wiped his hands on a rag and told me he needed to go into Auxerre, about fifty kilometers away, to get a part. When I offered him the key to the car, he smiled and said, "No, you drive. I'll ride in the back like a gentleman."

We hadn't spoken much since the night I'd found him struggling for the gun with Diane. It wasn't something I thought I could ask him about. But after we'd passed several kilometers in silence, he brought it up himself, asking me why I'd come into Diane's cabin that night.

It struck me odd and a little sad that even after years of sharing it with her he still called it Diane's cabin.

"Molly came and got me. Said you were fighting." I added, "It really frightened her," to absolve her of blame for mixing me up in their affairs.

I looked at Dilip in the rearview mirror. "Does Diane get like that often?"

For a long time he said nothing. When I thought I'd misjudged the moment, he said, "Sometimes. When she's drinking." His eyes shifted away. "Or when she thinks about Carbonne."

It had to make for a special kind of hell to love someone, knowing it's someone else she thinks of, someone else who shapes her life, even if it's someone she hates—the one who makes her hate herself.

"She ..." I couldn't find the words to shape the question.

"She was his girl. Yes."

It was a strange and disjointed conversation, him in the back seat, me in the front, not looking directly at each other, but both of us now and then glancing into the rearview mirror to make eye contact.

"And you knew her from back then, from when she was with Carbonne?"

Dilip paused, and I wondered if I was asking too much.

He shook his head. "No. From before that."

I didn't say anything, willing to let him continue or stop, as he wished.

"We lived in the same apartment building in a slum in Marseille."

"And you started working for—"

He spoke over me. "Who was that man looking for you yesterday?"

I don't know why his question took me by surprise. Everyone on the boat had to be asking themselves the same thing. But he needed to change the subject. And I needed to let him.

"His name's Dave. He's a detective." I knew that wasn't enough. "He works for my father."

Now it was Dilip's turn to look surprised. "Your father hired someone to come find you? Your family is that rich?"

"Yeah, we've got money."

"And your father wants you to come home so badly that he hired someone to find you."

"No."

"Then why is he looking for you?"

I couldn't bring myself to tell him more than half the truth. "I stole a lot of money from him."

He raised his eyebrows. "How much?"

"Enough that he'd miss it."

In the silence I could feel his surprise.

"I wanted to take from my father the only thing that he cares about—his money."

"So, this detective has come to arrest you."

"No. He can't. Not in France. But if he finds me he can have the French arrest me."

We passed a few moments in silence.

"If you took so much money, why are you broke?"

"After I took it, I didn't want it anymore." I saw his puzzled look. "It wasn't about having it. It was about taking it from him. And I decided to do the last thing in the world he would do with it. I gave it away. I'd walk into a charity somewhere—one for women maybe, or for kids—and leave a stack of money on the desk. Sometimes I'd just go up to people on the street and give them a hundred bucks, as if I was apologizing for having it. Which maybe I was. The funny thing is that it didn't seem to make them happy. They only looked at me like I was crazy, which also maybe I was. Sometimes I'd leave money in a church, just leave it there, like I was trying to prove that I had a soul—or thought I could buy one."

Dilip squinted at me through the mirror. "I don't think it works that way."

"No, I don't suppose."

I struggled to change the topic. "That ... That was your shrine. In the cabin."

"Yes."

I was ready to let it go, had only wanted to get us onto another subject, but he needed to talk about it. "When I was a little boy, back in Sri Lanka, I wanted to be a monk. I vowed that I would lead a life of peace and self-denial." He laughed in mockery of his dreams. "That's what Carbonne calls me, you know, the Monk."

He looked out the side window because he couldn't say this and look at anyone.

I reflected on the demons we all carried, wondered how we kept them from crushing us, wondered if they already had, preventing us from being who we wanted to be.

"I came to Europe fifteen years ago because my family needed money. When I first came, I thought I could earn enough in a couple of years to make things easier for them, and then go back. But I'd come on a tourist visa that wouldn't let me work, not legally. I wish I had met you then, when you were still rich," he said with a sad laugh. "I managed to get a couple of odd jobs, not enough to keep me alive, not a penny to send back." He took a breath, working up the nerve to say the rest. "One day I robbed a store. I didn't go in meaning to rob it. I asked for something in the back of this little grocery store, and when the owner went to look for it he left the till open. Before I could think, I reached over and took the money and ran out the door.

"I was sure someone would come after me. I should have known it was only my conscience trying to catch up. But I outran it. By the time I got back to my apartment I was sure the *flics* were right behind me. They would follow me up to my room, kick in the door and haul me off to prison. So I ran up the stairs and knocked on the door across the hall from mine. Diane's door. It didn't make much sense, but I was afraid to go back to my own room. And I didn't want to be alone."

"You knew her already?"

He shook his head. "Not really. We'd passed on the stairs, said a few words to each other. She was a *serveuse*, a waitress, which didn't bring her much. She wanted to be a model. She was very pretty, but she had found out, like me, that things were harder than they looked. There are lots of pretty women who want to have their pictures taken.

Like me, she was starving. Later, when we got to know each other, I asked her why she didn't move back with her family. She turned away and spit on the floor."

Dilip laughed as though it hurt. "I was a thief, a desperado. But when I got frightened I hid in a woman's room." He grimaced at the psychic wound, still fresh after the passage of years. "I told her what I'd done. I was afraid she'd throw me out. But she told me not to worry, to stay as long as I needed. So we sat and talked for a long time, long after it was clear no one was coming for me. It was like we'd both been holding back so much, searching for the right person to say it to. We talked about ourselves and who we wanted to be. We didn't need to say anything about how far we were from what we wanted.

"After a while I went back to my room. When I counted out the money I laughed to see how little I'd got away with. But it was enough that I could send some back home. Just a few euros, but it was something. I felt guilty about what I'd done, but it had been easy. And I'd helped my family. So I did it again. And again. I'd ask them for something in the back of the store and grab the money while their back was turned. I still thought of myself as a devout Buddhist. I told myself that the Buddha said life is an illusion. That meant that stealing was only another illusion, and as long as I didn't hurt anyone I could feel free to do it again.

"After I'd come to her apartment that day, Diane would occasionally knock on my door, or I'd knock on hers, just to talk for a few minutes. She didn't come in, and after that first time I didn't go into her apartment. We simply stood in the doorway and talked. Sometimes she'd been drinking. It was her way of getting through the day, the only way she could face anyone.

"One day a store owner caught me. He grabbed me by my shirt and hit me in the face. I couldn't hit him back. This wasn't from any virtue. I was just a coward. Or some part of me knew I had it coming. When he saw I wouldn't fight he let go and told me to get out. I ran away, feeling ashamed, not for trying to rob him but for being such a poor criminal.

"So I bought a gun. I vowed never to use it. I only wanted to intimidate people so they wouldn't fight back.

"It's hard to buy a pistol here, especially if you're a black man and you're here illegally. I finally got one from a man at a fish warehouse. I'd heard that the Mafia ran the place and that they were shipping out more drugs than fish. I didn't care. I just wanted the gun. It cost me everything I'd made that month. The part I didn't think about was that now the wrong people knew about me, knew enough to put their hooks into me."

Dilip told me his story in that lilting South Asian accent that made it all sound like a ballad, made his story of despair, loneliness and crime come off light as a song.

He'd turned his head away, looking out the window, lost in another time, another place. After a moment he picked up his story.

"Sometimes, she'd bring men up to her room. For half an hour, forty-minutes. I know she hated it. I hated it, but she was starving." He threw his hands out as if arguing, not with me but himself. "One day, one of her men got angry over something. Probably couldn't get it up and wanted to blame it on her. I heard him hit her. Before I could think, I was standing in her doorway with my gun in my hand. I told him to get out and never come back. He looked at Diane and called her a *putain*, a whore. I hit him with the pistol.

I'd told myself I would never harm anyone. But this was different." Dilip looked at me through the rearview mirror. "Or maybe I hit him because I hadn't frightened him when I came in. Even with a gun in my hand I didn't frighten anyone. So I grabbed him by the neck and pushed him out the door and threw his clothes down the stairs at him.

"I thought Diane would treat me like a hero, but she got mad, shouted at me to mind my own business. That hurt. Made me angry. I slammed the door behind me. Later that day she came to my door to say she was sorry. I invited her to have some tea. This was the first time she had entered my room. She saw my shrine. I told her about Buddhism, how we make ourselves unhappy by desiring, by wanting. I told her how the world we know is unreal, untrue. I told her all these things. Me, an armed robber. But she didn't laugh at me. That's when we started to ..." He struggled to get the word out. " ... to love each other. Everyone in the world despised us, but we never laughed at each other. We always saw each other as the better people we wanted to be.

"It must have been a couple of weeks later, I came back from a temporary job on the docks, dragging myself up the stairs. Before I got my door open she came out of her apartment. She was crying. A man had come and said his boss knew she was taking men up to her room, and now she'd have to work for his boss at one of his houses or he'd turn her over to the police. He told her all the girls in Marseille worked for him."

"This guy's boss was Carbonne?"

"Yes. And it was Serge who'd come to her door. When she told me what had happened, I said I would find this man, tell him she wouldn't do it. Diane only shook her head and made me promise to do nothing. I felt like she was asking me to be not a monk but a eunuch. She left the next day. She'd been my only friend. Now I was alone.

"I didn't know the same joke was going to be played on me. A couple of weeks after Diane left, a man came up to me on the street. He said he knew I had a gun, and what I did with it."

"How did he know?"

Dilip gave me a heavy lidded look that told me how dumb I was.

"They know everything," he said. "He told me I had to go to work for Carbonne too. If I didn't, he would denounce me to the police. He said I'd spend the rest of my life in prison. He followed me to my room and made me give him the gun. He saw my shrine and laughed. 'What are you, a monk?' Funny that he had called me the very thing I had turned my back on.

"So I had no more choice than Diane. I went to work for Carbonne. And, thanks to the guy who had taken my gun, everyone called me the Monk. My job was collecting protection money from small stores. Some of them were the same ones I had robbed in the past, and working for Carbonne was really the same thing, except I made more money than I had as a robber, enough that I could send some home regularly."

"What happened to Diane?" I asked.

"Serge saw she was a beauty. She was, back then." A smile played across his face, so full of regret that I had to look away. "So, instead of putting her into one of his houses, he brought her to Carbonne. Usually, the girls that Serge brought to him only lasted a month or two. Sometimes only a night. Diane stayed more than three years. His wife hated him for it.

"Carbonne's married?"

Dilip laughed at my surprise before again turning serious. "All of these gangsters are married. You're not a real man unless you have a wife and kids—and ignore them."

I thought of Serge talking about his family, about his son, and how he wanted to get back to them—and how weary he was of his work. It confirmed me in my notion that he was different from the others, and that my friendship for him was not misplaced.

"Once he'd decided to keep her, Carbonne needed someone to take her downtown when she shopped or went off to the beach, someone to be her bodyguard—and keep an eye on her. Diane had heard of a Sri Lankan, a petty criminal called the Monk who had gone to work for Carbonne, and knew it had to be me. She had Serge tell Carbonne to choose me. Diane didn't tell Serge we were close, or he would never have done it. With these people, you never tell them anything that shows you're vulnerable. Serge said fine. After all, I was the Monk, half-Buddhist, half-man."

Bitterness colored Dilip's voice even after a dozen years or more.

"I stayed with her every day for those three years. I looked after her, tried to keep her from drinking too much, heard her out when she complained about Carbonne, went with her everywhere she went. We became closer than before, even though I didn't dare touch her—maybe *because* I didn't touch her. When Carbonne finally turned her out for someone else it was because she'd grown sick of him, not the other way around. When he told her they were through she said she wouldn't go to one of his houses, no matter what he thought. She wouldn't let him just throw her away.

He would have killed a man for crossing him like that. From her he found it amusing. And in an odd way I think he was a little afraid of her, afraid of someone who would tell him no." Dilip shook his head chuckled, still awed at how she'd stood her ground. "That's when he set her up with the boat."

"He gave her her freedom."

"Freedom?" Dilip wagged his head equivocally. "A boat on a canal. She's easy to find. And he finds ways of telling her it's his boat, not hers. When he sent her off, he sent me with her, still in my old job, keeping an eye on her, making sure she didn't betray him in any way. At first I reported back to him every month. Then every three months. Eventually, he seemed to forgot about us. Until now."

I wanted to ask Dilip why he was telling me all this. Maybe it was fair exchange for even my truncated story. In any case, I was grateful, and a little mystified, that it was me he had trusted with his story. And I sensed, despite how much he had told me, he was holding back something important.

12

Luz, and the Killers Onboard

IF I'D TRULY FELT like a prisoner I suppose I would have been scratching out the passing days on the inside of the hull above my bunk. The truth is that I could have walked away. Maybe they would have decided that, like Brigitte, I knew too much and they would have come after me. Maybe not. In any case, there was a reason I stayed.

Whatever ambivalence I'd once felt about Brigitte had faded like those morning mists over the canal. I longed for her to stay on the boat as much as I wanted her keepers to leave. My daydream? A sudden bad guy crisis would force Carbonne to call his two thugs back to Marseille, leaving them uncertain what to do with Brigitte. I'd tell them, "Dudes, it's all right. Go ahead and go. I'll keep an eye on her for you." The part where they departed, beaming with gratitude, was where I knew I'd flipped from daydream into hallucination.

I didn't try to sneak up to her cabin at night. With Paul on one side and Sege on the other, I knew if we made the slightest sound they would hear us. If that happened, the best I could hope for was that they'd shoot me. The worst? That Diane would fire me without pay. Then they'd shoot me.

As it turned out, I had no need to go Brigitte's room. Two nights after her first visit, while I was scribbling a few words in my notebook, she came back to my tiny berth, stepping light as a butterfly on the deck above me, but not so silently that my heart didn't hear her. I put the notebook on the shelf beside my bed, got up from my bunk and opened the hatch before she tapped.

"You're so quiet," I whispered.

She didn't smile, but looked over her shoulder toward the main cabin, which remained dark, no sign that either Serge or Paul was awake. But her obvious fear put the chill into us both.

She came down the ladder into my berth, hugging herself against the cold, and got into my bunk. I got in beside her and reached up to turn out the light. She put her hand over mine. "Not yet. Let me see where you live." She looked around, nodding as if considering whether she should move in. "Cozy," she said.

"You're too kind."

"True." Her eyes smiled as her gaze fell on the shelf against the bulkhead. "Ah, what's this?"

Before I could stop her, she reached over and picked up my notebook.

"You keep a journal," she said, flipping through a few pages.

"No, that's not what—Brigitte, don't."

She must have thought I was only being shy about what I'd written. Her mood still light, she turned another page. On this one she stopped, and I knew what she had found.

"Who is Luz?"

"Who?" A lame evasion.

"Luz. You wrote her name here in the margin of this page."

"A girl I used to know."

"Used to?"

"Long ago."

"Where is she now?"

"I don't know," I said, which was true, more or less.

"Tell me about her."

"No, I really can't. Not now." She let me take the notebook from her hands and turn off the light.

We made love without a word, locked in a deep earnestness so different from the mischievous joy of a couple nights earlier. Afterward she leaned her head against my chest.

"I'm afraid," she said quietly.

"It's all right. You're here with me now."

What movie did I get that line from? She knew better than I did how empty my words were, knew how little I could do to protect her. She forgave me with a kiss.

"I need to get away from this boat, Kip."

I swallowed a selfish impulse to tell her I wanted her to stay. "How?"

She lay silently for a long time. "I don't know. Maybe I'll just run away one night. They watch me every minute during the day, but at night they think they're so alert that they'll wake up if I leave my room. I guess we're proving them wrong." She snorted her contempt for them.

"I'll take the car and we'll go away together. Maybe I can drive us to Brazil."

My little joke didn't make her smile. "No. For you it's too dangerous to go. For me it's too dangerous to stay." I could feel her think over the truth of what she'd said. Me? I wasn't thinking at all. The warmth of her body against mine made me content to live entirely in the senses.

"Some days I think this will all blow over," Brigitte said. "Marius will pay off the police, if he hasn't already, and they'll stop looking for me. When that happens he'll decide it's safe to send me to one of his brothels." She rolled onto her back, eyes turned to the darkness above us. "I'll die first."

The conviction in her voice shook me.

"If you run, they'll follow you."

"And they'll probably find me. But staying is worse. Worse than dying."

"Maybe we could ask Serge what they intend to do."

Her laugh made me feel like the class dunce.

"Why do you think Serge would tell either of us what Carbonne intended?"

"He's not like Paul. He's pretty decent in his way. Besides, how bad can he be if they call him the Fisherman?"

"The what?"

Suddenly uncertain, I repeated, "*Le pecheur.* The Fisherman. That's what Molly says they call him."

She blew out her breath in disbelief. "Oh, Kip, not *le pecheur.* He's *le pecher.* The Sinner. If Marius gives the order, he's the one who will kill me. And he'll kill you too if that's what Marius tells him to do."

How many ways could Brigitte make me see what kind of fool I was? I tried to reorder my thoughts about a man I'd come to like and whose gruff regard I'd come to prize as proof that I wasn't just some effete rich kid.

"No, Kip, you can't talk to Serge."

"Then Dilip."

"Dilip? He's no better than Serge."

"What do you mean? You just said Serge is a killer."

She had been lying on her back but now turned to me. "And you think Dilip isn't?"

"No, he's not."

My denial came quickly because I sensed I wasn't denying a lie, only trying to deny the truth.

"You don't understand how these people work." Though younger than me, Brigitte talked to me as if I were a child. "They start you at something small, something you might think you can walk away from. But they make sure you can't. Dilip was collecting protection money. They knew that someday someone would fight back. For Dilip it was a baker who hit him with a big metal pan. It knocked him down and nearly tore his ear off. The baker knew it was pointless, he would have to pay in the end. He only wanted to defend his pride a little before giving him the money. But Carbonne's people had given Dilip a gun. And a gun looks for a way to make you use it. When the butcher came at him again, Dilip panicked and shot him. Marius's men covered it up, but from then on he knew they would never let him walk away."

I thought of my conversation with Dilip that day in the car, how I'd felt he was holding something back. Though he could confess to leading a life of crime, he couldn't tell me he had taken a man's life. Just like I could tell him about stealing money, but not about hitting my father.

"If you stay on this boat long enough, with these people, you won't be able to walk away either. The police came once already. And you said nothing. That makes you complicit. And that man, the American who's after you, I don't know what you're running from, but believe me, unless you face it you'll have to run forever." She held me close, looked into my face. "Kip, you're not like the rest of us. Not yet. How long will that still be true?"

While I searched for an answer I knew I wouldn't find, she got up from the bed.

"It matters to you—that I'm different from them?"

"Yes. Very much."

I didn't know how to respond, other than to take her hand and hold it to my lips.

I asked her to come back. But she had already slipped her cotton nightgown over her head—retrieved the last vestige of her innocence?—and crawled up the ladder into the dark.

13

Love, Pure and Profane; Carbonne Redux

THE OCTOBER SUN SHONE in a thin blue sky, but it gave little warmth now and the clear, cold nights left a layer of ice on the inside of the steel hull in my unheated berth.

On a chilly morning with frost on the grass, Brigitte didn't come out on deck. Diane did, though only briefly. After snapping at Molly, snapping at Dilip and snapping at me, she turned on her heel and went back to her cabin. I should have realized what was up.

A little before noon I made a run for groceries and came back to find Molly fussing over a *salade nicoise* and looking fretfully out the galley window toward the towpath. Only one thing could cause this kind of tension.

As I put the groceries on the counter I said to Molly, "You're holding lunch until Carbonne shows up?"

"Clear off, ya bliddy fackwit!"

I can take a hint, at least when it's delivered like a slap in the face with a wet fish. I went up to the saloon for a book. Rather than risking Molly's further abuse by traipsing past her on the way back out, I crawled over the saloon's bench and went out through one of the tall windows, which opened outward like doors.

✕

About one o'clock I heard the sound of car tires on the towpath. As before, we all lined up on the well deck—Molly, Dilip, Diane with a shawl around her shoulders, me, and the two guards—everyone but Brigitte.

The short dark-haired guy who had come in the Citroen a week earlier got out from behind the wheel of the gray Mercedes. After turning around slowly, eyeing the empty countryside around us, he gave a querying look at Serge, who snorted and made a dismissive wave of his hand to let him know things were secure and to cut the theatrics. The driver twitched his shoulders to shake off Serge's disdain and opened the back door of the Mercedes.

If, two weeks earlier, Carbonne had strode on board with all the self-regard of God's older brother, he now appeared preoccupied, walking absently up the plank and giving Diane a perfunctory kiss on the cheek while they each murmured words of affection that struggled to rise to the level of even fake sincerity. He gave Molly a peck and glanced in my direction. But in fact he was looking past me toward Dilip. For a moment they regarded each other silently, communicating something only the two of them understood.

Stone-faced, he looked around the deck for Brigitte. When he didn't find her he turned to Serge, who cocked his head toward the main cabin.

As if waiting for this cue, Brigitte appeared with her suitcase and set it on the deck. Carbonne blew out a mirthless laugh and looked at Serge, who made a one-shouldered shrug that said he couldn't help what she thought.

Carbonne nodded at the suitcase. "Put it back in your room."

For a long moment she did nothing, refusing to accept the implication that she wasn't going anywhere. Finally, Carbonne himself picked up the suitcase and pushed Brigitte through the cabin doors toward her room.

The driver followed him onboard carrying a couple of suitcases. As he passed Serge and Paul he raised his chin in greeting. Serge replied with a scowl, and Paul muttered, "Welcome aboard, asshole."

Diane probably didn't want to have lunch with Carbonne any more than Brigitte did, but as Molly finished preparing the salad and took some onion soup off the burner, the *Celeste*'s mistress, grimly set the table for three.

Having learned by now when to make myself scarce, I drifted forward toward my berth. As I came to the bow, I found Carbonne's driver standing near the forward hatches with his suitcase in his hand, looking lost. When he saw me, he puffed out his chest to cover his uncertainty. Real tough guy stuff. He couldn't bring himself to ask where he was supposed to go, only lifting his eyebrows like a silent-film actor and thrusting his chin toward the two hatches in an inquiring way. I nodded toward the one opposite mine. He opened the hatch and snorted in disgust at the sight of his tiny, cramped quarters, then shot me a look as if I were to blame for his accommodations. I took my turn at shrugging and went down the ladder to my bunk, thinking I would steal some time to write.

For the hundredth time I told myself that my budding masterpiece would make the world understand my father and his kind, and know why I'd been forced to do what I had done.

As always, the words came slowly, as if traveling from a great distance to find me on this boat in a foreign land, far from the one I described. While I waited for them to arrive, I looked around my berth, its spare efficiency a hallmark of marine design, much like the small space on my father's thirty-foot sailing boat.

Memories intrude as they wish, with or without our bidding, and you write what comes. I felt myself back on the *Midas*—yes, that's what Father named his boat—sailing down the Hudson, the sun strong on our backs, my father, as always, at the helm.

The *Midas* carried no radio, and Father always left his phone at home when on the boat, letting him escape for a few hours from the demands of board members, bankers and rivals.

From a young age, Father had taught Elliot and me to sail, instructed us on the change of the prevailing winds as the seasons passed, and on the tidal forces that affected the current all the way to Albany. We absorbed the lessons dutifully, but refused to share in his enthusiasm. Like spacecraft fighting the gravity of an enormous planet, we resisted subsuming ourselves further into his Olympian persona. Once we'd acquired enough knowledge to be useful, he took one or the other of us with him—never both—onto the river.

We said little, Father's commands to me—crisp and short, brooking no questions—the only words spoken. As the afternoon wore on, his manner at the wheel relaxed. The tense, upright posture we knew at home gradually eased into something more relaxed, until he slouched comfortably in his chair, his normally laser-like gaze dimmed to half-light. His face softened and he would light the briar pipe he kept on board as we tacked our way upriver—the only occasion he smoked, outside the occasional "mine's bigger than yours" cigar with business associates.

My ease came more slowly and in fits. I feared letting my guard down, succumbing to his occasional fits of charm. So we shared the close quarters of the boat for the afternoon, but I made sure we didn't close the distance between us.

One fall afternoon when I was about ten or twelve years-old he told me we were going out on the river. I'd been fighting a nasty cold and tried to beg off, but Father put on his sternest demeanor and ignored my pleas. Before we'd been out on the water more than an hour, with me coughing and my nose running the whole time, I asked if I could go below and lie down. I expected him to refuse, reminding me again of the stoic Romans or the intrepid colonial stock from which he claimed we were descended, but he finally bit down on his pipe and nodded and I headed for my berth, feeling the familiar guilt of knowing I'd let him down.

Before long I heard the sound of rumbling in the galley and had no doubt Father had come below to fix some coffee to go with the brandy he kept on board, and was at the same time rehearsing the complaints he would make about my lack of fortitude once we got home. To my astonishment, though, he brought me a cup of tea and asked—gruffly of course—how I was feeling. He checked my forehead for fever, his hand cool and assured, then ran topside to make sure we were still on course. He soon returned below to ask if I wanted more tea. He sat down with me for a moment and told me the joke about the one-legged pirate. In spite of myself I laughed, and he smiled to see my spirits better. He actually tousled my hair before going back on deck. Later, he shouted at me for the way I tied off the boat as we moored at our dock. His earlier kindness had thrown me badly off-center and I been searching for a grudge to nurse. So, I was gratified by his unreasonableness at the end of the day.

This wasn't the man I wanted to write about, one capable of generous emotions, however momentary. I did not wish to deal with the ambiguous balance of debits and credits in my life with him. Unable for the moment to conjure up further enormities against decency by my father, and unwilling to cross out what I'd written about our voyage on the river,I threw my notebook on the floor and picked up a paperback to escape into what someone else had written of the world they knew.

I must have fallen asleep. I woke to see that the angle of the sun coming through the hatch had shifted. My growling stomach reminded me I hadn't had any lunch, so I wandered aft toward the crew galley to graze on whatever I could find.

As I crossed the well deck I was surprised to see Carbonne and Serge leaning against the rail, talking in muted tones. When they saw me they stopped, regarding me as I passed with a silence heavier than words.

The September afternoon had come on cool, but that wasn't made me shiver.

After I'd finished off some leftovers from the night before, I looked out toward the well deck to make sure Carbonne and Serge were no longer in sight, then climbed the five steps to the deck above, looking for Dilip.

I found him sitting in a chair facing aft, as he did when he wished to escape, making the rest of the boat and everyone on it go away for a while. Though I had come to talk, I couldn't find it in me to violate his solitude. I started to turn away, but he'd heard me come up and waved a hand at the other deck chair to let me know I should join him.

For a long time we both gazed silently down the canal, as if we didn't want to turn around and face where we might be headed.

Eventually, Dilip glanced at me before again turning away. "She told you, didn't she?"

"Who?"

He gave me a dead-eyed look. Shamed by the clumsiness of my evasion, I struggled to admit the truth. "I'm not sure what you ..."

"She told you I killed a man."

I took a long time. "Yeah. She did."

If I expected him to justify himself, rationalize homicide as an accident of circumstance, it only proved how little I knew him.

"I used to think that eating meat was the worst thing a Buddhist could do," he said. "It seems like a very small thing after killing a man. So now I eat meat too." It was a bitter joke and neither of us laughed. "When I was a boy I wanted to be a monk the same way other boys wanted to be cricket stars. I fell in love with the idea of living in the big temple by the lake, wearing a saffron robe, having everyone look at me with respect. As I got older I wanted the peace, the fullness of spirit I saw in the monks, the serenity. I wanted to smile at the world like the Buddha. Peace." He let the word hang in the air. "I'm a very emotional man. These tempers that come over me …" He expelled a sharp breath as if trying to rid himself of these storms. "I thought that if I could run away from the world and live in a monastery …"

He gritted his teeth as a wave of pain rolled through him. "You think I disliked Gallagher because he wormed his way into Diane's bed." He shook his head. "I knew he was never going to replace me in the sense that mattered. I hated him because he betrayed her. Gallagher is one of those people who preys on the weakness of others. I'm not sure what he was after. Maybe he thought she had money. Maybe he just wanted sex. But when she told him Carbonne was coming and why, when she asked him to help see her through it, he deserted. Diane puts on a tough exterior to hide how damaged she is inside. Gallagher's betrayal brought back all of her doubts about herself, all the ways she despises herself."

"Why does she hate herself like this?"

"When she was young her father … interfered with her. Another kind of betrayal. The worst kind. Carbonne broke what was left of her."

"And you love her."

Dilip watched a dove wing its way up the canal. He turned in his chair to see it pass overhead. When it had disappeared into the distance, he said, "Taking care of her is the only good thing I've done in my life. And she saved my life. If I had stayed in Marseille, stayed with Carbonne, I'd have been killed by some shopkeeper. Or by one of the gang. Or I'd have killed myself." He said all this while looking down the canal, as if he needed to say it to himself and I just happened to be within earshot. His eyes fierce, his voice oddly defensive, he said, "We've not made love since she lived in the room across from me."

He paused, wondering if I believed him.

I could think of nothing to say in reply. Yet, the abrupt and total silence demanded something, and he filled it in himself, his voice thick with emotion.

"It's the one thing I could do to prove to her I loved her, that I wanted nothing from her. It was my pledge to her. People like Gallagher sense the broken part in her and go straight at it. And she allows it because she cares nothing for herself. I try to tell her how she has within her a spark of the divine. How she is a part of the infinite. How ..." He looked away and bit his lip as if to keep from screaming—or weeping.

After a couple of cleansing breaths, he seemed calmer. "I've bedded other women. In Marseille, before I knew Diane." He shrugged. "And after. There was a cook before Molly. Even a couple of guests." Abashed, he hung his head. "They were like me, doing what they wished to do—from desire, maybe even from friendship. Not from weakness. And it was good. But Diane ..." For a long time he sat silently. "I came to Europe, thinking I would soon go back and present myself at the temple gate. Sometimes I still think that one day I'll do it, still take my vows. But for now I'm still half monk and half a man. And I have a parish of only one." He waggled his head. "I'm so far away."

I knew he meant something more than his distance from Sri Lanka.

With an abruptness that startled me he gripped my arm and said, "We're all on the run. You, me, everyone on this goddamn boat. We run from who we tell ourselves we want to be, when we should be running from who we are. Even Carbonne. He wants to be a real businessman. Serge, Paul, Diane, Molly, all of us, want to be someone else, live a different life. But we don't have the courage to make the effort. So we grow more and more unhappy. And that makes us do ugly, terrible things." He pulled me toward him. "Go home. Get away from here."

I leaned away, as if from a fire. "I … I can't. They'll arrest me."

"Then let them arrest you. You're trying to run from something. But you can't outrun it because you carry it inside you. Make your peace with what you've done. You'll be free then. Believe me, you're totally unprepared for this life. If you stay here you'll end up dead." He gave a look over his shoulder toward my berth in the bow, where Brigitte came to me at night. "You think nobody knows what you're doing?"

My mouth went dry.

He didn't scold me, or even try to warn me, my folly too obvious for either. He simply said, "He'll kill you if he finds out."

As suddenly as he had turned on me, Dilip fell silent, released my arm, and went back to gazing down the canal.

After a while he waved his hand again, this time telling me to leave.

If he hoped I would immediately walk off the boat and keep going, I disappointed him.

※

We motored down the canal a few miles then, late in the afternoon, moored for the night, I went into the saloon searching for a new book to read. To my surprise, I found Serge leafing through a paperback . He chuckled and waved the book carelessly. "Just something to kill the time," he said, as if I'd found him reading through a comic book.

It was in fact a novel by Marcel Pagnol, the great chronicler of life in the slums and dockyards of Marseille.

Did everyone have more sides than I assumed? It made me wonder, after talking with Dilip, of the dreams we all evaded, leading the lives we did. I thought of the son Serge had spoken of—my age, he'd said—and of his desire to get back home and spend more time with him.

※

Back in by berth, I read for a while and tried to nap, but a restless soul can't summon sleep.

I thought of my father. And I thought again of Luz.

Though I tried to lie to myself that I hadn't thought of her in ages, my memory of her lay behind everything, a canvas I had painted over many times only to see the image bleed through. If I'd loved her, and I told myself I had, the ardor I'd felt for her had long ago faded, even if the pain remained.

I don't believe my father had hated her, only what she was. "That Mexican," he called her, or, in a more generous mood, "That Latin girl of yours."

Of mine. Like a toy I'd bought instead of spending my money on something sensible. It didn't matter to my father that she attended the same prestigious school as I did, that she was smarter than me or that her family in Guadalajara was respectable and well-to-do.

"Well-to-do," he sniffed as if it were nothing more than a perilous step above disgrace.

He insisted I drop her, told me I refused to see she was a gold-digger. "An adventuress," he called her. Where in the hell did he drag that term up? He'd call her a flapper next. "This is not a deep relationship," he said with the complacency of the arrogant. "I'm sure I could give her enough money to break this thing off. She'd take it and run."

His smugness confirmed me in the certainty that I loved her deeply. When I came home for the term break I went into my father's study and told him I wanted to marry her.

Without looking up from his work, he said, "You won't."

Whether he meant I'd get over her, or she'd get over me, or that he would do something to end it I didn't know and didn't care. I shouted at him that he couldn't be more wrong about her, about me, about everything. He smiled.

During a brief armistice in this war I brought her home for the weekend. To my surprise—dare I say to my disappointment?—my father made himself the soul of cordiality, putting her at ease, solicitous of her at every turn. He spoke knowledgeably and without malice of Mexican politics, coined little witticisms to make her laugh. Several times she shot a puzzled glance at me, wondering why I had said such awful things about this sweet man. I could see my loss of esteem in her eye and knew my father had deliberately maneuvered me into this corner.

Mother, ever sensitive to the conflicts between father and me, beamed at his good behavior. I wanted to shout, "He's taking you in, too!" but I was too well bred to make a scene.

One morning during her visit, my brother Eliot and I drove into the city to pick up a suit he'd had made. When we returned I could hear Luz and my father talking in his study. As my brother and I passed by his door she came out. When she saw me she quickly turned her head away in a manner that made my heart clench.

Later, she wouldn't tell me what he had said to her, only that he held strong opinions and that she admired such qualities in a man. She told me he was quite different from the man I'd described. I tried to tell her it was all a smokescreen. The more I protested, the more I could see her recede from me.

At the end of the quarter she left school without warning and went home, saying only something about her mother falling ill.

My father had bought her off. He didn't need to tell me.

It was her betrayal, not his, that tormented me, the confirmation that he had been right about her from the beginning, and I had, all along, been a dunce.

He had offered her money and she had taken it. The squalidness cut like a knife. So I decided to do him one better. Both of us would take his money. If she was craven enough to accept her share, I was angry enough to steal mine, shake from my feet the dust of my father's home and leave.

Easiest thing in the world—or should have been. One morning I went into his study when he wasn't there and got out the checkbook he used for paying the help and other home expenses. Yeah, very old fashioned of him. He liked that the cooks and the maid and the gardeners and his driver had to come to him for their pay. They'd line up and he'd hand them their checks like an Old Testament patriarch. The good side of this was that it made it easy to get hold of some of his money. I simply wrote a check made out to myself and signed his name.

Life turns on small mistakes. I'd thought my father had gone into his office in the city that morning. I was wrong.

"What do you think you're doing?"

With a jolt that nearly made my heart stop, I looked up to see him standing in the doorway. A man who prided himself on his acquired aura of good-breeding—he was in truth a steamfitter's son—he didn't wish to show his loss of composure. But his foot tapped on the parquet like a machine gun.

As much as he loved his money, saw it as an extension of himself, validating who he was, I think his anger came less from me dipping into his accounts than from the fact that I would dare to sit in his chair. No one took his place.

"None of your business what I'm doing," I told him.

"It most certainly is. Get out from behind my desk."

His little white mustache quivered as he spoke.

I couldn't help but laugh. And that's what did it. He can't stand anyone laughing at him.

Quicker than I thought the old guy could move, he came across the room, grabbed me by the collar and tried to yank me out of his chair. I pushed him away and stood up. He snatched the check out of my hand and saw my name on it.

"How dare you," he said, like the villain in a melodrama. "If I decide you need money, I will be the one to write the check. And you'll take whatever I choose to give you."

"And keep me on your leash? No, I'm sick of it. Go ahead and sit in your damned chair and play the great man, but I've had it. You're not God. You're just a selfish old man."

He slapped me. What happened next came from reflex, and a lifetime of pent-up fury.

I punched him in the jaw, a short, cramped punch without much on it, but he reeled backwards and had to grab at his chair to keep from falling. He shook his head, tried to regain his bearings. I can't say which of us was more astonished.

Then he grabbed a gold paperweight, given to him by some Central American autocrat and raised it high, ready to crack me in the head with it. I could have backed away.

He was in no shape to come after me, but I hit him again, hard this time.

His eyes rolled up in his head and he fell like a chimney going over, hitting his head against the corner of the desk as he went down. He landed on the floor, eyes still open, only the whites showing, blood coming from his mouth and from where he'd hit his head against the desk.

A surge of vindication coursed through me, flushed immediately from me by a cold wash of absolute terror and, hidden in the shadow of my resentment and anger, a baffling surge of love and pity that nearly knocked me over.

I shouted, "Dad!" but he didn't respond, only stared sightlessly toward the ceiling, blood from the back of his head pooling on the floor. I picked up the phone that he used for the servants and called down to the kitchen. I told them, "Father's fallen in his study. I think he's had a stroke. He needs help."

I froze, overwhelmed with the certainty I'd killed him. Sweat popping out on my face, I stared down at the man I told myself I hated, half realizing that he'd made me despise myself for not standing up to him. Until now.

As the enormity of what I'd done sank in, a groan escaped from deep in my father's chest and he struggled like a crushed bug, trying to get to his feet. I don't know what scared me more, thinking he was dead or watching him resurrect himself. His unfocused gaze lighted on me and I saw, like the form of shark coming up from a great depth, the formation of a deep fury animating him, bringing him back to life.

The sound of footsteps came pounding up from the back of the house.

Panicked, I ran upstairs and got my passport, threw a few things in a suitcase and ran out a side door toward the garage. I took a car and drove like hell for our bank in Rhinebeck.

There, I presented the check and asked for the money in cash. When you're from a family like mine no one asks many questions about waiting for the check to clear. All smiles, the manager approved the transaction and personally handed over a couple of stacks of hundred dollar bills. He even shook my hand. Pushed by my barely-controlled hysteria, I nearly broke his hand and ran out the door.

Outside, I got on my phone and booked a first-class seat to Amsterdam for that night. I knew that in my rush I was leaving an easy trail to follow, but I was hoping it would take a while for anyone to piece things together, and by then I would have disappeared.

Still, when I landed I half-expected the police to arrest me at the gate. But there was no one waiting for me. I went through customs like anyone else and lied about how much cash I had on me. Almost no one actually checks that kind of thing. Within a few minutes I was out on the street and on the run. And all my running had brought me to a place from which I couldn't run anymore.

Yes, Dilip had held a lot back from me when he talked about his life in Marseille. And I'd held a lot back from him. We shared blood guilt, of greatly differing kinds but nevertheless there, and neither of us had been able to confess it to the other. I'd even made him think I'd spent Father's money out of a generous spirit, trying to get my karma straight. In fact, I was more like Lady Macbeth, trying to wash the blood from my hands. Eventually I'd gotten rid of the money but, as she found out, blood isn't so easily washed away.

Yet I'd achieved an odd sort of liberation. Throughout my life I'd wanted to be free of the family's money, find out who I was when I didn't have daddy's fortune to lean on. Now I had what I wanted. And I didn't know what to do next.

A real paradox, guilt and freedom, freedom and guilt. Maybe it's always like that. One comes with the other. It's a shame I'm not in school anymore. I could write a hell of a term paper on the subject. Anyway, for the first time in my life I had liberated myself straight into problems I couldn't buy my way out of.

"Kip!"

I jumped at the sound of Molly's voice calling down the open hatch.

"Yeah?"

"You need to come up. Diane wants you to serve at dinner."

"Wants me to *what*?"

"Come on. It's almost ready."

"Me?"

But she had already walked away.

14

The Ugly *Paisan*, Spilled Wine, and a New Bond

"DON'T YOU HAVE A BETTER SHIRT?"

I didn't tell Diane the shirt had cost two-hundred dollars before I'd worn it so thin you could read through it.

She turned to Molly. "Go ask Dilip for the white shirt I bought him in Paris. They're close enough in size."

Between anxious glances up the passageway, Diane gave me a rundown on the need to keep a white napkin over one arm, which side to serve from and which side to take away, apparently assuming I'd never eaten in a restaurant where the food didn't come with a plastic spoon. I rolled my eyes, wanting her to know I wasn't some rube, and let it slip out. "My family tips more than most families spend on food in a week."

It was a stupid thing to say and, given my appearance, I can't imagine why Diane would have believed me. Yet, she stopped and looked at me, perhaps sensing some truth behind my exaggeration.

People who serve the wealthy, as Diane and her crew did, can be the biggest snobs of all, and now she suddenly wasn't sure which caste I belonged to—rich kid or criminal on the run. It didn't occur to her that I might be both.

Molly returned with Dilip's shirt and Diane tied a chef's apron around me to disguise the way it billowed around me.

"All right, Mr. Rothschild," Diane murmured, "keep the wine glasses full and the dirty dishes cleared. Don't speak unless spoken to, and then only 'yes, sir' or 'no, sir.' Is that clear?"

"Why do you want someone to serve dinner all of a sudden? Why can't Molly do it?"

"It's his idea, not mine. And he doesn't want 'someone,' he wants you. Don't ask me why."

While I digested this disturbing news, a door opened in the passageway and Carbonne's voice growled at Brigitte, "*Vien ici.*" Come here. Said like a man calling a dog.

As always, Carbonne entered like a king, but a king with a lot on his mind, all of it unwelcome. Brigitte, pale and anxious, came in behind him, her hands clasped in front of her, her eyes cast down except to flick a furtive glance in my direction.

The big man took his seat at the head of the table. Dusk had fallen and Molly had lighted the two tall candles on the dining table. The soft light should have given the room a romantic glow, but in the wavering flames Carbonne's shadow danced against the walls like something out of a bad dream. Was it my imagination that made Brigitte's shadow flicker like a light about to go out?

Diane took her place across from Brigitte, her eyes darting between Carbonne and the younger girl as if she couldn't bear to look at either of them yet didn't know how to look away.

I brought the wine to the table.

"Ah, Skip, *mon vieux!*"

Carbonne threw his arms out in badly overplayed greeting. Behind his smile his eyes were flat and deadly. He knew my name, but took pleasure in acting as if he didn't, that I was too unimportant to remember. At that moment I wished I were anywhere in the world but on this boat being crowded by Marius Carbonne.

After I'd poured wine for Diane and Brigitte, I came around the table to Carbonne. He looked up at me with a smile that was all gleaming teeth and narrowed eyes, and spoke to me with a dangerous familiarity. "Serge tells me you're quite a guy. He's liked you."

Funny way to say it, implying that whatever fondness he'd had for me was a thing of the past.

Carbonne waved for the wine. "Serge's good opinion, that's a rare thing, my friend. You should be honored."

So why was I so uneasy?

While I poured Carbonne's glass, I glanced at Diane, hoping to find in her face some indication of what was going on. But she sat frozen, looking like a thoroughbred caught in a barn fire. I put the wine bottle back on the counter and waited to take a bowl of soup from Molly.

Behind me, Carbonne, with a bonhomie that rang as false as a cracked bell, addressed the two women. "Don't you two think he's quite a guy, our Skip? Yes? No? What's wrong, that you can't say anything? Brigitte, I'm sure you, of all of us, think he's an impressive young man, don't you?"

On the other side of the counter, Molly tried to act like everything was fine, but her hands shook as she handed me the soup. Under her breath I heard her whisper, "Fack."

Diane and Brigitte remained silent.

Carbonne blew out a breath. "Have you two forgotten how to talk. What's wrong? It's been an enjoyable week hasn't it? Yes? No?"

Diane made a smile. "It's been a long week, Marius. You know the police came."

Like a man batting at a mosquito, Carbonne waved his arm and scoffed. "The police. *Bof!* Don't worry about the police. They won't be back. That's been taken care of."

The mafioso caught the look between Diane and Brigitte.

"What? You don't think I can fix things like that anymore? You think I'm getting old?" An edge of menace colored his voice, but it quickly gave way to one of his phony expansive smiles. "So," he asked Diane, "has my girl behaved herself this week? Shall I take her home with me?"

He drew a finger under Brigitte's chin. She snapped her head back, then smiled to cover her reaction.

"She's been charming," Diane told him before adding. "But it's been hard on me financially, cancelling two parties of guests. So, yes, take her back home—if you feel that's what you want to do."

She and Carbonne sounded like divorced parents discussing custody arrangements. Carbonne put two fingers to his mouth and let out an ear-splitting whistle. "Paul!"

We could hear Paul throw open his door and slam it shut behind him. He stuck his head into the dining room. "Oui, patron?"

"There's a package in my room. On the side table. Get it."

Paul smiled, nodded—did everything but wag his tail and piddle on the floor, "*Oui, patron.*"

A moment later he reappeared carrying a package wrapped in brown paper and secured with a heavy rubber band. He set it down on the table next to Carbonne.

Humming to himself, Carbonne removed the rubber band, opened the package and retrieved two stacks of two-hundred euro notes. He pushed them toward Diane. "For your troubles, my love."

Whatever the tension around the table, Diane's sigh of gratitude rang true.

Pleased at her reaction, Carbonne spread his arms wide. "These are little things I like to do. Help my friends. I know where I came from. I was a poor boy. At heart, I'm still a *paisan* like Serge and Paul. Just a country boy." He looked at Paul. "Right?"

Paul said, "Sure thing, Boss."

"There. You see? Just a regular guy."

His young thug smiled at having made the right reply and *salaamed* his way out of the room.

Carbonne's mercurial moods made us all feel we were living inside a ticking bomb, but the rest of the dinner passed smoothly. The napkin didn't fall off my arm, I didn't pass wind, and I didn't spill the soup in anyone's lap, however attractive the thought.

Still, every time I came around the table—serving the main course, the salad, the cheese—I felt Carbonne's eyes on me, the watch spring of his foul temper winding tighter and tighter while he overpraised my service and repeated his certainty about my upstanding character, each word carrying an ugly wad of menace.

A wave of fear rolled through me. If, as Dilip had warned me, Serge and Paul knew of Brigitte's visits to my bed, and one of them had told Carbonne, she and I might both end up dead.

Carbonne picked up his table knife and tapped Brigitte sharply on the hand.

"What do you think, my little cauliflower? Is Serge right? Is Skip quite a guy? Are you *impressed* with him?"

She rubbed her hand where Carbonne had hit her, her eyes seeking a place where she wouldn't have to look at any of us, but there was no such place.

"I haven't thought about it."

The sinister tone of his laugh made my heart drop to my socks. "Maybe you should, eh?" He pointed the tip of his knife toward me as if judging the distance to my chest. "Actually, he doesn't look like much, does he? And I don't think he's very bright. But Serge, well, Serge says he's quite a guy." His eyes fell on me, shrewd, assessing. "And I'll bet he's not just some *paisan*, like me. No, he thinks he's something special. Maybe he is. Are you something special, Skip?"

I set out the dessert plates, trying to keep my hands from shaking from equal measures of anger and fear.

"I wouldn't know."

Carbonne chuckled like a dog growling and looked at the two women. "He wouldn't know. Didn't I tell you he wasn't very bright?" Enjoying himself as he played to Diane and Brigitte, he asked, "What does your father do, Skip?"

Not my favorite topic. But I remembered what Brigitte said about how Carbonne yearned to be a real businessman, and told him, "My family owns two shipbuilding companies," aiming it at him like an arrow.

Idiot that I was, I wanted to show him up, make him angry. What I got instead surprised me. For an instant Carbonne's face went blank before sagging into the expression of a little boy made to feel small, a little boy with his nose pressed to the window of a party to which he wasn't invited.

His voice sounded hollow and I could barely hear him say to me, "You're lying."

The temperature in the room dropped ten degrees. Blinking in the thick silence, Diane managed a smile and put her hand on his. "He's joking with you, Marius. He's just making a little joke. Why would he be working on my boat if he were a rich man's son?" But she had to be thinking of the crack I'd made about my family's wealth. Her sidelong look made me understand she was now inclined to believe me. And she had to be puzzling over the same question she had asked of Carbonne. What was I doing here?

It was a little pathetic how Diane's pat on the hand appeared to reassure Carbonne. She might as well have patted him on the head like a mother to her frightened boy. Who would have thought this mafioso kingpin could so easily have the props knocked out from under him, simply because my daddy had money? But Brigitte had told me how his insecurity ate at him, and how his insecurity about coming up short in the eyes of the legitimate world was what made him dangerous.

Laboring to recover the tough façade he'd maintained only moments earlier, he again rapped Brigitte's hand with his knife, harder this time, and choked out, "You say you haven't thought about it? About what a treasure we have in Skip. Think about it now and tell me."

She said nothing.

His tone grew hard. "Tell me."

"Marius, leave the girl alone!"

Diane looked more surprised than Carbonne at her own outburst. Brigitte's face went blank in astonishment. For an instant the two women regarded each other without the wall of malice they had erected between them.

Were they aware of Carbonne studying them? It was he who benefited from their animosity toward each other and who least wanted that wall to come down—and he who most needed to feel in charge.

The meal neared its end. Carbonne seemed to have recovered his *amour propre*. He leaned back in his chair with a show of satisfaction and threw his napkin on the table like the guy waving the checkered flag at the end of a brutal endurance race.

I cleared the table and began to breathe normally for the first time since they'd sat down. But as I handed the plates to Molly, the big man said with false amiability, "What are you doing, Skip? Can't you see my glass is empty? No, don't look at Diane. Come, fill my glass." With every word his voice took on a sharper edge, cutting deeper into the thick layer of menace built up during the dinner. "Don't stand there like an imbecile."

As I tilted the bottle over his glass he clamped my forearm in his hand.

Feeling my self-restraint giving way, I grunted in the back of my throat.

Diane looked at me sharply, her eyes pleading with me to maintain my control.

So I kept quiet and gave him a generous pour. When I tried to step away, though, Carbonne kept his grip on my arm. Unable to withdraw my hand, the wine continued to pour.

"No, Skip, don't be stingy. Fill it up."

He looked me in the eye as the wine spilled over the lip of his glass, running down the stem, puddling across the table.

"You oaf! Look what you're doing!" He shouted. In the next moment, his voice grew dangerously mild, though his grip on my arm was turning my hand numb. "I'm very disappointed in you, Skip."

The pool of wine spread across the table, dripping onto the floor, red as blood.

"Let go of me, you bastard," I said, abruptly twisting my wrist enough to escape his grip and set the bottle down on the table.

I looked into Carbonne's eyes and saw my death looking back at me.

Gripping his table knife as if he wanted to strangle it, he bit out each word. "The last man who called me that, I slit him from his chest to his prick."

Frightened for me, terrified for herself, Diane jumped from her chair and laid a hand on Carbonne's arm. "You were hurting him, *mon amour*. You don't know your own strength. You're so strong." She attempted a flirtatious laugh, but it sounded more like someone coughing up blood. "Look, he's apologizing."

Carbonne hadn't taken his eyes off me. "Is that what you're doing? Apologizing?"

I thought of the words I could throw in his face, bait him into a fight. But I said, "Sure."

I owed Diane that much.

Carbonne's ragged breathing, the heaving of his chest, slowly eased as he worked to regain his pose as the great man he wished to be, rather than the thug he was. For the span of two deep breaths his eyes remained fixed on mine, letting me know what he could have done, might still do.

"Fine," he said, his voice barely audible. Then, "Fine!" as if he had made up his mind about something.

I was still too angry to feel scared. That would come later.

Carbonne chuckled like a man enjoying the prospect of whatever happened to me next. "Serge was right. You're quite a guy. Kip."

With that, he threw his arms out, putting one around Diane's waist as she stood next to him, the other gripping Brigitte's shoulders. With a leering wink, he looked down the passageway toward the guest rooms. "Come, let us enjoy ourselves!"

It took a moment for Carbonne's invitation to register on Diane. When the words hit, she made a sickly grin, painful to watch.

"Why, Marius, it's not a good time for me. I ..." She whispered something in his ear.

He blew out a breath. "I don't care."

Diane wrenched a coy laugh out of herself. "Well, I do."

"Marius, it's not right."

Both Diane and Carbonne turned toward Brigitte. I couldn't tell which of them she'd most surprised by her words.

Carbonne glowered at the younger girl. "Shut up. She can speak for herself."

"She just did."

For a moment I thought he would strike her, his anger so clear. It had been a tough meal for the big guy and he had to work hard to maintain any appearance of equanimity, any impression that he was still in control. He looked at Diane and then Molly and then me and finally only grunted unhappily. "All right." He rose from his chair and grabbed Brigitte by the arm. "Come on. You'll have to make up for the both of you." He made an ugly laugh and pushed her down the passageway to their room, slamming the door behind them.

A wave of jealousy and rage pulsed through me, strong enough that I didn't see coming the punch that Diane aimed at my chest.

"What the hell were you trying to do?"

"I got tired of him pushing me around."

"Then you're tired of living. Do you understand how dangerous he is?"

At that moment I didn't care and she could see it.

"You can pretend all you want about being a rich boy from America, but I see nothing but some fool in raggedy clothes. No! Shut your mouth. I don't want to hear it. You may think getting yourself killed is your business, but I'm not going to let you ruin me at the same time. Everything you do reflects on me."

"I'm not willing to just take whatever abuse he wants to dish out. Maybe you are."

"Yes, I am! Because this boat is all I have, and he can take it away from me and leave me back on the street. All because of you."

I looked at Molly, who glared back at me, her anger at me clear enough that she didn't need to say anything. I thought of her dream of a little restaurant in a quiet town, thought of what Dilip had said about all of us running from the lives we wanted to live—me perhaps most of all, because I'd never known what I wanted except to make my father unhappy, which I'd begun to understand was not much of a life ambition.

"You two stuck up for each other," I said.

She tossed her head in annoyance. "What?"

"You and Brigitte. You protected each other."

"You're mistaken," she said without conviction.

"I heard you. First you, then her, and—"

"Then you heard a pair of fools. That's all."

"She says he'll kill her in the end."

I expected a nasty comeback about how Brigitte had known what she was getting herself into.

Instead, she looked toward their room. "He'd never ..." But her assurance failed her and she stared down the dark passageway a long time before saying to me, "Get out."

※

I climbed onto the deck above the main cabin and waited for Molly to appear for her nightly smoke.

I didn't have long to wait. She came up on deck, saw me and stopped. For a moment we regarded each other along the span of the deck. Then she turned and walked away.

As discussions go, it was short and eloquent, telling me everything I needed to know about my status on the boat.

I considered drawing a refreshing bath of self-pity. But who was finally at fault? I'd allowed Gallagher—that crapulous Irishman!—to hoodwink me into taking a job that could only lead to trouble. And, whatever my excuses, I had freely chosen to stay. Now I lived a life that played out like a ghastly parody of everything I'd known before. Of the crew, my only real friend was a homicidal monk. My boss, Diane, tried every day to drink herself into oblivion in order to forget that she owed everything to a murderous crime lord. And the girl I loved was, in her own eyes, nothing but a gilded courtesan.

I felt a great yearning to save Brigitte from these people, this life. Yet, if Dilip was right, if Serge, and now Carbonne, knew of Brigitte's visits to my bed, I'd have my hands plenty full just trying to save myself.

With these disturbing thoughts spinning through my head, I slid down onto the bow deck—and felt my heart contract into a piece of coal.

Standing motionless in the faint moonlight, Carbonne's driver looked like he'd spent the evening waiting for me to appear, though I swear he hadn't been there when I went up to talk to Molly.

"What do you want?" I asked him.

Moonlight surrounding him like a sinister halo, he shifted his feet, cocked his head to one side and continued to stare at me stone-faced, the Buster Keaton of gangsters.

I was suddenly grateful Molly had refused to speak to me. No doubt we would both have said things the little bastard could take back to Carbonne. On the other hand, what could I say that would land me in deeper trouble than I was in already?

Naturally, given my talent for taking any hole I've fallen into and digging it deeper, I decided to share my reflections with this little creep.

"Not much point spying on me. It's a small boat. You know where to find me. And if you want to know what I'm thinking, just ask."

He thrust his hands in his pockets, turned his head to one side and spit into the canal. He favored me with one more narrow-eyed scowl then scuttled down to his berth like a cockroach.

I looked down the open hatch into the dark hole of my own berth—yeah, it was about six feet deep—and swallowed hard before climbing down and going to bed.

15

"By God, I Will Kill You"

I WOKE TO A SCREAM.

I shot upright in my berth, holding my breath, straining to hear. Nothing but silence. Baffled, I wrote off the cry as nothing more than a dream or a distant train whistle and lay back down.

The second scream, very close and very loud, ended with the smack of a blow. I jumped from my bed and clambered up the ladder wearing nothing but the t-shirt and shorts I'd worn to bed.

A light came on in Paul's room, shining around the edges of his closed door.

From where I stood, near the bow, I heard a guttural voice come from the main cabin, words unclear, then Brigitte shouting, "No!" followed by the sound of her bedroom door being thrown open and Carbonne's voice, clearer now, "*Putain!*" Whore! followed by the grunting and thrashing of a struggle.

Paul opened his door, the light spilling out, revealing Carbonne and Brigitte wrestling in the passageway.

Not wanting to take the time to run the length of the cabin and come in through the galley, I crossed the bow to the main cabin, pried open one of the saloon windows and jumped in.

Paul heard me land on the deck of the saloon. Gun in hand, he crossed to the doorway to block my way.

The sight of his gun only made me angry. I ran straight at him and put a shoulder into his chest that sent him flying. My shoulder would hurt for days, and I managed to trip over him as I tried to reach Brigitte but, migod, it was satisfying.

By the time I got to my feet a light had come on in the galley followed by the sight of Diane standing at the end of the passageway, her face distorted by anger and drink. I supposed she had come to plead with Carbonne, tell him not to hurt Brigitte, or even, in her bitterness, tell Brigitte to straighten up and take her medicine. But the time for talking had passed. In her hand she held Dilip's pistol, aimed at Carbonne's chest.

"Leave her alone, Marius! Leave her alone or, by God, I will kill you!"

Carbonne shouted back, "Get out of here, or I'll take care of you, too!" and took a wild swing at her that missed by a couple of feet.

The sound of the shot filled the narrow passage like a bomb.

I doubt that Diane could ever have managed to align her fear and rage with the barrel of the gun long enough to shoot him. In any case, it didn't matter, as Dilip had come up behind her an instant before she pulled the trigger and deflected her arm upward, sending the bullet into the ceiling tiles, which disintegrated in an explosion of dust and chaff.

Carbonne froze in astonishment, struggling to grasp the fact that Diane would try to shoot him. Until that moment he may have actually thought she half-believed the terms of endearment she showered on him, as he perhaps half-believed his own. Confronted with her hatred, a corner of his world crashed down with the ceiling tiles.

While Carbonne gaped at Diane, Brigitte took the opportunity to bring her raised fist down on his ear. The great *capo* jumped away, yelping in pain.

I might have indulged a suicidal impulse to laugh, but at that moment a blow from behind knocked me against the side of the passageway as Paul rushed past to shove Carbonne back into his room, out of the line of fire. Blocking the doorway, he spun around and raised his gun, pointing it first at Diane then Brigitte then, lingeringly, on me.

But the fight was already over. Dilip had wrestled the gun from Diane's hand, just as he had that evening in her room. In the same moment that Dilip spoiled her shot Serge came out of his room and threw a bear-hug around her, pinning her arms to her sides. Her legs buckled and only his grip on her kept her from falling.

Sobbing, she repeated, "No, no, no," as if her words might somehow rewind the present back to a better past. To the days she lived across the hall from Dilip?

Dilip put his hand on the barrel of Paul's pistol and pushed it aside. "Put your gun away."

Paul looked to Serge, who told him, "Do what he says."

Everyone took a deep breath.

Carbonne had fallen back on the bed when Paul pushed him into his room. Now he rose and walked unsteadily to the doorway.

"Get out of my way," he said, shoving Paul aside.

Whatever his gruff words and forceful-seeming gesture, Carbonne appeared old and shaken, his face red, his cheek scratched by Brigitte's nails. Absently, his mouth hanging open, he licked his lips and looked at the scene around him. He had to be reflecting on what would have happened if Dilip hadn't interfered with Diane's aim.

When his eyes lighted on Brigitte, he grabbed her by the arm and yanked her past him into their room. For the second time that night, he glared at me in a way that made me feel he was looking down into my grave. Still, I couldn't get rid of the thought that if I blew on him hard enough the great Mafia chief would fall over.

Perhaps he saw in our eyes how he appeared because he stood up straight, striking a pathetic imitation of his Sun King persona. It didn't last. Lost and depressed, he turned to Serge and gave him a weary lift of his chin.

Serge pushed Diane toward Dilip. "Everyone out."

As Dilip led her away, Diane threw a last despairing glance toward Carbonne. "Leave her alone, Marius. *Mon amour*? Please, for me, don't harm her any more than you've already done."

Carbonne snorted and turned away.

Molly, who had run in from her room to see what was going on, followed Diane and Dilip out. Carbonne, back bent and head thrust forward like an old man, shut the door behind him. I might have feared for Brigitte, but for the moment I was sure she was more than his match.

Serge waved Paul back to his room. "You heard the boss. Go back to bed." As he passed, Paul took the opportunity to slug me in the side of the head, but in the cramped space he could only manage a glancing blow, knocking me against the side of the passageway instead of onto the deck. Lucky me.

Serge snickered at Paul's ineptitude, then turned serious. "You too, *con*."

It was only one more measure of my cluelessness that I felt hurt he would use this most vulgar of French terms on me. But when I turned to go back to my berth, I saw it wasn't directed at me but at Carbonne's driver, who stood in the doorway of the saloon, his gun trained on me.

The little thug considered Serge's order, then shrugged and went out through the open saloon window by which we'd both entered.

Serge stood in the passageway and shook his head at me. "You're a fool, *mon vieux*. You know that, yes?"

He seemed to be talking about more than my running in to save Brigitte, but I asked, "What was I supposed to do?"

Like a saint praying for patience, he raised his eyes to what was left of the ceiling.

"Stop thinking with your dick. You think you can trust her? You think she's not just looking out for herself?"

Every nerve in me told me he was wrong, but I couldn't think of a reply that wouldn't make me sound like a love-struck schoolboy.

He spat on the floor. "You had your chance, you know."

"What do you mean?"

"You could have been one of us. But you fucked it up."

Was I more shaken that someone like Serge thought I might want to be a gangster, or by the fact that for a vanishing moment the idea held its appeal? For an instant I entertained the seductive notion of living outside all the rules, being a killer and a thief, like everyone else on board.

"But you fucked it up," Serge repeated.

He spoke with regret, but I was grateful for the reprieve. Whatever my crimes, I would not be one of them.

16

Exit Carbonne, I Fight for My Life

A FRANTIC TAPPING above my berth jolted me awake the next morning. Wondering what the inarticulate Morse Code on my hatch would bring me this time, I stumbled out of bed to find Brigitte kneeling on the deck above me, her hands trembling.

"He's gone!" she said.

"What? Who's gone?"

"Marius. He left while I was asleep."

I climbed up a couple of rungs and saw that the space near the towpath where the Mercedes had been parked stood empty.

"He's gone with his driver," Brigitte said. "And everyone else is still here."

"Good riddance," I said.

Though Carbonne had come with the intent of taking Brigitte and his henchmen back to Marseille, he had apparently changed his mind and left them all behind. With Serge and Paul still on board, I felt like a prisoner whose parole has been denied. Still, I couldn't understand her panic.

Brigitte rapped her knuckles on the deck in frustration. "You don't understand," she hissed.

"Okay, he's left. I still don't see why you're—" It hit me. When she explained to me how she had ended up out of Carbonne's favor, she mentioned that he disappeared whenever he ordered his men to commit a crime—like killing someone.

"Jesus."

"Kip, you've got to get me out of here. And you have to leave, too. He will never forget what happened last night, how we made him look weak. He can stand anything but that."

I breathed open-mouthed, trying to take it all in.

"Where would we go?" I asked. "We're broke."

She looked over her shoulder toward the taxi. "Do you have enough gas to get us to Paris?"

This was no moment to quibble over the difference between gas and diesel.

"I'm not sure. Maybe. But what would we do once we get there?"

"I have friends in Paris. They have money. But we have to go. Now. While everyone's still asleep. You've got the keys?" At the sound of footsteps in the passageway she turned and looked over her shoulder. "*Zut!*"

Through a porthole in the main cabin, we saw Serge coming out of his room, heading for the galley.

"Ah, too late! Too late!" she cried. "I have to go."

"Wait!" I whispered. "Listen, I'll think of something. We'll talk this evening."

"We don't have that much time." Panting with fear, she crawled back into the cabin through the saloon window.

※

The boat came awake slowly, all of us preoccupied and anxious after the previous night's mayhem. Coffee mug steaming in his hand, Dilip opened the hatch on the well deck and tinkered with the engine. Molly rattled pans in the kitchen, preparing breakfast. Diane was nowhere in sight.

Trying to look casual, I ambled into the galley and nodded to Serge, who sat at the table with his coffee. No "*mon vieux*" this morning. No wink and a smile. Only a cold, wordless regard over the top of his coffee mug.

Molly stood at the sink, her back to me. "I'll go get some bread," I told her.

Without turning around, Molly bit off, "Do whatever you want."

My mind resisted thinking things were as bad as Brigitte insisted. Despite their faults, their crimes, these people had become my world. I belonged, not because of my name or the family wealth, but simply for being part of the crew. All this would somehow blow over. Still, it helped to have the keys in my pocket.

"We don't need any bread this morning." Serge poked his knife at the bit of baguette on the table. "We'll make do with yesterday's."

Molly cocked her head in surprise. More than anyone else on board, Serge insisted on having his bread fresh. After Brigitte's warnings and the fight the night before, after Carbonne's abrupt departure, it was Serge's claim that he didn't want fresh bread that brought home to me the danger we were in.

※

The rest of the day passed in near silence, everyone walking quietly, speaking in whispers, as if someone very close lay deathly ill. I hoped my instinct was right, that Serge and Paul wouldn't do anything to us in broad daylight.

I looked for a chance to speak to Brigitte but couldn't find her. I couldn't think she was trying to avoid me, but wherever I was, that's where she wasn't.

At lunchtime I made my own sandwich while Molly gave me the silent treatment. I retreated to the crew galley, where I tried to talk to Dilip. He gave me a thin-lipped, "Later," and disappeared into Diane's cabin.

Late in the morning, I finally found Brigitte, bundled in a deck chair on the upper deck, a blanket wrapped around her, covering everything but her eyes, which stared anxiously into space, giving no sign she saw me. Serge's insidious question came back to me, asking me why I thought I could trust her. I wanted to say I simply knew that she loved me as I loved her. But his corrosive words ate at me.

✕

Late that afternoon a cold north wind came up, pushing dark clouds before it, turning the day dim as dusk.

Under towers of advancing clouds, evening settled early over the canal. I saw through my hatch that the lights had come on in the saloon. Of all of us on the boat, only Brigitte spent any time there.

Silently, I crept up the ladder, crossed the bit of deck and crouched near the tall windows of the saloon. Brigitte sat only inches away, a book in her lap. With the pads of my fingers, I tapped on the window. She jumped and spun around. I put my finger to my lips to keep her from yelping.

She looked down the passageway to make sure neither Paul nor Serge were near, then pushed the window open a hand's width.

"Kip, I'm so frightened."

"It'll be dark in a little while. Are you ready?"

She nodded, her eyes shining.

"I can jump to the bank from the bow. Can you do that? Otherwise they'll see us heading toward the plank."

"I think so."

"You'll have to. I'll get my backpack. Take a bag with whatever you'll need."

I looked through the gloom toward the towpath and the taxi. "The taxi's diesel motor makes a hell of a racket. Hopefully, we'll be gone before they can do anything about it. And without the car they can't follow us."

Footsteps sounded on the walkway that ran along the outside of the main cabin. Someone was coming toward the bow. Brigitte hurriedly closed the window while I jumped away.

A voice called, "Kip."

It was Molly.

"Yeah?" I fought to make my voice sound natural.

"Serge changed his mind. He wants you to go get some bread."

In my mind I had already leaped from the boat and taken off with Brigitte. It rattled me to be yanked back. "Now? It's dinner time. The bakeries have all closed."

"He says there's an *epicerie* near the bridge up ahead. They should have something left."

"It won't be fresh," I argued.

"He wants bread, so go get some bread." She started to walk away, then said. "And he wants the key to the car. He says you can take a bicycle."

"Why does he want the key? Is he going somewhere?"

"Give him the key and get going."

I slapped my pockets. "I've been looking for the key all afternoon. I think I dropped it somewhere in my room."

"Oh, for fack's sake. Just get the bike and go!" she said and retreated toward her galley to start dinner.

I fetched a baseball cap from my pack, grabbed the bread bag from the crew galley and wheeled one of the bikes from the aft deck down the plank.

The wind died and a heavy rain began to fall. As Molly would say, "Fack."

The thick clouds made the dusk as dim as night. The bike had no light, and once I got a few yards from the boat only the sound of the grit under the bike's tires assured me I was still on the towpath. I looked for the bridge Molly had mentioned but couldn't see much of anything through the rain. I put my head down and pedaled hard, the rain dripping from the bill of my cap.

Even if I'd been sitting up straight I doubt I would have seen the figure that came running out of the darkness. He hit me broadside, knocking me off the bike. I landed on my back in the grass, no more than a couple of feet from the edge of the canal, with the bike on top of me. My attacker leaped at me and landed on top of the bike.

It's true what they say about an adrenaline rush. Seized by a strength I'd never before possessed, I shoved the bike off my chest with him on it, rolled away and scrambled to my feet.

He came at me low, growling like a dog.

It's hard to dodge someone you can barely see. Though I tried to leap away, he managed to clip me with one arm and I slipped to my knees on the rain-slick grass. Before I could get up, he jumped on me and tried to roll me toward the canal.

With a cry that came from the pit of my gut, I threw him off and jumped to my feet, unsteady from fear and surprise, but strong with the determination to stay alive.

In the dark and the rain I could just make him out, circling for position. My hat had fallen off when he knocked me down and, with the rain in my eyes, everything appeared fractured and blurry.

I only now registered that when he had leaped on top of me I'd caught the smell of cheap cologne. Things came clear. This wasn't some random robber but Paul, and he'd been told to kill me.

With the speed of a fear-fueled mind I understood that he hadn't stabbed or shot me because he needed my death to look like an accident, that I'd somehow ridden into the canal in the dark and the rain, panicked in the eye-high water, and drowned. Not likely, but why would anyone think otherwise?

As we circled each other, his hesitancy lent me a dram of confidence. I wasn't as easy a mark as he'd thought. Still, he was an experienced fighter and, despite my martial arts classes in prep school, I was not. I had only the advantage of knowing I was fighting for my life.

While he tried to decide how best to tackle me, I had time to shake away the worst of my fear and think about what I had to do. I could see him more clearly now, maybe six, seven feet away, crouched low, his arms out to his sides.

When he ran at me again I was ready. Calling on the muscle memory of my old karate classes, I made a jump kick to his face. I missed my mark, but hit him in the throat. Better yet.

With a comic "oof!" he fell to the ground.

I would never have imagined that I would owe my life to his fear of water. The bank sloped here and he began to slip into the canal. With a horrified screech, he scrambled to his feet, spun around and backed away from the edge of the canal. I couldn't have asked for a better target. I kicked him in the back and he went down hard. He didn't, as I'd hoped, slip into the canal, but you can't have everything. Before he could do more than rise to one elbow, I leaped the short distance between us and kicked him again, this time in the side of the head. He collapsed on the grass and lay still. I only regretted I wasn't wearing heavier shoes.

Soaked by the rain and sweating with fear, I left the bike on the ground and ran for the lights of the *Celeste*, hoping to get there in time.

I thumped up the plank and ran through the galley toward Brigitte's room, pausing only long enough to shove Molly aside and grab the first weapon that came to hand, a mallet-like meat tenderizer. I was too deadly earnest to laugh at the absurdity.

Brigitte would owe her life, and I mine, to Serge's professional thoroughness. He had her face down on the floor, tying her hands behind her, a knee in her back, a gag already in her mouth.

He must have thought I was Paul coming back on board after killing that pesky American because he hardly looked up as I rushed through the open door. He only had time to register his surprise—did I catch a small smile of admiration?—as I whacked him in the side of the head with the meat tenderizer, breaking it in two from the force of the blow.

In the movies the bad guy immediately falls over when the good guy wallops him like that, but for several horrifying seconds Serge simply froze, his head and upper body tilted at an odd angle, as if posing for a statue. Just as I wondered if I should hit him again, though I held only the handle of the broken meat tenderizer, he slowly tipped over onto the floor unconscious, his eyes open but blank—like my father's when he'd fallen to the floor of the study.

I untied Brigitte's hands and removed the gag. She didn't cry or say my name, only held me tight.

I brought her to her feet and gently pulled her hands away.

"Come on. We've got to get out of here."

Worrying every moment that Serge would regain consciousness or Paul would recover enough to run back to the boat, I went out through the saloon window and down to my berth, grabbed some clothes and my notebook and stuffed them into my backpack.

I returned to Brigitte's room and found her standing with her back to the wall, her bag pressed to her chest, watching in horror as Serge's hands and feet twitched as if trying to figure out how to get up.

"Let's go." I grabbed her by the hand and ran for the galley.

And there we found Dilip standing in the door, blocking our way. I tried to read his face, looking for the killer or the priest, but his features betrayed nothing. For an eternity that lasted maybe five seconds we stared at each other across the galley.

"Is he dead?"

I shook my head, "No."

"And you think you're going to take the car and drive away."

I squared my shoulders and stood up straight. "Yes."

I wondered where his loyalties lay. Was I looking at my friend or at the gangster monk?

"Dilip, we need to get out of here. You know that."

He licked his lips and shook his head. "No."

"Dilip, we can't be here when Serge comes to."

"But you don't care what danger you're putting Diane in by leaving. Carbonne will blame everything on her."

"Better he should blame the incompetence of his two goons."

I saw a movement in the darkness behind Dilip. Diane stepped into the light spilling from the galley and stood in the doorway behind Dilip, a shawl over her head against the rain. Where I thought to find anger over our attempt to flee, I found only resignation. Perhaps she had always known things would end like this.

"You've stirred the hornet's nest," she sighed, "and now you run away to let us get stung."

"If we stay, they'll kill us." For some reason, I felt the need to add, "I'm sorry."

She shrugged. It didn't matter to her how I felt.

"I knew I should have never hired you." To Brigitte, she said. "Don't ever let him catch you." Then she turned to Dilip, "Let them go."

"No, Diane. Carbonne will—"

"Dilip, let them go."

"No! If they're gone, Carbonne will punish you for what they've done."

"Dilip, he's right, Marius will have them killed. I can't have their deaths on my conscience. As for me, I'll take my chances."

Dilip bit his lip in anxiety and frustration but didn't move.

We stood like this for some time, the rain pounding on the steel deck above us. It was heavy enough that he could later claim he hadn't heard me coming back on board after Paul attacked me, didn't hear the taxi start up or drive away. He would tell Molly to say she was in her room and didn't hear anything either.

He regarded Diane unhappily, then stepped out of the way.

I held Brigitte by the arm and we ran down the plank to the taxi and drove away in the rain.

17

We Leave the Floating World

WE DROVE FAST—and went nowhere. After weeks on the canal, our world had shrunk to the waterway's narrow bounds. Even as we tried to escape we only sped along the towpath, like a couple of lab rats unable to jump from their maze. Too anxious to speak, both of us looking over our shoulders through the rain, we jounced along the rutted track, gravel pinging against the bottom of the car, the old taxi's suspensions groaning at every bump.

We'd put several miles behind us before I eased my death grip on the wheel and began to breathe normally. Fighting the irrational fear compelling us forward—neither Serge nor Paul were in any condition to follow us, even if they'd had the means—I slowed the car to a stop.

Brigitte asked "What's wrong?"

"Nothing. There's no one behind us."

Reluctant to fully believe we had outrun our danger, at least for the moment, she gripped my arm and looked into the darkness behind us.

"It's okay," I told her. "We got away."

She turned back around, her face dimly lighted by the dashboard lights, and said quietly, "For now."

"For now."

"Marius won't allow us to escape."

"We don't need his permission." The lingering fear that twisted her smile testified to how much she remained in his thrall. "He'll come after us," I said, "but if we're lucky, and he's not, he won't get us."

She nodded, only half-believing. I didn't choose to tell her that I had in fact been running for months, pursued by the image of my father's sightless eyes, and by the man in the gray suit, trying to track me down. Dangerous as he was, Marius Carbonne was just one more guy in line.

For the span of a few breaths I listened to the rattling diesel and the pounding of the rain on the roof and took stock. The *Celeste* lay well behind us, though Serge or Paul or even Diane, might already be on the phone to Carbonne. Ahead of us ... My mind stopped, unable to picture what waited in front of us, but certain that we had to keep moving.

I put the car in gear and glanced at the dash. The fuel gauge trembled just above empty.

Ahead of us, a small stone bridge carried a country road across the canal. I drove up the towpath to where it intersected the road and stopped. Ahead of us lay further miles of the towpath that would keep us locked onto the canal, taking us nowhere we wanted to go. Behind us, the *Celeste* and death.

I eased down on the accelerator and turned onto the bridge. As if waking from a dream, I pressed harder on the pedal, then harder still, and I felt for the first time in weeks that we were truly escaping the gravity of the floating world in which we'd been living.

After perhaps twenty minutes we came into a small town with a filling station still open. Brigitte had no money, but

I still had most of the tip given to me a lifetime ago by the guests from New York.

While I filled up, Brigitte got out of the car and wandered along the pavement, looking down the road in the direction from which we'd come. The rain had slowed to a drizzle.

We had escaped the canal, but I feared we had also outrun something else. Freed of our forced intimacy, an emotional letdown left each of us looking at the other a little too clearly.

As I put the cap back on the tank Brigitte scuffed her way back toward the car. For some reason the grit of the pavement against the soles of her shoes irritated the nerve that connected my ear to my gut.

Peering into the darkness behind us and the darkness ahead, she asked, "Where do we go now?"

Her question surprised me.

"Didn't you say you had rich friends in Paris?"

Her eyes popped in surprise as if she'd forgotten about them. "Yes. I only meant ..." She seemed unable to identify what she meant.

Unsettled by her response, I asked, "How far are we from Paris?"

She looked away. "I don't know."

"What do you mean, you don't know?"

"I don't know where we are," she snapped.

I paid for the diesel, told Brigitte to get in the car and turned down the highway in a likely seeming direction.

A few kilometers down the road, a sign indicated we were driving toward Autun.

"Zut!" Brigitte slapped the dash in frustration.

"What?"

"We're going the wrong way."

"You're sure?"

"You have to turn around and go back."

The irritation in her voice set me on edge. "I thought you didn't know where we were."

"I only know we're going the wrong way."

I jerked the car into a u-turn. Brigitte braced herself against the dash at the violence of the turn and gave me a look.

"It's not like it's my fault," I told her. "This isn't my country."

"And you think I know every road and village in France?"

We sped down the highway in the direction we'd just come, both of us in a mood as dark as the road.

I couldn't help thinking that Serge and Paul should have done things the other way around. If Serge had been the one to jump me in the dark I'd be dead now, and so would Brigitte. But he'd said once he was too old to work outside in the rain. So he had left the outdoor work to Paul and we were still alive.

After passing through the village again, I asked her, "Where in Paris do your friends live?"

She looked at me, her face full of resentment, as if being held to a promise she didn't want to keep. "Place des Vosges. You know where it is?"

"Yeah."

They were the last words we exchanged until, a couple of hours later, we drove into Paris by the Porte d'Orleans.

✳

It was past midnight and the rain had stopped and traffic was light. Still, tooling up the Boulevard St. Michel in a

London taxi felt like driving a moving bullseye through the middle of Paris. In my worried state it seemed everyone we passed noted the car and its direction.

We crossed the Seine near the burned out hulk of Notre Dame and turned down the rue de Rivoli. A couple hundred yards beyond the Hotel de Ville, Brigitte told me to turn up a side street and park in front of a row of darkened shops.

She got out of the car and walked up the dark street. I followed.

We passed under a narrow arch and came into the Place des Vosges, a modest square centered on a green park edged by an iron fence, itself surrounded on all four sides by narrow streets. Above these streets rose tall and elegant brick-faced residences from the 17th century, once the homes of aristocrats, now broken up into apartments for the merely rich.

Brigitte led me into the cloister-like arcade that runs along three sides of the square. Our footsteps echoed within its low, vaulted ceiling as we hugged the row of shuttered shops and darkened restaurants facing on the park.

As we walked, Brigitte kept her eyes on the row of buildings on the opposite side of the square. At this hour, only a couple of lights still burned in the windows.

I leaned into her and asked, "Which one belongs to your—"

"Ssh!"

Backing deeper into the shadows, she pointed to a lighted window on the third floor of the building opposite us. At this angle I could see only the upper shelves of tall bookcases and the ornate plasterwork running along the edge of the ceiling. From where we stood in the cold, it looked warm and inviting.

"That's the one?"

She nodded.

"Okay." I took her arm and walked out from under the cover of the arcade.

Brigitte wrenched her arm free. "Stop!" She pulled me back into the cover of the arcade's pillars.

"What?"

The anguish in her face reminded me that, despite our long mutual confessions in my berth, I barely knew her, understood little of her life.

When she didn't speak, I said, "We can't stay out here all night." I took her arm, more gently this time, and led her across the dark square toward the building's entrance. For a long time she regarded the row of buttons with names written beside them before finally pressing the button next to the name Beaulieu.

I had started to think no one would answer when a woman's voice came out of the speaker next to the door. "Yes? Who is it?" she asked mildly, as if having someone ring her doorbell after midnight was the most common thing in the world.

Rather than answering, Brigitte looked at me with a strange pleading in her eyes. When I said nothing she turned back to the speaker. "It's me. Marie-Therese."

My mouth dropped as I tried to take in what I was hearing.

The voice asked, "Marie-Therese?"

Brigitte leaned into the speaker, her eyes fixed on me, searching for my reaction. "Marie-Therese Aubert."

Is it only in dreams that we see a familiar figure suddenly turn into someone else entirely? I stood back and looked at this stranger, bewildered, and a little frightened. I fought an impulse to go back to the car and drive away without her. But I had tied my fate to hers and would have to see it through.

Through the speaker came another voice, a man's, muffled, as if someone had put a hand over the receiver at the other end. After a short, sharp exchange, he asked, "What do you want?"

"I need to talk to you. I'm in trouble."

Again, an exchange of words at the other end, louder but still unintelligible.

"That is no affair of ours," he said. When Brigitte—for so I still thought of her—made no reply, the man added grudgingly, "I'm sorry."

Brigitte leaned into the speaker. "Please, Monsieur Beaulieu."

Unsure where to go, but convinced this was leading nowhere, I started to walk away, hoping she would follow.

At that moment a buzzer sounded and the door clicked open.

A broad, carpeted staircase led us past two other apartments—only one per floor, speaking to the wealth of the residents—until we came to the tall, elegantly carved wooden door on the third floor.

Brigitte—Marie-Therese?—knocked softly.

The door opened to reveal a short, fit, gray-haired man in dark slacks, a dress shirt and a silk cravat.

That impressed me. A silk cravat at midnight.

The unwelcoming look he laid on Brigitte grew deeper when he saw me standing behind her. He started to shut the door. Brigitte laid a hand on my arm. "No, please, Monsieur Beaulieu. He's my friend. He saved my life. He has no idea who you are."

The man's frown turned into white-lipped displeasure, but he stood away from the door and allowed us to enter, though no further than the foyer. The door remained open behind us to make clear how tentative was our welcome. Behind him stood a woman, also gray-haired, taller than her husband, in a simple, elegant blue dress.

"What is it you want?" the man asked, his tone making clear that, whatever it was, we weren't going to get it.

"I'm in trouble, Monsieur Beaulieu—Alain."

He huffed dismissively at the familiarity. "So you said." He nodded toward his wife. "We read the papers."

Brigitte asked, "The papers?"

I realized she hadn't seen a newspaper or a smartphone in a couple of weeks. She had no idea she had become notorious as the mafioso's missing girlfriend.

"Your photo is in the tabloids. They give you a different name, but we recognized you. 'Gangster's Mistress Missing' they say. I'm surprised to find you still alive." He didn't seem pleased about it.

"I don't know anything about the papers." She shook her head as she tried to take in this unsettling news. "I need your help."

Beaulieu raised his chin. "You chose your path. Andre made it clear that you left him behind to live your life on the arm of a criminal." He gestured toward his wife to make clear he was speaking for both of them. "What you are doing now is of no consequence to us. I let you in the door only for madam's sake."

In the silence that followed, his wife stepped closer to him and laid a hand on his arm. "Alain," she said softly.

Was she more sympathetic, or only concerned about maintaining an appearance of *noblesse oblige*? Whatever her intent, her husband turned to her and quietly spoke a few cross words in her ear. When he'd finished, she held his eyes. He huffed in exasperation, but asked Brigitte, "What do you want from us?"

"It's late. We've come a long way. We need a place to stay."

Beaulieu scoffed. "Be serious."

With a look toward us that we might take as apologetic, his wife again laid her hand on his arm. He looked down at her hand, and with a sigh regarded Brigitte again.

"I suppose you have no money."

Brigitte lowered her eyes and shook her head.

I'd never witnessed a conversation in which the parties so clearly wished not to be speaking to each other.

"And you are—how do you say?—on the run."

She nodded.

"I should call the police." But his tone said he wouldn't.

Expelling an unhappy breath, he picked up a wallet from a table next to the door, extracted three one-hundred euro notes and thrust them at Brigitte.

"Here."

Brigitte raised her head and, her voice failing, whispered, "Thank you, Monsieur Beaulieu." She looked at his wife. "Thank you, Chantal."

Beaulieu put his hand to the door.

"I have no more time for you."

We hardly had time to step out before he shut the door behind us.

Brigitte folded the money in her hand and ran down the staircase. Before she had reached the floor below she stopped, leaned against the wall, wrapped her arms around her head and wept, the tears streaming down her face.

I came down the steps and put my arms around her.

"Oh, Kip. I used to be a good girl. Really, I did."

With a deep shudder, she ran her sleeve across her face to dry her tears.

I leaned my head against hers. "Who are they?"

It took her some time to speak around the lump in her throat. "The parents of the boy who took me to Marseille."

"The one who brought you to that party, and watched you leave with Carbonne."

She looked up toward the Beaulieus' apartment with its warm lights, its tall bookcases, its silk cravats at midnight. "We used to be such good friends."

She thrust at me the euros Beaulieu had given her. "Here, you take it. I can't ..."

I stuffed the bills in my pocket, led her downstairs and onto the street.

It felt much colder than only a few minutes earlier, though the question of what we were to do next hit me harder than the cold. I nodded toward the iron-fenced park in the middle of the square. "We could curl up on a bench," I said, not sure if I was joking.

Brigitte managed a smile. "They lock it at dark."

I don't know what was funny about this, but we both laughed.

"I guess we can sleep in the car."

The force of her "No!" reminded me of the distinctive look of the taxi, and her fear we'd be spotted.

I tried to reassure her. "Carbonne's in Marseille. Hundreds of kilometers from here."

She looked around the darkened square. "There are people like Marius in every big city. They know each other, do favors—when they're not killing each other. He has contacts in Paris. With my picture in the paper, even the police are looking for us. And some of them work for him."

"You must have other friends in Paris. Someone."

"No. I'm not from here."

That took me by surprise. For some reason, I had always thought she was a Parisienne. I realized once more how little I knew her. I'd somehow assumed her family was of that circle of the monied and well-placed to which the Beaulieus clearly belonged. But Alain Beaulieu's patronizing tone, one I well recognized as the manner in which the wealthy spoke to their lessers, made me think otherwise, leaving me more lost than ever.

"Kip, you must know people here. You said you lived here."

"Only a couple of months. It was summer. I was in a cheap hotel. People came and went."

"There must be someone."

A thought occurred to me. I rejected it, tried to think of something else, and finally had to accept it.

"Come on," I said, and started toward the car.

"Where are we going?"

"Montmartre."

18

Arab Hospitality and the Judas Kiss

STEEP AND NARROW, the rue Muller ends in a long staircase leading up the eastern slope of the old artist's colony of Montmartre. On summer evenings guitar players stroll from one restaurant to another, serenading the diners at the outdoor tables, giving to the scene the atmosphere of a street fair. On a cold night in autumn the street is deserted and the wind whips along its empty sidewalks.

I parked like a Parisian, with two wheels on the sidewalk to keep from blocking the street—never mind about blocking the sidewalk—and led Brigitte to a wooden door scarred by time and neglect. I pressed the buzzer next to the names Sebti and Badaoui. Nothing. I pressed again, longer.

A man's sleepy voice croaked inquisitively.

I leaned into the speaker. "It's Kip Weston."

The silence grew so long I thought he'd gone back to bed.

"Who?"

"Kip Weston."

As at the Beaulieus' an hour earlier, we heard a second voice in the background and a rapid conversation, this time in Arabic. Its tone lacked the hostility of our greeting on the Place des Vosges, but made up for it with a larger factor of "What in the hell?"

Finally, the background voice laughed and said something that included the word "American," then shouted, "Keep! Yes, come up!"

Despite the good-natured wildness of the two Moroccans who'd been drinking with me on that fatal evening when Gallagher walked into the bar, I recalled in them vestiges of the old-fashioned propriety instilled by their upbringing.

"I've got a girl with me."

A pause, then, "*Mabrouk!*" Congratulations.

The buzzer sounded and I pushed the door open. In a hopeful gesture, I'd already grabbed my backpack from the car. Now I slung it over my shoulder and led Brigitte across the dismal foyer and up the worn treads of the wooden staircase leading to the fifth floor apartment.

Though, to my mind, I'd barely known them, Mohamed Sebti and Hassan Badaoui greeted me like a long-lost brother.

"You would like some tea," stated Hassan, the shorter and darker of the two.

Exhausted, wanting nothing but a place to sleep and a safe harbor, I could only smile and say thanks. After I'd made introductions, Mohamed, tall and hefty, with big arms and a soft belly, swept a hand toward the sagging sofa and insisted we sit.

"We are so glad you have come to visit."

There's nothing like Arab hospitality. No questions about why we had come or what we might ask of them, just Hassan bringing a tray of cookies and tea and expressions of gratitude for having awakened them in the middle of the night.

Only when we'd finished the cookies, had drunk a second cup of tea and happily given in to Hassan's insistence that we each take a bowl of soup, did Mohamed again thank us for coming and ask to what they owed the honor of our visit.

I told them we were in trouble.

"With the police?" Mohamed asked, betraying no concern, only curiosity.

"Worse."

The young Moroccans raised their eyebrows but asked for no explanation.

"Then you must stay with us," Mohamed said.

I glanced at Brigitte before saying to our hosts, "It's possible our presence could put you in danger."

Mohamed put his hand over his heart and made a slight bow. No matter.

Whatever their expressions of generosity, I knew the possibility of trouble had to worry them. As Arabs living in France, despised by half the population, their lives were already difficult enough. Any brush with trouble could lead to jail and swift deportation. But they refused to betray any concern.

It took us some effort to turn down the offer of their twin beds shoehorned into the apartment's single tiny bedroom. After a slight hesitation, Hassan adopted an air of indulgent sophistication, "You can push them together if you wish," though he couldn't look at me as he said it.

We persuaded them that we wouldn't hear of it. Brigitte would sleep on the sofa with a blanket and I would take a Moroccan sheepskin and the floor.

Though the chance that anyone was looking for us yet seemed remote, Brigitte insisted we couldn't put Sebti and Hassan at risk by leaving the London taxi in front of their place. So I went down to the street, moved the car to find an even smaller street a few blocks away and walked back.

It must have been two o'clock before our hosts told us they had to work in the morning—Mohamed, as I recalled, as a street sweeper, Hassan in a shawarma shop a few blocks away.

We turned off the lights and Brigitte settled on the couch under her wool blanket while I wrapped myself in the heavy sheepskin on the floor next to her. Though exhausted, we were too keyed up to sleep. Soon, the darkness grew weighted with words that needed saying. She shifted on the couch and looked down at me.

"I'm sorry I've put you in the middle of this."

"I did it with my eyes open." Not entirely true, but no point whining now.

"And I've involved your friends."

"They're not complaining." I let some time go by. "Marie-Therese?"

She made what sounded like a laugh. "Yes. A name like an Austrian princess."

"And Carbonne made you change it."

She turned over and lay on her back, looking up at the ceiling. "No. I wanted to make an impression on a powerful man. I told him my name was Brigitte. It sounded more like southern France. Sexier. The Beaulieus are right. Much more than you, I did it with my eyes open."

"And how do you think of yourself? Which name do you call yourself when you're alone?"

"Outside, it is Brigitte. Inside me, I'm still Marie-Therese. It's Brigitte you met and got you into trouble. You should keep that in mind."

I smiled.

"And you?" she asked. "How should I think of you? Diane was right. Kip is not a name."

"You don't want to know."

She rolled over on her side, looked down at me and waited.

I spit out the hated word. "Wilfred."

"What?"

"You heard me."

"Wilfred? Wilfred!"

She put her hand over her mouth to cover her laugh.

"It's not like I chose it."

"Wilfred!"

"Mother insisted," I pleaded. "She said the name's a family tradition. I told her, so's astigmatism, and I don't see any point in passing either of them along."

"Kip," she said, and repeated it more softly to restore the equilibrium between us. "What are we going to do?"

"We're safe here for a couple of days. Maybe Carbonne will stop looking for us. Maybe he's not looking for us at all."

I deserved the mocking snort I got.

"That day when we gave Paul the slip in that village," I said, "We should have done like you said. Run away and flown to Brazil."

"If we'd had the money I'd have done it." She rolled onto her back and looked at the ceiling. "That was the day we went to the church." I could hear her smile. "The day we walked up the aisle together."

In this darkness it was a happy memory. "Yes, the day we walked up the aisle together." I worked to form the next part. "The church ... That day when you dove into the canal, you told me you were ..."

"A spiritual being." It made us both shy to talk like this, and she spoke very quietly. "It's nothing I decided. It's something I realized. Marius considered me his property. A thing he owned. Like his cars, his mansion, his yacht. Every day I could feel myself becoming just that, a thing. He owned my body and he'd stolen my freedom and he wouldn't be happy until he'd stolen me from myself. But I decided, no, he couldn't own my spirit. I vowed I would not let it die. It was the only thing left to me, and I would not let him have it. He could do whatever he wanted to my body. Take it here, take it there. Fuck it. Even kill it. But he could not have my spirit. That belongs to me."

The power of her hushed voice carried the force of her words.

We lay in the dark for a long time, our faith in each other slowly recovering. Eventually, Brigitte needed to broach a subject we had stayed away from.

"I've told you so much, Kip, but you've never told me anything about the thing you're hiding from, the thing that makes you run. Who is the man who came looking for you on the boat?"

I wasn't sure I could tell her the truth, but my silence had become a form of lie, and the longer I refused to say anything the deeper the lie went. So I told her the whole story—my theft, the fight with my father, how I fled, and had been fleeing ever since. I told her of the guests from New York and how close they came to realizing I was the one they had read about in the papers back home.

For a long time Brigitte said nothing. When she finally spoke she went straight to the heart of it. "And the more we've run from what we've done—and what we've become—the faster we've run straight into evil. We can't get away because when we run that evil turns and comes after us."

"Dilip said the same thing, except that we carry the evil in us. That's why we can't get away."

"We aren't living the lives we want to live."

And how similar her words were to Molly's. Are there only a few simple ideas in this world to guide our lives, and we refuse to follow them?

"How do we get out of this mess?" I asked.

"I don't know, Kip. I'm so afraid it will catch us."

In the dark, I reached out and found her hand. We lay like that for a long time before falling asleep.

※

Mohamed and Hassan were gone by the time we woke, and we had their tiny apartment to ourselves. Throughout the long, slow day we dozed, made love on my sheepskin and lay naked in the sun coming through the window, our idyll made more precious by the danger we feared waited for us on the street.

In the afternoon we dared to run downstairs to a little grocery store, looking both ways as we crossed the street as if searching for a sniper, which, for all we knew, we were. After buying a few things we ran back, clutching our groceries to our chests.

Brigitte and I made dinner that night. We pulled the tiny table to the sofa because there weren't enough chairs for all of us. After Mohamed said a blessing over the meal, we enjoyed lamb chops and green beans and salad and shared a bottle of wine I'd picked up for cheap. Back during the summer they had both insisted nothing in the Koran expressly prohibited alcohol, and they now sipped modestly, with impish smiles, as they told stories of Morocco and their adventures as small boys. We told them of our uneventful day and I made fun of our daring dash across the street for groceries.

They both laughed, but Hassan said, "I kept my eye out this morning and this evening," squinting and swiveling his head to show how assiduously he had scoped things out, "and I can assure you, there is no one waiting in the streets for you."

We slept better that night.

※

The next day we woke in time to make coffee for our hosts and see them off to work, telling them we would again make dinner that night.

We had hardly shut the door behind them when Mohamed came bounding back up the steps and stuck his head in the apartment. "There is no one in the street looking for you. You are safe now," he said, inadvertently undercutting his message by adding the traditional "Inshallah." God willing.

It was a gracious gesture and he spoke with a smile, but when he'd shut the door behind him Brigitte said he was trying to tell us there was no need for us to stay longer. When I told her she was imagining it, she said, "We're putting them in danger."

Despite Mohamed's assurances, when I went back to the store later that morning I looked up and down the rue Muller before crossing to the little grocery store, and looked once more after I'd bought some dinner and got ready to run back.

Of course, like a lovesick teenager, I had to glance up toward the apartment, hoping to catch a glimpse of Brigitte at our window. As with most wishes, I was surprised when it came true. She stood, half hidden behind the curtain, looking down at the street. I started to wave but stopped. She wasn't looking at me. I tried to follow her gaze, but from where I stood, just inside the door of the grocery store, the angle wasn't right and all I could see was that she was looking somewhere off to my left, in the direction of the steps that led up to the top of Montmartre. She stood there for some time, then shook her head at something—someone?—and started to retreat from the window. As she did, she saw me standing in the doorway of the grocery looking up at her. Startled, she jumped back, but immediately recovered herself and smiled and waved. Yet her smile looked forced and her wave as wooden as a beauty queen's.

As I crossed the street I looked in the direction of the stairs but found only the empty street.

When I got up to the apartment Brigitte seemed distracted, repeatedly brushing her hair aside and speaking in half sentences. I put an arm around her, less to reassure her than myself. She didn't exactly throw it off, but made an awkward laugh and pulled away, then busied herself unpacking the groceries, keeping her back to me. I could see her hands shaking. I tried to read her face by looking through the back of her head, which, okay, would make anyone nervous. So I didn't blame her when she playfully—or semi-playfully—threw a washrag at my face and said she had left her bag in the car and needed to go down and get it.

"I need to change my underwear, brush my teeth," she said.

"Brush your teeth? Haven't you got—"

"I've been using yours."

"Oh, yuck!" She laughed and I felt a little better about her, about us. "Are you sure it's safe, going out there?"

"I know I've been nervous, jumping at shadows. But I think it's all right now." She tried to laugh. "Do you think I'd go out there if I didn't think so?"

"Let me come with you."

"No!" She stepped back, her expression apologetic about the fierceness of her refusal. "I'm sorry. I'm still a little on edge. Just tell me where the car is."

If I didn't feel as assured about our safety as she did, I trusted her judgment on all things gangsterish and decided there was no point insisting. I told her where I'd parked. "Be quick. Don't hang around. Grab what you need and come back."

"Of course."

Before she went out she put her arms around me and kissed me on the lips, a long lingering kiss, as if trying to make it something to remember.

19

A Knife From the Shadows

FOR THE FIRST TIME in a couple of days I got out my notebook and dug a pen from the bottom of my backpack. I set the notebook on the table and stared at it, unable to write a word. I flipped through the disjointed pages I had told myself I would stitch together to form a searing denunciation of my father and those like him, all of them grasping misers, evil to the core.

Now the notion seemed ridiculous. When held up against the real thing, when compared to Marius Carbonne, my father's iniquities looked thin and timid. He wasn't evil, just narrow and mean. A garden variety bastard. My grudges and resentments appeared increasingly like adolescent rebellion rather than the militant righteousness in which I'd clothed my actions.

The truth was that in vowing to indict my father's shortcomings I had only discovered my own. I had wanted to insist on my independence, get free of my past and stand on my own two feet. In fact, I only needed to figure out how get free of myself.

I should live so long.

Really.

I closed my notebook and looked at my watch. Brigitte's dash down to the car and back should have taken ten minutes, fifteen at most. She'd been gone half an hour.

I got up from the table and looked out the window. No sign of her. Trying to tell myself I was unconcerned, I made a cup of coffee and sat at the window. But a trickle of anxiety curled around my chest even as I manufactured plausible reasons for her failure to return. When I had finally dismissed the last of them and decided I had to go down and look for her I heard the key in the lock and Brigitte came in with a sack of groceries, and no bag.

"Where are your things?"

She set down the groceries and put her arms around me. "Oh, Kip, I got scared. I know it's ridiculous, but I thought someone was watching the car and ..." She shrugged to hide her embarrassment.

"You were gone nearly an hour."

"I stood a block away and watched the car for a long time. Then I bought some groceries. You see?" she waved at the groceries as a token of her good faith.

"And you saw someone keeping an eye on the car?"

"Yes. Well, maybe." She laughed, embarrassed. "I don't know. I couldn't make myself go up to the car. So I went to the store and bought a few more things for dinner." She smiled in a way I would have found charming a couple of days earlier.

"You were afraid someone was watching the car, but you weren't afraid someone would see you walking around on the street?"

"I know it sounds foolish."

"What about your bag, those other things you said you needed?"

Unable to look at me, she pulled the key to the car from her pocket and held it out to me.

"Could you go? I got scared, that's all. I know it's ridiculous, but ..."

I took a deep breath and tried to tell myself it was all pretty natural. She'd been on the edge of panic for days—for weeks. I shouldn't be surprised at her loss of nerve.

I took the key. "Sure."

※

From newly formed habit, I stood at the door of the building and looked up and down the street before stepping outside. Truthfully, I wasn't sure what I was looking for, but decided it wasn't there.

It took only a few minutes to walk the three blocks to where I'd parked the London taxi. I figured I could grab her stuff and get back to the apartment without drawing attention to myself.

When I got in sight of the car, though, I stopped. There, on the other side of the street, a tall skinny kid, maybe seventeen or eighteen, leaned against the fender of the car. While I ducked into a doorway he looked around—up the sidewalk, down the street—casually, not as if keeping an eye out for anyone. But he didn't go away either.

Caught between conflicting urges to run back to the safety of the apartment and to dismiss the kid as nothing more than a loiterer, I continued to watch him for a few minutes, certain his presence was the reason Brigitte had thought someone was watching the car.

He pulled out his phone, made a call. Though my feet wanted to run back to the apartment, I forced myself to come out from the doorway I'd been hiding in and start down the sidewalk. The tall, skinny guy looked at me and straightened up, no longer leaning against the car. My heart felt funny in my chest. I crossed the street and continued walking toward him.

The kid ended his call and watched me, not alarmed, just watching. Of course, if he had a gun I was the one who should be alarmed.

As I got within a few yards, he reached into his pocket.

I stopped.

He pulled out a packet of cigarettes, lit one, and ground the match under his heel. Then he walked away.

I shook my head at the state of my nerves, mistaking this underfed vagrant for a gangster. My hands still trembling, it took me a moment to get the key in the lock and open the car door.

The guy with the knife must have been hiding in a doorway.

He came at me quick as a cat, betrayed only by his image reflected in the windshield.

Already keyed up, I sprang away from the car like a pogo stick.

I wish I could say that, with my boundless courage and dragon-fly reflexes, I stood my ground and decked the guy, then took his knife and carved my initials in his forehead. What I did was turn and run like hell.

The guy, someone I'd never seen, chased me for a block, but I was younger and faster, not to mention better motivated, and I quickly left him behind. Another thing that was pretty easy: Figuring out something stunk like hell, because when I'd looked in the car I could see Brigitte's bag wasn't there.

If my hands had shaken when I opened the car door, it looked like I had Parkinson's by the time I got back to the apartment. I couldn't get the key in the door and had to ring for the concierge, who buzzed me in and stuck her head out the door of her ground-floor apartment as I ran past her and up the stairs.

Brigitte looked astonished as she opened the door to my knock.

"Surprised to see me?" I gasped after dashing up the stairs.

She took a step back, then with a tremor that shook her whole body, jumped across the room and threw her arms around me.

"Oh, Kip!"

I stiff-armed her. "Get away from me."

In the space of maybe two seconds a wild array of emotions played across her face. It's anyone's guess which ones were true. I decided I didn't care.

"You set me up to get killed," I told her.

"No!" Her shock appeared genuine. But so had so much else. "No!" she repeated. As she saw the look in my face. "Kip, you have to believe me."

"Sure I do."

Again, she opened her arms and took a step toward me. I put up my hand.

"Where's your bag?"

How many times had I seen her hang her head as she did now? Play acting, I told myself.

"It's downstairs," she said, her voice a whisper. "I hid it in a corner."

"You lied to me about the bag, sent me off to get it when you knew someone would jump me."

"No! I mean yes, but—"

"Well, that makes it clear."

"Kip, you don't understand."

"I think I do. You saw someone you recognized this morning. I watched you looking out the window at him."

"Kip, I had no idea—"

"You saw someone and—"

She swung her arms around her head as if her hair was on fire. "Yes! All right! I saw a man I'd seen before. He came to Marseille once with the *capo* of a mob here in Paris. I told you, they all know each other. I knew Marius would call someone here, get in touch with contacts in every big city, asking everyone to keep an eye out for us. They found the car and searched the neighborhood for us. This man, the one I'd seen before, must have seen us crossing the street together yesterday. Or maybe someone else saw us, knew we matched the description, and they sent this man over here to be sure. I don't know. But I recognized him standing near the steps when you went to the store." She crossed her arms and pouted. "I told you we shouldn't have gone out yesterday."

"You're saying it's my fault. That's really good. This morning you said you were going after your things, which gave you enough time to go meet this guy and agree to give me up in exchange for your own skin. I don't know why it took you so long. I'd have thought it would be a pretty simple deal to—"

"No!" In her anger she picked up an ashtray and threw it at me, the glass shattering against the wall behind me. "I saved your life!"

That set me back a step.

"What do you mean?" I meant to sound tough, but it came out like I felt, confused.

"Kip, we have to get out of here. They know where we are."

"I'm not going anywhere until you tell me the truth about what's going on."

"All right, yes, I saw someone I knew and I knew they'd found us. It's me Marius wants. You're just someone who made him look bad once. He kills people for that, but he wants me back. So I went down and talked to this man. I told him I'd let them take me back to Marius if they let you go."

I laughed in her face. "I'm supposed to believe that?" Yet I halfway did. It's a dangerous thing, falling in love. You make a hostage of your own heart. Vulnerability like that breeds distrust almost as easily as love.

"Don't tell me they were going to let me to get away like—"

"Shut up!" She waited for me. "He said Marius told them to kill you and take me back to him, where he would deal with me." For a moment she went speechless at the terror of the thought, then continued. "But this man's boss didn't want to kill anyone just on Marius's say so."

"So you didn't really save my—"

"*Shut! Up!* I told this man that if they took me back to Marseille, Marius would be satisfied. He said all right. They would beat you and tell Marius that would have to be good enough. They wouldn't kill anyone."

"The guy came at me with a knife."

Brigitte's face went slack. "No." She said it so quietly I could hardly hear her. "He promised."

I believed her. I didn't believe her. I believed her. Like picking petals off a daisy. But my life was at stake.

"We have to get out of here," she whispered, and repeated to herself, "We have to get out of here."

I looked at the door of the apartment as if gunmen were already on the other side, knocking it down. "Do you think they'll come up here?" I couldn't bring myself to add, "And kill us?"

"I don't know." She seemed dazed. This was what fear could do. "I think maybe they'll wait for us to come out rather than run up after us. At least for a while."

"I'm not going to stand here waiting for them to make up their minds. Maybe there's a back way out of here."

"They might know about it."

"They might not."

She raised her head and looked at me. I could see her pulling herself together. "All right. We'll go. Get your backpack."

I folded up my notebook, grabbed my bag and we ran downstairs. Brigitte pushed the buzzer for the concierge's apartment.

A large sixtyish woman in an old housedress came to the door wiping her hands on a kitchen towel and looking put out. "Yes?"

"Bonjour, madame," Brigitte said with her sweetest smile.

Sensing Brigitte wanted a favor, the woman's face turned stony enough for a place on Mount Rushmore.

"Madame, is there a back door to this building?"

The woman curled her lip. "Who are you?"

Brigitte took my arm and leaned her head on my shoulder. "Mohamed and Hassan gave us their room for the day. But my boyfriend found out, and he's waiting outside."

The concierge looked at me and sniffed. "So that's why you ran up the stairs so fast. I might have known." She tossed her head and muttered something unpleasant about Mohamed and Hassan. "What's any of this to me?"

"He's very angry, madam. Crazy." Brigitte gave the woman her best just-us-girls smile. "You know how it is."

I doubted she did.

"I really don't want a scene," Brigitte said, glancing at the door with a look of anxiety I found real enough. "He can get violent. I'm afraid of what will happen if I open the door. I've seen him go after everyone in sight when he's like this."

The woman only half believed her, but half was good enough. She waggled her head and flicked her hand toward a metal door at the back corner of the foyer. "That's the way I go to put the garbage out on the back street," she said, leaving the impression that this included us.

With an apologetic smile in my direction, Brigitte grabbed her bag from where she'd hidden it in a corner of the foyer. We threw open the metal door and ran to the end of the narrow passage between our building and the one next to it. Standing between the two buildings, we peeked out onto the street.

An old man was walking his dog along the sidewalk, keeping up a muttering monologue with the beast as the two of them tottered along. Other than that, the street was empty.

"What do we do now?" I asked.

"You steal a car and we leave the city."

"What? I don't know how to steal a car."

She seemed genuinely surprised. "I thought every man knew how to steal a car."

"I majored in literature, not grand theft auto. You've been hanging too long with the wrong crowd."

"Then we'll go get the taxi."

"You're kidding, right? They'll be watching it."

"No. They'll think we're too smart to go back to the car."

"Well, I guess we'll show them, won't we?"

"Bus, metro, taxi. None of them gets us out of the city. We need a car."

"Trains."

"You have enough money for two train tickets?"

I sighed.

"Do you have a better idea?" she asked.

"So, you say we should run down the street, jump in the London taxi and drive off. And go where? If we stay in Paris they'll find us."

Brigitte let out a deep sigh. "I know a place we can go."

"I see. We come to Paris, which is full of gangsters waiting for us because, all along, you have a safer place to go."

"Yes."

"This is nuts."

But she was right about one thing, I didn't have a better plan. I followed her toward the car, feeling like we were taking a short walk to the gallows.

When we came around the corner of the street where I'd parked the car Brigitte hissed, "*Merde!*" and pulled me into the same doorway I'd hidden in earlier that morning.

"What?"

"There's someone watching the car."

I nearly bit through my tongue to keep from shouting, "I told you so." But I couldn't help saying, "So they believed we *were* stupid enough to come back."

"Quiet!"

"It's the same guy you talked with earlier?"

"No."

"Then how do you know he's—"

"I just know."

"I don't see anyone."

"You didn't see the man with the knife either. Get back in here." Brigitte took my arm and yanked me back from where I was peering down the street. "The last they saw you, you were running up the street. I'll tell them I don't know where you are, but I'm ready to go back to Marius."

"You're just going to walk up to whoever you think is looking for us."

"It's the only way to get out of here."

"You know what will happen if you're wrong."

She didn't choose to hear me. "And I'll tell them Marius will be upset if we don't get his London taxi back to him."

I could tell she was making this up as she went. "Really? The taxi?"

"Yes. I'll say he loves the London taxi."

"Taxi or no taxi, they'll want to take you to their boss first, yes? Whoever is waiting for us can't just drive you down to Marseille without someone's okay."

"Okay, but I'll insist we have to go in the taxi."

"I don't get it about the taxi."

"Just give me the key."

Struggling against a great lump of dread in my gut, I handed over the key and watched her walk away while I stood in the doorway and wondered if she'd only found a new way to set me up. She walked slowly down the middle of the quiet street. When no one came out of the shadows to accost her, I began to think she'd simply imagined a bad guy had an eye on the car—or that this was all a clever way to allow her to drive off and leave me standing there.

I'd nearly decided to run out of the doorway, grab her and take the key back when a man appeared from a narrow passage between two buildings.

Brigitte stopped and let him approach.

For a couple of minutes they talked in the middle of the street. Or, rather, Brigitte talked and the man, a heavyset guy in a cheap suit, no tie, waggled his head and shrugged. Anyone passing by might have thought they were neighbors who happened to run into each other. Eventually, the man seemed okay with whatever she'd said and held his hand out for the key. Brigitte pulled back and said something. He laughed and shook his head and again held out his hand, palm up. She drew the key back and nodded at the car, apparently insisting she drive. His hand still out, the man shook his head. Brigitte crossed her arms, the key tucked against her chest.

With an exasperated, "*Bof!*" that I could hear all the way up the street, he forced a laugh and gave in. While he walked around to the passenger side, Brigitte threw her bag in the car and got behind the wheel. The guy pulled a phone from his coat pocket, probably telling someone that he had the girl.

He was still punching in the number when Brigitte started the car and pulled away from the curb.

The man in the cheap suit dropped his phone and grabbed for the car door. He managed to get it open but couldn't get in before she veered into a parked car, scraping the man from the door like putty off a knife. This stuff is funny in movies, but when the guy has a gun it's pretty scary.

For an ugly moment I thought she might drive right past me, but she waved her arm at me to get in and hit the brakes. The still-open side door nearly swung off its hinges. I hopped in, threw my bag in the back, and glanced down the street. The big guy had got to his feet and pulled out a pistol. I was about to yell at Brigitte to duck when the man thought better of it, put the gun back in his pocket and ran toward the phone he'd dropped on the sidewalk.

The door, dented where she sideswiped the other car, didn't want to close and I had to hold it shut with one hand while I grabbed the back of the seat with the other to keep from falling out as we careened down the street, Brigitte driving like a mouse with a cat after her.

Finally able to slam the door shut, I asked, "Where are you going?"

"I don't know! I don't know how to get out of town!"

"Oh, for crying out loud. Where are you trying to go?"

"Normandy."

"Normandy? That's like saying we're heading for Texas. Normandy's huge."

"Near Bayeux. How do I get out of the city?"

I knew the area around Montmartre pretty well, but with Brigitte driving like Bonnie and Clyde it took me a moment to get oriented and direct her onto the *peripherique*, a freeway that rings Paris. We drove along the freeway for a few miles then took a road heading northwest, toward Bayeux, staying off the main highways.

It was late in the afternoon before we could bring ourselves to stop running long enough to park in an alley behind a small town bistro. We went in and asked for a table at the back, far from the windows, though the idea that Carbonne or his allies would have a spy in every small town in France was pretty loopy. Still, we kept our heads down except to glance anxiously at everyone who came through the door.

I again asked Brigitte where we were going, but she only shook her head. While we waited for our order she put her hand over mine. I didn't pull back, but I didn't return the squeeze she gave me either.

What was the point in asking her if she really believed the gangbangers in Paris would have been satisfied with beating the shit out of me? My trust in Brigitte had fallen low enough that I wondered if they had even made such a promise. I could drive myself crazy trying to figure it out, and there was a part of me that didn't want to know.

We ate a quick, cheap lunch, sandwiches and fries and coffee and went to the counter to pay up. When I opened my wallet I saw in its thin contents nothing but bad news. We'd have to stop for fuel soon. After that I'd be broke.

I paid the bill and we went out behind the building to the car.

Brigitte said she was too tired to drive any further. The danger we'd dodged in the street, the tension of our escape from Paris had worn me out too. I wondered if I would spend the rest of my life running.

We agreed to take a quick nap before getting back out on the road. After all, no one would think to look for us here. Still, I felt better when I got behind the wheel and locked the car doors.

※

A fist pounding on the car door sent my heart into my throat. I opened my eyes to find a face filling the side window, contracted with fury. Brigitte stifled a scream.

The man grabbed at the door handle, raging at me, the words coming too fast for me to make out.

I'd left the key in the ignition and only needed to push the start button. I threw the car into reverse but in my panic let the clutch out too fast. The engine coughed and died.

Still shouting, the man continued to pound on my window.

I pushed the start button again, but now Brigitte put a hand on my arm and gave me a shaky smile.

"You're blocking the door to his garage. He wants us to move so he can get his car out."

"He doesn't want to kill me?"

"Actually, I think he does. But if you'll move the car it will be all right."

I looked again and saw the man for what he was. Not a gangster. Just a little old man in a faded suit coat that hung nearly to his knees. I smiled in relief, which only made him angrier.

I backed out of the alley, nosed the car onto the main road and followed the signs toward Caen and Bayeux. It was the fourth of October and the dusk came early. I turned on the headlights. Within a few minutes we were again driving through fields and hedges.

20

Marie-Therese, a Visitor, and a Gun

THEY SAY FRANCE is a nation of villages. I believe it. Every couple of kilometers we entered another little town with a long name and a longer history. Yet many of the villages appeared to be dying. Empty houses and shuttered stores faced on neglected streets. In a couple places even the bakeries had folded. In France that means the end.

We searched for road signs. Sometimes they didn't point to either of the cities I was looking for. But Brigitte seemed to know where we were now and would tell me which road to take.

Well after dark, we came into a town a little larger than the rest and I saw that the signs to Caen and Bayeux now pointed in different directions, which told me we must be getting close. I nudged the turn signal, ready to follow the road toward Bayeux. Brigitte stopped me.

"No. Turn here." She pointed me down one street, then onto another. Moments later we were out of town and back into the countryside.

After a few minutes she said, "There. Turn," pointing toward a narrow farm lane.

A sign gave the name of some hamlet further down the road, the sign not written in normal block letters but in the italics the French use to indicate a place so small it's only a shaky step above imaginary. We were well and truly out in the sticks.

Driving slowly down a potholed lane in the dark, I'd made less than a kilometer, no more than half a mile, when Brigitte said, "Turn in here."

Since leaving Paris she had given me little idea of where we were going but, whatever I'd imagined, I hadn't expected this, an old single-story stone farmhouse and a barn, both surrounded by a high stone wall, making it, like so many French country farmhouses, look like a small fortress.

I pulled in through the narrow gate and stopped. Still uncertain that this was truly our destination, I left the car idling until Brigitte put a hand on my arm and I turned it off. Yet she didn't get out. We sat there for some time, listening to the motor pinging as it cooled. Brigitte stared at the house until I began to wonder if we'd come all this way only to look at the place.

Taking a deep breath, she got out of the car, leaving the door open, as if she might yet get back in and tell me to drive off. For maybe a full minute she stood only a few feet from the car, looking at the stone farmhouse.

A curtain moved. A face appeared at a window. The curtain fell shut. Brigitte made a gesture for me to follow her and started toward the house.

As I got out of the car I caught the unmistakable smell of cows. When Brigitte had made that remark about how Carbonne thought being a gangster was as easy as raising cows in Normandy, it hadn't occurred to me she was talking about home.

Brigitte approached the door of the farmhouse. Before she could raise her hand to knock, the door opened, spilling light into our eyes. In the doorway stood two backlit figures, a man and a woman.

For what felt like an eternity no one moved. Then the woman—short, round, an apron around her waist—shouldered past the man and threw her arms around Brigitte.

"Ah, Marie-Therese," she sighed, as if these were the words she might say with her dying breath.

The man behind her put his arms around them both. At the same time he looked over their heads and regarded me coolly.

Brigitte choked out, "Mama. Papa."

After several wordless moments her mother backed away and pulled her into the house, still holding her hands as if afraid she might fly away. I came in behind them, feeling not unwelcome but under scrutiny, an unknown quantity.

Brigitte made hurried introductions. "Mama, Papa, this is a friend of mine, Kip Weston. Kip, my parents, Jacques and Madeline Aubert."

Her father shook my hand in that quick, single-pump way the French do. I could see in his face the same question Diane had asked weeks earlier, "This is a name, Kip?"

Their age surprised me, both of them gray haired, her father already stooped at the shoulders, Brigitte clearly the gift of their later life.

Her hands fluttering like birds, her mother said, "Have you eaten? No, you're starving, I can see."

Brigitte tried to tell her that we'd eaten only a couple hours earlier, but her mother had made up her mind before she asked the question. A moment later we heard the sound of pans shifting on the stove and the chopping of vegetables.

Her husband waved us toward a solid, old-fashioned sofa while he settled into the leather-covered armchair that had long ago molded itself to his form.

Father and daughter regarded each other with a wavering mix of emotions until Brigitte looked away.

"I'm so happy to see you, Papa," she said, though in fact she couldn't look at him.

Her father leaned forward in his chair, his hands clasped in front of him. "And we are happy you have come home. It has been a long time. Nearly a year?" he said, his reproach gentle but clear. "It's been months since you last called. We called you and left messages, but ..." He spread his hands, letting the unspoken question hang in the air.

"Oh, Papa, I'm so sorry, but my life has been terribly busy. I hardly have a moment to myself."

"Of course." The sadness in his smile spoke of love and the resignation of a father who knows his daughter has left home for good. "You told us you've been working for a businessman. Your work is interesting? He treats you well?"

Apparently, they weren't the sort to read the papers or their reaction to our appearance would have been different. Or, more likely, they'd read something about a Brigitte Del Ray without any idea it was their daughter.

"Yes, Papa, he ... he treats me well," she said. The look on her face belied her words, but he didn't press.

"And what has happened to your friend, Andre?"

I recognized the name of the boyfriend whose parents we had spoken to in the Place des Vosges, the one who had taken her to Marseille.

Again, she could not look at him. "He went back to Paris."

"Ah."

Some kind of disappointment there. Had her parents been fond of him? Perhaps they had thought that this Andre would be her ticket to a higher social status than farmer's daughter.

Her father turned to me. "But you are not this businessman who keeps our daughter so engaged."

I smiled, taking the question as a small joke, though his curiosity about who I was, especially who I was to his daughter, couldn't have been more serious. "No, Monsieur Aubert." I knew better than to get all American on him and call him by his first name. "I'm just—"

I don't know what Brigitte thought I might say, but she put her hand on my arm to keep me from saying it. "We are friends," she said. In the security of her own home she looked at me with a warmth I felt genuine. Despite everything I'd gone through that day, my doubts about her, my suspicions, once more melted away.

"I see." Her father allowed me an indulgent smile and rose from his chair. "You must have things to bring in. Shall I help you?"

"No, Papa, we can get them." She looked at me before asking her father, "But ... I know this sounds silly, but can we park our car in the barn?"

The meaning of her request escaped him for a moment. When he understood, his lingering happiness at his daughter's return faded and his expression turned grave as he looked from his daughter to me and back again. He would not ask for an explanation, but it was clear she had not come back drawn by love of family and home, but because she was in danger and needed to hide. And I was somehow a part of it.

Monsieur Aubert looked toward his wife in the kitchen, his face softened by nostalgia for that innocent time of only a few moments earlier, before our arrival had put an end to it. He waggled his head, accepting the possibility that, by welcoming us in, he and his wife had put themselves at risk.

Brigitte could see he understood and, lips trembling, smiled. She had not wanted to do this to them. She had only come home because she had no good choice left. Who was it who said that home is where, when you have to go there, they have to take you in?

"Yes, certainly," her father said. "Park in the garage."

We went outside. Brigitte opened the doors to the barn and I drove in. I grabbed our bags from the back seat, handed Brigitte hers and nodded toward her parents' house. "If they ask, am I your boyfriend?" I tried to say it lightly.

"I don't know."

"How long will we stay here?"

"I don't know."

"And where do we go when we leave?" I didn't care if she saw my impatience.

"I don't know, I don't know, I don't know!" She twisted away, then as quickly turned back and threw her arms around me. It struck me that her sudden embrace had less to do with affection than to make me stop asking questions.

Uncertain what I felt or what I could promise, I put my arms around her too.

My only question was a practical one. "What should I call you?"

"Don't call me anything. I have no name anymore. You know Brigitte. They only know Marie-Therese. I'm both. I'm neither." The pain lacerating her voice moved me more than any words could. We held each other yet more tightly and kissed, not from love, though it was there, or even desire, which we shared too, but like two half-drowned creatures trying to breathe life into each other.

We closed the barn doors and went back into the house, where it was warm and smelled of dinner on the stove. Her mother had fried up some potatoes and made a large omelette with herbs. Simple and delicious. She was tempted to stay and watch us eat, but her husband lifted his eyebrows in a meaningful way, and she retreated with him toward the main room, allowing us a few minutes together.

We looked around the big kitchen—the stove from a different century, the pots and pans hanging from the ceiling, the big chopping table in the middle of the room—aware that we were each seeing something different; for me a quaint kitchen steeped in tradition, for her, home.

"You grew up in this house?"

"Yes. My grandfather passed it on to my father, as his own father had before him. Six generations we've been here. When Papa dies it will go to my brother."

The surprise on my face made her laugh. "Yes, I have a brother. Marcel. He's eleven years older than me. He and his wife live in the village we drove through just before we came here. He drives trucks and helps Papa when he can." She gave me a lopsided grin, that ended in a sigh. "I was supposed to marry a nice farm boy. And stay close to home."

When we finished eating, we rejoined her parents in the main room. Her father looked at us over the top of the local newspaper he was reading. Her mother set aside her book. "You both look tired. You don't need to stay up with the old folks." She smiled at her daughter, "Your room is always ready for you."

While Madame Aubert took Brigitte back to her room, Monsieur Aubert led me through the kitchen to a room not much bigger than my berth on the *Celeste*, with a cot and a table and a tiny window.

"There's a toilet off the kitchen," he told me and started to leave, but stopped and worked a bit of dirt from under his fingernails, as if his next words had no importance. "It's true she's been working for a businessman in Marseille?"

I told him yes, but he could tell there was much more than that.

"And you are ... protecting her?"

"Yes, I guess so."

"Even from us."

I started to apologize, but he waved a hand to stop me. "Maybe later she will feel she can tell us. For now, I'm glad she has someone." He looked at me from under his brow. "You are her boyfriend?"

"I ... I'm not sure."

For the first time since we'd arrived he smiled with real humor, then sighed, "Ah, Marie-Therese," with loving exasperation. "Well, I must be off to bed. Farm work starts early."

"Can I help you?"

"You know how to milk a cow?"

"No. But ... "

He raised a forestalling hand. "Then I think you had better sleep in."

The glint in his eyes told me I'd been accepted, maybe only in a conditional, tentative sort of way, but accepted.

"Good night, Kip."

"Good night, Monsieur Aubert."

※

In the middle of the night I woke from a dream of killing my father. No matter how often I told mysself that I'd left him alive and furious, the dreams would not go away. I lay awake for a long time.

✳

In the morning I came out of my room to the smell of breakfast cooking and the sight of Madame Aubert poking sausages around in a frying pan.

"Good morning, Kip. You slept well?"

"Yes." I lied to make her happy.

"Marie-Therese will be out in a moment," she announced cheerily as she bent down to pull an egg casserole from the oven.

In fact, her daughter already stood in the doorway, wearing a long blue dress with green embroidery and a smile as shy as a country bride. I had never seen her in a dress before. It made her look very young and fresh.

I thought of her standing on the cold metal deck of my berth in her modest cotton nightgown and understood now I had been glimpsing her true self.

"Good morning, Marie-Therese."

She laughed at how I called her by her real name and made a little pirouette, the skirts of her dress billowing slightly.

"You like?"

I pictured her in her cabin on the boat, lounging in her negligee, or on deck in her bikini and sunglasses, and thought how much I preferred her like this.

"It makes you look like a spiritual being."

Her laughter died in a look of wonder. She knew I was saying everything between us was good.

Madame Aubert, who had been busy pretending she wasn't listening, smiled.

After breakfast I went out to find some way to help her father. Though I hardly knew which end of a cow to milk, I found I could feed the cattle and muck out the stalls without too much supervision. My shoulder still hurt from when I had knocked down Paul on the boat a hundred years earlier, but I enjoyed the work and the clean air and the autumn sun.

Brigitte changed into blue jeans and an old sweatshirt and came out to help, taking pails of milk and pouring them into a tank. Every time she passed me she smirked and shook her head at the dubious quality of my work, but she also seemed pleased, and I knew she wanted me to impress her father.

While she watched me becoming a farmhand I watched her re-becoming Marie-Therese. And I knew, when she completed her metamorphosis and finally left Brigitte behind, I would have to leave.

Unless.

Unless I turned myself into the farm boy she needed me to be. If she could become Marie-Therese again, I could again become Wilfred—a preposterous name back home, but maybe acceptable on a Norman farm. I mean, if they could name her brother Marcel ...

Her parents had gotten to an age where they napped after lunch, allowing Brigitte and me time to sit at the kitchen table and talk freely. We soon turned to the true reason she had come home. The contentment she had shown that morning faded to gray.

"We can't stay here, Kip. My parents don't deserve this, the danger we bring with us."

"Nobody will find us here," I said, though I wondered how I could know that. "The car's hidden, so even if Diane wants to call the police and report it stolen, tries to find us that way, no one will spot it."

Reluctant to accept our safety as real for fear of jinxing it, she said, "The man in the gray suit. He won't give up. He'll find you."

That took the wind out of me.

"What's wrong?" she asked.

"I had a dream last night, a nightmare, about killing my father."

"This man is still looking for you and hasn't gone to the police. That tells me your father's still alive."

"And that's why he hasn't given up. He's still answering to my father. When he finds me, that's when he calls the police."

She thought this over for a long time before saying what we both knew to be the truth. "We can't stay."

Which caused me to again bring up the question we had been asking ourselves from the moment we drove away from the boat. "And go where?"

"You thought I was joking when I said we should run away to Brazil."

"Part of me knew you were serious."

"But not the part that would let you come with me."

"It was the part that has no money that couldn't go with you." Reluctantly, I asked, "Your parents do well? Maybe we could borrow some money." I felt ashamed even as I said it.

"They're farmers. They are rich only in debt."

"Too bad I didn't get Diane to pay me before we left."

It wasn't much of a joke and she didn't give me much of a laugh. "Yes," she said. "And a shame Marius gave that stack of money to Diane and not to me that last evening before he left." The memory of the boat jogged something in her. "Kip, I'm sorry for the way I was then, parading past you with nothing on."

"Actually, I kind of enjoyed it."

"You know what I mean. I shouldn't have acted that way. I don't know why I did."

"You did it so I'd react, so you would have someone other than gangsters pay attention to you. The funny thing is I liked you best in your nightgown—except maybe for when you took it off."

Acting scandalized, she shot a look toward her parents' room then laughed and punched me in the shoulder. My eyes holding hers, I nodded toward my tiny room in the back. It did me good to see she was tempted, but she said, "No. We're under my parents' roof, and I have to respect that. They would never let us sleep together here unless we were married."

"Well ..."

For a moment, we looked at each other, until the distance between us no longer existed, each of us entirely absorbed in the other. It was too much. We both laughed and pulled back from something we didn't know how to think about yet. Then the sound of her father coughing and rising from bed made us instinctively put distance between us, like teenagers afraid to be caught holding hands.

※

The rhythm of the afternoon proved more relaxed than the morning. Her father and I finished up some light chores and he called an end to the work day. He didn't thank me or compliment me on my work, but he gave me an appreciative slap on the back that meant more than compliments.

At dinner, we talked like old friends. They spoke a bit about people I didn't know and her mother told a few stories about her daughter's childhood that made me laugh. Brigitte reddened and said, "Please, mama."

With every word they spoke Brigitte slipped more comfortably into being Marie-Therese.

Brigitte and her mother were rinsing the dishes in the kitchen and Monsieur Aubert had wandered off to the freezer at the back of the house to get some ice cream when a knock sounded at the door.

"Kip, would you answer that? It's probably our son." Madame Aubert's request made me feel a part of the household. I enjoyed thinking that I might soon be calling her Madeline, her husband Jacques.

Our impatient visitor knocked again. I raised the old-fashioned latch and opened the door.

Two thoughts flashed simultaneously through my mind. First, it struck me odd that a man with a gun would bother to knock. And, second, I could never have imagined it would be Dilip coming into the house with a pistol in his hand.

21

The Gun Seeks New Hands

DUMBSTRUCK, I STEPPED BACK from the door and held my hands away from my body. Dilip looked quickly around the room and put the muzzle of the pistol against my chest. "Where is she?"

"Dilip—"

"Where is she?"

From the kitchen, Madame Aubert called, "Who is it, Kip?"

It took me a moment to find my voice. "A friend."

Dilip gave me a wild look, thinking I was mocking him.

Brigitte's mother came into the room, wiping her hands on a towel. Her welcoming smile vanished at the sight of a dark-skinned stranger in her house. She shook her head, less in fear than confusion.

"Yes? What is it you want?"

Then she saw the gun, and the towel fell from her hands.

With an urgency bordering on hysteria, Dilip again asked me, "Where is she?"

Madame Aubert started to back toward the kitchen. Dilip turned the gun from me to her. His voice quiet but charged with emotion, he ordered her, "Get back in here."

Did Brigitte sense the disturbance in the order of her home? Or, despite Dilip's near-whisper, she thought she heard a familiar voice. Whatever it was, she came out of the kitchen. Even before she saw the gun, her sharp intake of breath punctuated the silence. She put a hand around her mother's waist and directed her toward a corner of the room, well away from us.

"Dilip," she said, keeping her voice even, "what are you doing here?"

Dilip waved the gun toward her. "Where's the taxi?"

"In the barn," she said. "Why?"

"You're taking the taxi and coming with me back to the boat."

Brigitte clasped her hands in front of her. "No, Dilip, I can't."

Taken aback, he blinked. However this scene had played out in his mind, it had apparently not occurred to him that she would simply refuse.

Trying to force things back on the track he wanted, he trained the gun on her.

"Marius is blaming everything on Diane. He says he's going to take the boat away from her. He'll throw her off with nothing. He'll come up from Marseille and beat her—or have Serge or Paul beat her for him. Then he'll take everything away. I warned you, I can't let that happen. I won't let it happen."

With marvelous calm, Brigitte said, "Dilip, you know if I go back he'll kill me."

"He said he'd never kill a woman. He told me that." But he slid his eyes away from her, both of them knowing how little Carbonne's promises meant. He pointed the gun toward me again. "Get the car."

"What are you going to do, Dilip, hold the gun on us the whole way back? That's what you'll have to do."

Hearing voices, Monsieur Aubert came into the room, the carton of ice cream in his hand.

"What is everyone doing in here?"

Then he too saw the gun. His first reaction was to look at me, his face hard with accusation. His voice barely under control, he asked, Dilip. "By what right do you come into my house and threaten my family?"

"Be quiet!" Dilip shouted.

Though we all stood at gunpoint, it was Dilip who seemed desperate, reeling at the edge of self-control.

Monsieur Aubert drew himself up to his full height, his stoop gone. "I demand that you leave my house immediately."

My god, the man had guts.

"Be quiet!" Dilip fairly screamed the words. "Or I'll shoot your daughter."

Brigitte stepped between her father and Dilip, the anguish on her face painful to see.

"No, Dilip, you won't. You're too good."

"Diane's in danger and it's my fault! I should never have let you leave the boat."

"You had to, or watch them kill us. You know that."

"I have to protect Diane! Giving you to Marius is the only way to do that." Swept by riptides of anger, fear, panic, I thought he might pull the trigger without meaning to.

Brigitte must have seen it too, but she took a step toward him. "Then protect her. Take her away from that boat and from that life. She has the money Marius gave her. Start a new life. As long as she stays on the boat, she's his hostage."

As Brigitte spoke, Dilip slowly lowered the gun, but now caught himself and leveled it unsteadily at her. "Stop it!"

I tried to get us off the track we were rushing down.

"How did you find us?"

Brigitte answered for him. "Marius knew my last name. Dilip did too. I'd mentioned I came from a village near Bayeux. It would have been easy."

Dilip blinked in confusion as we talked around him, sensing he was losing control of a scene he had thought he and his gun would dominate.

"If you need us to drive you to the boat, how did you get here?" I asked, adding to his dislocation by demanding answers of him.

The look he gave me bore as much confusion as annoyance. "I hitched into Auxerre this morning, took a train to Bayeux."

For the first time since he had come in, his voice sounded almost natural. The Dilip I knew.

"And you took a taxi here?" Brigitte asked.

It might have seemed comic, giving him the third degree while he threatened to shoot us, but he only flicked his hand impatiently. "To the village. I walked from there. I didn't want the driver to know where I was going."

In his fading resolve, the hand with the gun sank once more, as if its weight increased with his realization of what he was doing.

"Dilip," I said, trying to recall our old manner with each other. "You know we can't go with you."

"Then, help me ..." He raised the gun again, his hand trembling.

"What are you going to do, kill all four of us? How does that help Diane? Brigitte's right, this isn't who you are."

Her parents exchanged a puzzled glance, wondering why I called their Marie-Therese by this strange name.

"You can't save Diane this way," I told him. "If you two keep trying to make Marius happy, you'll only drive the both of you deeper into hell."

More to himself than to us, he muttered, "She told me not to come after you, but ..." In his anger and frustration Dilip waved the gun around, but his menace lacked assurance now. "You two will come with me or I'll shoot all of you!" he shouted. None of us believed him anymore, but he seemed to feel better for saying it.

For some time—ten seconds? fifteen?—no one said anything, Dilip's frightened panting the only sound.

The kettle on the stove began to whistle, adding its note of alarm. Madame Aubert started toward the kitchen, but stopped and asked, "Does anyone want a cup of tea?"

Dilip growled in frustration. "Stay where you are."

The whistling pot protested further, its growing pitch matching the tension in the room.

In the end, he sighed and hung his head in defeat. "Go turn it off."

"Are you sure you don't want a cup of—"

"Just turn it off."

Dilip tilted his head back, the light catching the tears in his eyes.

Brigitte touched his arm. He jumped.

"Dilip ..."

"What am I going to do?" he cried.

"Where are Serge and Paul?"

He shrugged as if it didn't matter.

"When you left, Marius made them go back to Marseille." He drew a hand across his forehead. "Then Serge called

Diane and told her they'd found you in Paris, but you'd gotten away. I was sure I knew where you'd gone."

I reached out to Dilip, but it was too much and he turned the gun on me. I stopped and put my hands up. "Dilip, go back to the boat and take Diane away. Everyone needs to leave that boat—you, me, Diane, all of us."

"I can't. She can't. She doesn't have anything else."

"Maybe Molly could find a place where Diane can cook. She's a wonderful cook."

"Molly left the same night you did. She'd had enough. She won't be back."

I pictured her little restaurant in a small town, and her apartment above. Would she make that part of her life come true now? I hoped so.

Dilip had told me he was an emotional man. Now he paid for his anger with a depression equal to its weight. His face drawn, his shoulders slumped in exhaustion, he stared into space.

"I couldn't find you," he said to no one, already trying out the line he would give Carbonne. "You'd already left. I tried, but I couldn't find you." Abruptly, he raised the gun and pointed it at me, but now the gesture lacked menace, reduced to a means of getting my attention. "Give me the keys to the taxi."

"I can't, Dilip. Maybe you can tell Carbonne you couldn't find us. But if you have the car he won't believe you. He'll just send someone else here to kill us. And we'll have no car to get away."

Dilip looked at the gun in his hand until none of us had eyes for anything else. Half a minute ticked by, the world reduced to a hand and a gun. Then he slowly turned it around in his hand, the barrel resting in his palm. Without a word, he stretched out his hand, offering the gun to me. I could only stare at it, a killer's weapon waiting to make a killer of whoever took it.

He read my hesitation and barked, "Take it!"

"Dilip, I don't want—"

"Take it! You've chosen your path. You're going to need it now." More quietly, he said, "You have to take it."

I tried to tell myself he was wrong. But the truth was too large to escape. I could only ask myself at what moment I could have still turned around, taken another direction that led somewhere other than here. The truth was that there were many such moments, starting with the decision to take my father's money. And I had chosen wrongly every time.

I reached out my hand and took the butt of the gun. Dilip let go and stepped back. It was mine now. I hefted the pistol. "But this isn't your gun."

"It's Serge's. I took it after you knocked him out."

"Why didn't Serge ask for it back?"

"I told him you threw it in the canal." Dilip allowed himself the ghost of a smile. "Be careful, Kip. I've told you. You think you have the gun. But it has you. It will look for ways to force you to use it. Believe me. I know."

Dilip looked toward the open door behind him, felt the cold wind. Had he known since he set off from the *Celeste* that it would end like this? Probably so. But he knew he had to try. And he had failed, as he knew he would.

Quietly, he said, "I have to go."

We offered to drive him to Bayeux, but he refused, saying only, "I'll go back the way I came."

He rubbed his hands together, adjusting to losing the weight of the gun. Without a word, he left through the open door, back into the night.

It took a while for any of us to move, all of us still trying to grasp what had happened. Eventually, I crossed the room to shut the door behind him.

"And you can keep going." Monsieur Aubert's voice carried every dram of the outrage that had been building in him. "You come to our home and put us all in danger. Men come into our house, hold guns on us."

I wanted to tell him it was really just the one, but I knew that would only make things worse.

"Go away and leave us in peace."

"No, Papa." Brigitte took his hands, but he ignored her, his eyes on me. "No. It's me who put him in danger, not the other way around. Coming here wasn't his idea. It was mine. I told him to come with me. He has risked his life to keep me safe."

The hostility in his eyes remained. Whatever the truth of what she said, he didn't want to hear it.

"He won't spend another night in this house," he said, his eyes fixed on me, making sure I got the message.

"He'll go in the morning, Papa. And I'll go with him."

Startled, Monsieur Aubert looked at this stranger, his daughter. "No. You will stay home with your mother and me."

"I can't stay, Papa. It's me they want. If I stay, someone else will come, someone far more dangerous than Dilip."

Her father's confusion, his inability to protect his daughter from something he couldn't understand made him angry. "What have you done? Who is this man who wants to kill you?"

"It's too long a story, and if I told you everything it would break your heart. I have to leave, Papa, and you have to let me go."

Her father brushed her hands away, breathing hard. The color left his face and he staggered as he turned away from us.

Brigitte said, "We came together, and we'll leave together."

Wanting to appear in control, but desperate now, her father refused to look at me, but told her, "He goes. Tomorrow. You stay."

But there was no conviction in his words. Like Dilip, he knew he had lost before he spoke, knew we would leave because we had no choice, just as we had come because we had no choice. Having only barely regained his daughter, he would lose her again.

It was still dark when I woke to the sound of Monsieur Aubert opening the barn doors to milk the cows. I rose quickly and went out to help him, but he ignored me except to turn his back whenever I came near.

Breakfast passed like the first meal after someone's death. Her back against the stove, Madame Aubert looked blankly at the floor, unable to find the words that might console us or herself.

We packed our few things and went outside to get the car out of the garage. Madame Aubert followed us out to the farmyard and took her daughter in her arms.

"When will you be back?"

"I don't know, Mama."

"Will it be a long time?"

"I don't know."

"I'm afraid you'll never come back."

"Don't think like that, Mama."

Brigitte had set her bag on the ground to hug her mother. I got out of the car to throw it in the back seat, to let her know it was time to go. Madame Aubert released her daughter and gave me a hug too, squeezing me hard to let me know how badly she wanted her daughter back.

Brigitte stood for a long time in the open door of the car, one foot in, one foot still home. She looked toward the house, toward the barn, toward the wooden gates that led toward the green fields beyond.

Madame Aubert sighed. "Your father can't come right now. He's busy getting the cows into the pasture." She spoke as if this were perfectly reasonable.

"He won't even say goodbye?"

Scuffing her toe against the ground as if something at her feet had taken her attention, she said, "He's too upset."

"He's disappointed in me."

"No." Her mother clasped her hands tightly under her chin in an attitude of prayer. "He's afraid for you. When you come back again he'll be all right."

"Yes. When I come back again."

Her mother gave her another hug, fleeting and light, and slipped some money into Brigitte's hand, folding her own hands over her daughter's to seal the act.

"Goodbye, Marie-Therese."

"*Au revoir*, Mama." Until I see you again.

Brigitte got in the car and we drove away.

22

"We Must Be Mad"

WE WENT BACK through villages we'd passed through two days earlier. But I soon turned south toward Le Mans and Orleans and the Loire. The farmland rolled by, the apple orchards bright with fall colors, the stubble of the harvested wheat fields a dusky gold. Neither of us paid much attention to the scenery, our minds ranging far ahead to the end of our journey and what would happen when we got there.

As we had driven away from her home, I asked the question I had asked her, and myself, so many times. "Where are we going?"

It took her a moment to work up the nerve to tell me, "Back to the *Celeste*." She cut me off before I could speak. "We have to. We have no money. Diane does. We won't be able to do anything, go anywhere, until she gives us what she has."

Through my disbelief, I managed to say, "She won't do it."

"She'll have to. I thought about it all last night. It was the only answer I could find."

"Do you really think Diane will give us the money Carbonne gave her?"

"You have a gun."

"I'm not going to shoot her. She knows that."

"The gun makes it easier for her. She can't just give us the money. But she can let us rob her, say we held her at gunpoint."

"You make it sound like she's looking for excuses to give us the money she says she needs for herself."

She turned on me. "You don't understand the shame we share! Diane and me. That we've allowed this to happen to us, the fear that it's our own fault. You can't know how much Marie-Therese despises Brigitte, or how part of Diane hates the other part of herself. That's the bond between us, and it's a difficult one because it's between the parts of ourselves that we despise. She will give us the money so she can buy off part of that shame. She can free herself by letting me go free."

"And if she doesn't?"

Brigitte shrugged at the obvious. "Then you hit her with the pistol and we take the money." She saw my reaction. "You'll have to. Then we'll go someplace they'll never find us. Otherwise ..."

She stopped because no one can easily speak about the possibility of their own death.

"And Dilip won't stop her from giving us the money?"

"He won't be there. Even if he found a taxi last night, by the time he got to Bayeux, the last train would have gone. He'd have to wait until morning for a train to Paris. Then he'd need to get across the city to the Gare de Lyon and wait for the next train to Auxerre."

"And from Auxerre he'd have to get another taxi."

"We should be there hours ahead of him."

"But somebody may be waiting for us on the boat."

"No. They won't think we're stupid enough to—" She put her hand over her mouth.

"They know exactly how stupid we are." I threw back my head and shouted, "We must be mad!"

Brigitte said nothing.

That might have been a good moment to pull over and think again about what we were doing. Instead, I sped up. Whatever was going to happen, I needed it to happen soon.

Before noon we'd got through Auxerre and were heading for the canal. However much I'd told myself I wanted to get there as fast as I could, my hands were sweating.

A few miles south of Auxerre we came to a village I recognized. A moment later the canal appeared a hundred yards to our left. A commercial barge carrying a load of gravel glided slowly toward Paris, its prow breaking the mirror-like surface of the still water. It all looked so familiar, so beautiful, so sinister. I turned off the main road and found a bridge over the canal and turned down the towpath, entering once more the world I swore I'd put behind me.

The boat hadn't moved since we'd left. With no guests, no crew, it had ceased its endless circling and lay still, simply floating.

I stopped the car a hundred yards from the boat, right about where Paul jumped me in the rain. We watched and waited, though neither of us could have said for what. There were no cars in sight, no one on deck, no movement of any kind, only a fisherman trying his luck in the stream on the opposite side of the canal. After a couple of minutes, I put the car back in gear and we rolled slowly up to the *Celeste*.

I'd thought Diane would recognize the distinctive burbling of the taxi's diesel engine and come out to look.

But no one appeared on deck. The boat looked deserted, but the plank was down, extending its uncertain invitation.

After I'd turned off the car all was silent until, like eyes adjusting to darkness, we could pick out the quiet lapping of water against the hull, the sound of a distant tractor plowing wheat stubble into the earth, a crow calling out its warning at our appearance and, finally, drifting through Diane's door, the sound of Edith Piaf singing. "*Je Ne Regrette Rien.*" I regret nothing.

Everyone who could flee had fled. Only the *Celeste*'s last prisoner, crushed under the weight of her regrets, was still on board.

I tucked the gun in my waistband, like Paul—Serge would have warned me I was going to blow my ass off—and pulled my shirttail over it. Quiet as cats, we walked up the plank and onto the well deck. Though I thought she'd be in her cabin, we found Diane in the galley, her back to us, stirring a pot.

How is it we sense the presence of someone behind us in an otherwise empty room? Whatever the reason, Diane stiffened, raised her head and turned to us, her eyes glassy and unfocused. She'd been drinking.

After looking at us wordlessly for several long beats, she drawled, "Well, look who's back." A confused frown clouded her face. "Where's Dilip?"

"He's not with us," I told her.

"So, he didn't find you" she said, her voice lilting in misplaced good humor. "I told him not to bother looking, but he thought if he brought you back Marius wouldn't do anything to me." She chuckled, "Oh, foolish boy," and leaned against the stove to remain steady on her wobbling legs. "He loves me, you know, Dilip does."

"Yes."

"Can you imagine anything sillier?" She looked at me, momentarily serious. "We never make love. Not once since we came to the boat. He thinks this leaves our love more pure. Pure," she scoffed. "Me."

"Yes, he told me."

"He did?" Baffled, Diane gave her head a little shake, either losing her train of thought or unwilling to complete it. "He's a saint, you know, the only saint I've ever known, but he doesn't believe it. He thinks of the things he's done in his past, and he can't get beyond them." I felt my face flush at this description of my own sins. "Well, saint or not, I guess he couldn't find you."

"He did."

This seemed too much for her to take in. She closed her eyes and gripped the edge of the counter.

"Then where is he?"

"He's coming back by train. When he found us we told him we wouldn't come back with him. He knew he couldn't force us, and he left."

Diane arched an eyebrow like a melodrama villain. "Yet you did come back—and without him."

"We decided after he left that we needed to see you."

"See me?" Delicate as a debutante, she put her outstretched fingers against the base of her throat. "Ah, you were afraid I was lonely." She dropped the act. "No. You want something. Why else would you take the risk?"

She looked at us both, but only Brigitte could invoke the bond between them, a bond neither of them wanted nor could deny.

She again took a step toward Diane and held out her hand. Diane regarded it as she would a dead fish. "You know the kind of danger we're in," she said. "We need money to get away."

"You've come to a funny place to get it."

"Marius gave you that stacks of euros."

Diane tossed her head and declared, "That was for boarding you and Serge and that cretin, Paul. And for canceling two tours. I earned that money. Oh, how I earned it." Whatever her words, her eyes searched us like a judge who wishes to rule a certain way but needs the lawyers to make the right argument.

Brigitte extended her hand. Diane recoiled, but Brigitte spoke over her fear, pleading. "Diane, you know Marius better than I ever will. You know he won't give up. It's become personal. I've made him lose face. He won't let me get away with that."

Diane flicked a glance toward the empty canal, anything to avoid looking in the particular mirror that was Brigitte's face. When she spoke again, her voice had lost the ironic distance she wore like armor. Without it, she seemed lost. "Marius ..." Saying his name stopped her voice for an instant, like someone whose soul has faltered after invoking the devil. "Marius believes you'll go to the police. Especially after Serge and Paul failed to ..." She cocked her chin toward the towpath and the spot where Paul had tried to kill me. "That's what he's always been afraid of, that someone will betray him to the police, ones he can't bribe, and everyone will see him for what he is, just another hoodlum, someone who can't make it in the real world."

"I haven't talked to the police. I won't. I don't trust them."

"Why should he believe that? You hate him."

"No more than you."

Engaged in a bout of psychic combat, the women looked at each other without blinking.

Diane turned away first, covering her retreat with an awkward laugh. Brigitte pressed her advantage. "Help us get away, Diane. Tell them we held a gun on you, forced you."

Brigitte must have sensed the weight of the gun pressing against my back, waiting for me to draw it out, and shook her head at me before turning back to Diane.

Diane took an unsteady step away from us. "Marius says he only wants you back where he can keep an eye on you. He says he's still fond of you." Diane raised her chin defiantly, daring Brigitte—or herself—to disbelieve.

They exchanged a few words in that dialect of the south, words I couldn't understand. It ended with her saying, "Diane, Marius will never know you helped us get away. He'll leave you in peace."

She had plucked the wrong note. Her face distorted with drink and fear and anger, Diane shot her words at Brigitte like bullets. "Don't take me for a fool. You know he'll never leave me in peace. It's about you today. Tomorrow, next month, a year from now, it will be about something else. I'll never escape him." She drew a shaky hand across her face, forced on herself a fragile calm more frightening than her anger. "Fine. I'll get you some money. Then go away and never bother me again."

Brigitte sighed, both relieved and ashamed for having provoked this unhappy woman into doing what she didn't want to do.

"We have a bag in the car," she said. "I'll go get it."

Diane's laugh made us both flinch. "You think I keep that kind of money on the boat? What children. Marius may work in cash. I do not."

Confused, Brigitte asked, "Then how—"

"It's in my bank. In Dijon."

When I finally reached for something it wasn't the gun, but the key to the car. "How long will it take us to get there?"

Diane's mouth curdled in disgust. "I should never have hired you. It all started to go bad from that day."

"Maybe you're right."

"Now, give me the key," she said and held out her hand.

"What?"

"Give me the key. I'm going by myself."

I looked at Brigitte, who seemed as startled as I was.

I told Diane, "I don't think you're in any condition to drive."

"I'll decide what condition I'm in. And I'll be damned if I'm going to ride in that car with you. It's my car, and I'll do with it what I please. You can wait here."

"Why should we believe you'll come back?" I asked.

"Because you don't have any choice. If you force me to stay, you don't get your money. If you want me to go get it, I'll go without either of you tiresome people tagging along. I can't stand the sight of either of you."

The logic of a drunk is difficult to penetrate and I had no wish to follow Diane down the rabbit hole of her thinking.

"One of us has to go with you," Brigitte said. "We don't trust you."

"You think I trust you? Look at you. Which one of you would trust the other to come back with the money?"

Our silence shocked both of us. Diane snorted and made a crooked smile that showed her satisfaction.

Brigitte dropped into one of the chairs at the table, her head in her hands. "I'm sick of arguing with her. Give her the key. We can stay here."

Certain I was doing the wrong thing, I handed the key to Diane. She wobbled down the plank and drove away.

"You've driven around here," she said, "How long do you think we'll have to wait?"

I leaned against the stove. "An hour and a half there, an hour and a half back. Plus however long it takes her at the bank. I wonder if Dilip will be here before she returns."

"Do you think she'll even come back?" Brigitte asked.

"Where else is she going to go? She's not going to run away and leave us with her boat."

"Why not?"

The question didn't surprise me half so much as the fact that I didn't have an answer. "She wouldn't leave Dilip behind," I said, wondering which of us I was trying to convince.

We looked up the empty towpath, our mood as bleak as the gray skies and grayer water.

We ate some of the soup Diane had been making and talked a little about where we would go from here, discussing the advantages of Brazil or Thailand or Morocco, or even just Belgium, until we could hardly breathe for the nonsense we were uttering.

If Diane came back with the money—if she came back at all—we were, in a sense, still defeated, having no choice but to keep running, hoping we could somehow outrun Marius Carbonne's long arms and short henchmen.

After we'd eaten, Brigitte said she hadn't slept well the night before, and went back to her cabin, saying she wanted to take a nap. If she wanted me to come with her she gave no hint of it. In our present mood, any lovemaking now would only lay down another layer of make-believe on a relationship that couldn't carry much more.

Left alone, I grew restless. Unlike Brigitte, I had no intention of retreating to my old berth. I couldn't have slept anyway. Instead, I took a book from the saloon and wandered aft, taking Dilip's chair. I propped my feet on the low railing and waited.

There are people who relish being left along with their thoughts. But my thoughts were all bad company, and my unquiet mind did not allow me to read. I could only sit and watch the sun make its slow arc toward the west.

Lost in thought, I didn't register at first that for the last few seconds I had been hearing the distinctive rumble of the London taxi. I looked up to find the boxy black car approaching along the towpath. Diane had been gone longer than I'd thought she would, more like four hours than three, but she had returned.

In my uneasier moments, I'd pictured her returning with someone else in the car, her supposed trip to Dijon nothing more than an opportunity to pick up one of Carbonne's men and bring him back with her—as if he had mobsters posted in every city throughout Burgundy, like Fed Ex trucks. But she returned as she had left, alone.

Diane got out of the car, a thick paper-wrapped bundle in her hand, and came on board. She saw me on the deck above her. "Go get the girl. Bring her to my cabin."

"Wouldn't it be easier to take care of this in the main cabin?" I asked.

"Do as I say."

I tapped at Brigitte's door and went in. I found her lying on the bed in the darkened room, fully clothed, eyes fixed on the ceiling.

"Diane's back," I told her. "She wants to meet in her cabin."

Even in the dim light bending around the closed blinds, I could see she felt as uneasy about it as I did. "In her cabin?"

"Yes."

"Kip, I'm frightened."

"Me, too."

"We get the money, and then we run. Where? And what do we do when we get there?"

"Stay alive."

"That's it?"

"That'll have to be enough for now." I sat on the edge of the bed, and she put her arms around me.

"What if we just stayed here, like this?"

We both smiled at the silliness of the question. "I'd develop a cramp." I took her hand. "Come on. We'd better get going. Get out of here while we can."

23

The Reckoning

THE UNMADE BED, the clothes strewn on the floor, the nearly empty gin bottle on the night stand all spoke to the disorder that came over Diane in Dilip's absence, said how much she needed him to hold off the disintegration that lurked within.

Only the shrine remained untouched, the Buddha's beatific smile unchanged, the unlighted candles waiting for Dilip's return. I noticed how clean he kept the backing mirror, to enhance the light given off by the candles and, no doubt, to bring the worshiper to look into that mirror and regard the illusion of self.

At Diane's direction, Brigitte and I sat in two small chairs pushed up against the bulkhead under one of the room's two portholes. She appeared agitated, stepping toward us, then away, running a hand through her hair.

"It needs music, doesn't it?" she said, A bizarre suggestion, but we didn't feel in a position to say no. The CD of her beloved Edith Piaf had ended, but she restarted it, and cranked up the volume.

"I've brought ten thousand euros. I don't know where it is you think you're going, but that should be enough to get you there. Wherever it is, don't come back. I never want to see either of you again."

No point mentioning that we felt the same.

She looked down at the bundle of euro notes as a mother might regard a child she was about to bury. After a long pause, she looked up and, to our befuddlement, launched into a long soliloquy about her life and hard times as mistress of the *Celeste*, her laughably small profit margin, her expenses for upkeep, the dreary and irritating guests, how difficult it was to find good help these days—this last accompanied by a dagger-like gaze in my direction—all of it played to the background of Edith Piaf's lamentations.

Reciting these burdens and affronts only appeared to upset her further. She stood up, sat down, licked her lips, until I wondered if she'd plummeted over some mental tipping point and we were watching her descend into madness.

Eventually, her tirade ran itself down, leaving her standing on the other side of the cabin, gazing through the porthole, exhausted.

It was Dilip's shrine that gave us the warning of what we'd walked into. Though small, the mirror that backed his homely altar stood just high enough on the chest of drawers to reflect a slice of the world outside the *Celeste*. What I saw changed everything.

I jumped from my chair and grabbed Brigitte by the arm. "Come on! We've got to get out of here!"

Confused, Brigitte pulled back. "What?"

Too late, Diane realized what I'd seen and tried to get between us and the door, but I stiff-armed her and ran out.

Brigitte looked around in confusion, but she hadn't seen what I'd seen. The mirror behind Dilip's shrine had allowed me a flickering sight of the long gray Mercedes quietly pulling alongside the boat, the sound of its engine covered by Diane's music.

I shoved Brigitte toward the door. "It's Carbonne!"

She ran with me out of the cabin, both of us pushed by the vanishing hope that we might somehow get off the boat before anyone could cut off our escape.

We were already too late. We'd got as far as the top of the plank when we found Serge positioned at its foot, a gun in his hand. For a wild moment I thought of pulling the pistol out of my waistband, but I knew I'd be dead before I even figured which end the bullets came out of.

With a wave of his gun, Serge moved us away from the plank. After a quick glance up the towpath, checking for witnesses—the fisherman on the opposite bank of the canal had left hours ago—he strode up the plank and onto the boat, followed by Marius Carbonne.

Instinctively, Brigitte and I raised our hands.

Serge growled, "Put your hands down." He again looked around to see if anyone was watching us. Reassured, he glanced over his shoulder toward Carbonne, who nodded toward the main cabin. Serge underlined the *capo's* gesture with a wave of his gun, and we backed toward the cabin's glass door.

As the two gangsters came aboard, Diane appeared in her doorway, hands in the pockets of her sweater, her eyes following us as we shuffled toward the main cabin.

For a fleeting moment, I considered diving off the other side of the boat into the canal. But the thought of Serge shooting me in the back as I swam away, of ending my life with a mouthful of filthy water, was more than I could bear. And I knew that I couldn't desert Brigitte. So, still holding hands, we backed into the cabin, even as I feared we would never come out of it alive.

Once inside, Marius murmured something to Serge, who prodded us toward the saloon, a room with fewer windows than the galley and less chance of witnesses.

We marched down the passageway, passing under the hole in the ceiling where Diane's shot had gone astray. At that moment I badly wished she hadn't missed.

When we got to the saloon, Brigitte and I turned to face Serge and Carbonne. Diane had followed and stood behind them in the doorway.

I waited for Serge to search us, to find his gun tucked in my pants and laugh at me for dreaming I was tough enough to use it. But they apparently couldn't imagine that either of us posed any kind of threat and did nothing.

We regarded each other dumbly, the silence so deep I swear I could hear myself sweat. Free now from prying eyes, I wondered if Serge would simply open fire and kill us both where we stood. After all, it was his job, nothing personal. But it wouldn't be that quick or that simple.

Leering, his mouth practically watering, Carbonne reached out and pinched the flesh of Brigitte's arm. "As lovely as ever," he said, his voice weighted with lust and derision.

Before I could think, I stepped between them, putting Brigitte behind me, out of his reach. I wondered if he had put his hands on her to provoke me. If so, he probably hadn't thought it would be this easy.

His mouth twisted in a sadist's smile. "Ah, protecting your woman. How touching. I'm impressed. Really." With exquisite slowness, he looked her up and down, his eyes like a pair of hands. "But you're young and stupid and want to play the hero." He actually winked at me, a leering, contemptuous gesture that I wanted to kick down his throat. "She's terrific in bed, isn't she? The things she knows ... A little too thin, though, don't you think? No ass." He made an obscene thrust of his hips. "It's much better when it's the two of them." he said, cocking his head toward Diane. "Now, *that's* worth living for." He nodded toward Brigitte, "She's not."

"You're disgusting, Marius."

Though I expected him to explode at Diane's words, Carbonne only laughed.

To me, he said, "That was impressive, getting between us. Very heroic. You've got a real pair." He looked across the room to Serge and said, "But he's going to die anyway."

Over his shoulder, he said to Diane, "I almost forgot to thank you for calling to let me know they were here. Of all places." Smiling at Brigitte, Carbonne added, "And I'm so happy I could come in time to see you. I was in Paris when Diane called. I'd flown up from Marseille when Serge called to tell me they'd found you. He was sure you'd be in our hands by lunchtime. So, I came all the way to Paris, only to find you'd gotten away." He made a childish pout. "You can imagine my disappointment. I never doubted we would find you again. I only wondered how long it would take. I don't like to be away from Marseille." He threw his hands out and let them fall back, slapping against his thighs. "But it all ended happily, didn't it? Diane called, and we rushed down from Paris as fast as we could."

Carbonne grinned at Brigitte and tapped me on the shoulder as if he were cutting in at a dance. I looked him in the eye and didn't budge. With a little shake of his head at my chutzpah, he waved toward Serge, who inclined the barrel of his pistol toward my chest.

I suppose I could have refused to move, maybe even pushed Carbonne back, and died right there. But to be alive is to hope, and I was still alive. I stepped aside.

He ran his hands down Brigitte, stroked her arm, kneaded the flesh of her waist. With a glance at me, he drew the back of his hand down her breast.

"You'll come back with me?" he asked.

Brigitte lowered her head and whispered, "Yes."

"That's good. Of course things can't be as they were. You understand that. When you come back you will go where Jeanne went."

"No, Marius!" Diane cried. "You promised. Over the phone, you promised."

"Promised?" He looked toward Serge to join in his laugh, and frowned when he didn't. "I never promise. I only take negotiating positions."

Diane wouldn't be put off. She thrust her hands deeper into her pockets. "And the boat? You said you'd give me the title to the boat if I handed her over."

Carbonne made a face. "Did I? Well, we'll see."

"Marius ..."

He wasn't listening. He ran a finger along Brigitte's throat, his face inches from hers. "I can't trust this one anymore. She knows that, but knows she'll be safe—or at least she'll still be alive." He laughed. "But, no, she'll no longer live in my house." He brightened. "Besides, I've already found someone else. Very young. Very sweet." To Brigitte he whispered, "As innocent now as you once were. She is de-lic-ious." He sighed from deep in his throat.

Brigitte raised her chin, like Joan of Arc heading for the pyre. "No! I won't go. Not like that."

His teeth clenched, his voice barely under control, Carbonne whispered, "Don't tell me no, *ma petite*. You don't say no to me."

I was no longer afraid, only angry.

"Why should she trust you?" I shot the words at Carbonne. "I don't care what you say, you were going to have Serge kill her here on the boat the night we got away."

Carbonne closed his eyes to demonstrate how sorely I tried his patience.

"No, Serge was only going to bring her back to Marseille. She resisted. So he had to tie her up." He waggled his head equivocally. "You, on the other hand, I meant to kill. But, Paul, as he always does, stepped on his dick and ..." He shrugged at the difficulties of finding good help these days. "You're pretty good, you know that? You've been keeping ahead of a private detective for months, I'm told. You stood up to Paul, gave him the slip once. You beat him in a fair fight the other night, knocked out Serge, and got away to Paris. Then, when we thought we had you, you slipped away again. Yes, you're really quite a guy. Serge even told me I should hire you. He thinks highly of you, he really does. But you're full of romantic nonsense. You wouldn't be any good to me."

My anger made me reckless. "You're full of it."

I wanted to get under his skin, and I succeeded.

No one could miss the look in his eyes or mistake the quality of the silence that descended on us, the sort of charged silence that ends in a gunshot. I watched Serge's finger on the trigger of his pistol. Again, I thought of the gun in my waistband.

Brigitte's voice cut through my impulse to commit suicide-by-Serge.

"Oh, yes, you have your code, Marius, your macho pose. But that code only applies to what you do, not to what you have other people do for you. You'll kill me without needing to pull the trigger yourself, and that will make it all right."

Carbonne actually looked hurt. Brigitte had wounded the big guy's feelings. I might have laughed, but that would have been the end of me.

"I don't kill women. I don't have them killed." He sounded defensive.

"Yes, you do. You kill us all in the end because you hate women. You'll kill me the way you killed Jeanne."

"I didn't kill Jeanne."

"Yes you did! When you took me as your whore you sent Jeanne off to one of your brothels because, like all of us stupid enough to come near you, she knew too much for you to let her free." She spit the words out with every dram of the contempt that filled her—contempt for Carbonne, contempt for herself. "You'll say she killed herself and you had nothing to do with it. But when she jumped out the window of your hotel, you might as well have pushed her." She pointed at Diane. "And even her. You've put her where you can torture her forever."

"Be quiet," Diane snapped, shushing Brigitte not because she was wrong but because she was right. She looked to Carbonne. "Marius you promised. You did." Then, more plaintively, "*Mon amour.*"

Carbonne gave no sign he had heard Diane, but grabbed Brigitte and pulled her toward him. She snatched her arm back. "Get away from me."

Propelled by love and anger and folly, I jumped toward Carbonne and pushed him in the chest, knocking him back a step.

"Leave her alone," I told him.

All Carbonne's pretense of control fell away. His face went white with fury. That's what happens when a weak man gets shown up in front of others. He glared at me with death in his eyes.

I wished I remembered how to pray. A strange calm came over me. This would be the end. All the worries and fears that had formed my life had no meaning now. But as Carbonne turned toward Serge to order him to kill me, Brigitte spat in his face. I was probably as shocked as Carbonne, and also terribly moved. She was making clear that if we were going down, we were going down together.

With a vicious backhand to the side of her face, Carbonne knocked Brigitte reeling across the saloon, crashing into the bookcase before falling onto the bench that ran along its base.

His eyes burning into Brigitte's, he said to Serge, "If she wants to die that badly, let her die. Shoot her!"

His gun still trained on me, Serge shook his head. "No, *patron.*"

A look of confusion passed over Carbonne's face, as if he couldn't register Serge's refusal. "I said shoot her!"

"No."

"Who do you think you're talking to, some kind of—?" But as he shouted at Serge, he saw Diane and fell speechless. The *Celeste*'s mistress had finally taken her hand out of her pocket. In it, she held Dilip's pistol.

"Leave her alone or I'll shoot you."

He actually staggered in his bafflement. "You think I'm afraid of Dilip's pea-shooter?" This time his laughter sounded genuine. "You didn't shoot me when you had the chance last week. You won't do it now." Turning to Serge, Carbonne barked, "Give me that," grabbed Serge's gun, and turned on Brigitte.

From the long bench on which she'd fallen, Brigitte stared at him open-mouthed.

Carbonne raised the pistol.

The flat crack of the gunshot reverberated sharply in the little room.

With an explosive, "Ah!" Carbonne arched his body as he took the bullet from Diane's gun in the back.

Gritting in pain and astonishment, he lurched around to face Diane. His face wore the expression of a wounded child, betrayed by those who should have loved him. He whispered to Diane in that strange dialect they shared, one that might not have been regional, as I had supposed, but belonging to those who lived in the province of the disappointed and the damned.

I'll never know what Diane said in reply, but I couldn't miss the contempt in her voice as she spat it out.

Carbonne's face hardened into its accustomed mask, the one he'd worn for decades to hide the Maurice Carbonne he had left behind many years ago, and he pulled the trigger again, this time in earnest.

Diane took the bullet in her chest and fell heavily against the doorway before collapsing onto the floor without a sound. In the shock of the moment, I had my chance. I fell to my knees and drew my gun.

Though Diane's shot had left him gasping, Carbonne was still on his feet. He turned again toward Brigitte, ready now to kill.

I pulled the trigger. Nothing happened. I pulled it again. Only a click.

At the sound of the firing pin hitting the empty chamber, Carbonne turned and saw me with the gun. With a backwards glance at Brigitte, he trained his gun on me. I can still see its muzzle pointed at the space between my eyes.

Panicked, I pulled the trigger again. Nothing. My last thought: This isn't fair. I'm not a gangster. I don't even know how to fire the pistol. Then the explosion rocked the room.

I looked up, uncomprehending, as Carbonne spun across the saloon and into one of the tall windows, which shattered under his weight before he fell back into Brigitte and rolled onto the floor. He twitched a bit and made a gurgling sound that I hope I'll never hear again. Then he lay still, eyes wide with astonishment. It shook me badly to think how much he looked like my father did when I knocked him down.

Out of the corner of my eye I saw a man step over Diane and come into the saloon.

He'd always looked good in that gray suit, a touch of style behind the steely professionalism, a combination Father liked. And the suit went well with the dark gun in his hand, the one with which he had shot Marius Carbonne. He kept his gun on Carbonne as he kicked the big man's gun from his hand. But there was no need. Carbonne was dead.

He trained the gun on Serge, but Serge shook his head and held his hands away from his body to show they were empty. It was over.

The man in the gray suit let out a long uneven breath, put his gun on safety and tucked it back into the holster under his arm. He was an Iraq war vet and he'd probably seen worse, but his hands were shaking.

He looked down to where I was still kneeling on the floor, the pistol in my hand.

"Hi, Kip."

He always liked to come on all laconic that way.

"Hi, Dave."

It might have been the banality of our exchange that penetrated Brigitte's shock and woke her to the horror around her. On TV, in the movies, we see this kind of scene all the time, and maybe that helps us think it's almost normal. But it's not, no matter how much you try to tell yourself you've seen it before.

Brigitte let out a sort of strangled scream. And then she went quiet. As her cry faded I heard, like its grim echo, a shuddering gasp for breath.

Diane was still alive.

My legs too shaky to let me stand, I crawled across the floor to where she lay near the door. Her chest, the floor, were covered in blood, her face ghastly white, yet composed. Her eyelids fluttered and I think she knew it was me who held her head. She tried to speak, but her lips only twitched wordlessly. Thinking she might wish to express some last word of love for Dilip, or remorse for her life, or regret for shooting a man, even one as evil as Marius Carbonne, I leaned over her, my ear near her mouth.

Her words were almost inaudible. "I got him, didn't I?"

With someone else, I might have tried to ease the burden of taking a human life, told her how the fatal shot had come from someone else. Instead, I said, "Yeah, you got him."

The corners of her mouth turned up in a faint smile and she whispered, "That's taken care of then." With a long sigh, she let her life go.

Over the ringing in my ears I heard the voice of Edith Piaf drifting through the boat, the lyrics like a prayer for absolution after a life so filled with regret.

My own hold on the scene around me, of what had happened in those few seconds of violence, wobbled frighteningly. I felt I was floating, only lightly connected to the earth.

Dave saw it. "You okay, Kip?"

A buffer surrounded me as if I were wrapped in cotton, keeping reality at a distance as I woke from a dream. The buffer and the dream faded quickly, though, and I was forced to return to the scene around me.

"Yeah, I'm okay." I glanced at Carbonne, and quickly looked away from his staring eyes. "Is he ...?"

"Dead?" Dave nodded at Carbonne's body sprawled on the floor. "Yeah."

But my mind was elsewhere. "No. I mean my father."

"Your dad?" He screwed up his face in puzzlement. "No. The old man's okay." He saw the look on my face. "You mean, all this time you thought he was dead? That you'd ..."

"Killed him? No, not really. Not ... But I was always afraid maybe the wound to his head was more serious than it looked. You read about people seeming to be okay, then ... with an injury like that...."

A guy like Dave can't show a lot of softness, but he'd known me most of my life and said gently, "Jesus. No, Kip. You only broke his jaw. They had to wire it shut. Couldn't say a word for six weeks." He bit his lip to keep from smiling at the memory of my father speechless. "He had to write down what he wanted me to do. No, he's alive and kicking. He's okay, Kip." He cocked his head toward the passageway. "Come on, we got to get out of here."

I tried to take it in and could not, couldn't so quickly release the guilt that had driven every move I'd made, every word I'd said. I'd struck my father, a crime that shakes the foundation of everything good and decent. I'd left him bleeding on the floor and then stolen his money. And I'd come to cherish that guilt, which both haunted and animated me.

Now I somehow had to let it go. My father was all right. I'd stood up to him and both of us had survived. Almost instantly, I felt the joy and relief one gets from escaping a nightmare that seemed absolutely real until it vanished on waking. At the same time I shook under a sudden surge of emptiness.

"He lay there with his eyes open. And the blood...."

"Jesus, Kip. All this time, you—"

I tried to smile, say the next thing lightly, but I couldn't pull it off. "Did any of this ... Our fight. The way I ran off with his money. Did any of it...?"

"Change him? Nah. He's the same old bird." He looked at me narrowly and cocked his head to one side. "He wanted me to find you, bring you back home. That's why I've been trying to do for months."

When I didn't say anything, he added, "He loves you, you know."

It wasn't what I wanted to hear. It was exactly what I wanted to hear. "He's got a funny way of showing it," I said. "And the money I took? I thought he'd kill me for that."

"It's money. He'll make more." Dave took a deep breath and looked at the scene around us. "Look, we got to get out of here. I haven't got the type of visa that lets me kill people while I'm here." He tried to smile, but I finally saw that he, too, was badly shaken.

His gun trained on Serge, he said to me, "I don't think your friend's in any position to call the police on us, is he?"

I started to tell Dave that Serge was no friend of mine, but stopped myself. In some weird way, I knew he was. I translated Dave's question for Serge. Serge looked at Carbonne, his contempt for his boss clearer than I'd ever seen, and shook his head. "No. I'm through with all this. All of it."

Brigitte had slowly got to her feet, still in shock, but pulling herself together.

Dave nodded at her and asked me, "And her?"

"She's with me."

Dave frowned at the complication. "All right." He put his gun back in his shoulder holster and pulled me to my feet. "Come on."

Dave leading me, I turned toward Brigitte and held out my hand and she took it.

When we came to the doorway of the saloon we stopped, confronted by Diane's body. We all looked down at the mistress of the boat, and its longest-serving prisoner, finally free now. She and Carbonne lay silently, their eyes staring at the outrage of how their lives had ended.

I turned back to Serge, "We can't just leave them here like this."

He regarded the bodies of the two people he had known so well, perhaps feeling complicit in how it had all ended. "No. We can't."

"Is there some way to ...?"

"I'll take care of it, *mon vieux*. There's a guy in Paris who will take them away."

"And for God's sake, don't bury her next to him." I could barely get the words out.

"I'll make sure."

"Bury her someplace where there might be room for Dilip next to her one day."

"Of course."

I tried to smile at my friend, the Sinner. He'd been ready to see me killed that rainy night. But I was sure he'd taken no pleasure in it. He was just doing his job. A hell of a job to have.

"Now you can get back to your family, to your son," I said to him.

"I suppose so." In the sadness of his smile he looked old and tired. He was a professional killer whose refusal to shoot a young woman had precipitated the death of his boss and of the one woman in the world for whom his boss had any respect.

We stepped over Diane and headed down the passageway.

We'd got as far as the galley when I stopped again and asked Dave, "I won't get arrested when I go back?"

"Nah, your old man told the police it was a misunderstanding. It got in the paper somehow, but there won't be any charges."

He was telling me that nothing I did mattered, had no consequences.

He saw the look on my face. "This is turning into a hell of a day for you, isn't it? But there you go. People are funny. Funny as hell," he said, summarizing, I suppose, his entire philosophy on life. "Come on."

But a thought that had been dancing around the periphery of my mind came into sudden focus. "What are you doing here?"

"I just told you. I'm supposed to get you back home."

"No. I mean what are you doing here? Now. How could you know I was here?"

"I didn't. Not at first. I was in Paris, thinking I might still find your trail there. Like I say, I'd come back and forth a couple of times. This time I decided to call your friend

Gallagher again. Good guy. Very helpful. He's the one who told me about the boat, how maybe you were working here."

"Fuck. Him."

"Whatever you say, chief." Dave raised his eyebrows but didn't ask what it was about. "Anyway, this Gallagher guy said he still thought you were working on the *Celeste*. I guess you know I'd already come by once. Everybody said they'd never heard of you. They said it so quickly I didn't quite buy it. But I didn't see any trace of you, so I left." He waggled his head. "Anyway, I was still wondering if you were around the boat. When I couldn't get a lead on you anywhere else, I hired a guy a couple of days ago to watch the boat, keep an eye open."

It hit me. "That fisherman on the other bank."

"Yeah. He saw you and the girl show up this morning and phoned me. I came as fast as I could." It didn't need saying that he couldn't have come two minutes later and found me alive.

"Let's go, Kip. I've got a car. I can drive us to Paris and get a flight out tonight.

All these months I'd thought of myself as a criminal, living a desperado's life in expiation of my sins. In fact, I'd been a coward and fled over what was finally a small thing. The bodies in the saloon testified to the evil I had fallen into by running, not from my crimes but from myself. It all caught up with me at once. I collapsed into one of the dining room chairs, dropped my head and wept.

From whatever recess where it had been hiding, I recalled the memory of my mother at my bedside, folding my hands into a reverent position, teaching me to say, "And if I should die before I wake ..." Had I finally awakened? How much had my slumber cost me, cost others? It was terrifying to think that, from here, I might have to go through life fully aware.

When I'd stopped crying, Dave coughed, embarrassed, and nodded toward the plank and his car, parked on the towpath. The idea finally penetrated, that I was supposed to keep running, this time running back to the place where I had started, running for a different reason now, but still running.

For what seemed like several minutes but was probably no more than a few seconds, I forced myself to see what I needed to do.

"No. I can't go. Not yet," I said. I waved my hand in front of my face, brushing away the last cobwebs of who I thought I'd been the last few months.

Dave laughed, trying to tell himself—tell me—I was kidding. "Kip, we gotta get out of here."

"No." I listened to myself, nearly as puzzled as Dave by what I was saying. "No, I have to stay a little longer."

"Well, that's great. You going to let me know when you're ready to go?"

"Running away from my father, running toward my father. It's all the same thing. Either way, I'm letting it be about him, letting him set the tone of my life." I took a deep cleansing breath. "Maybe I'll come back when I've worked it out. But for now I can't."

Dave raised his arms in frustration. "For chrissake, Weston ..."

As I searched for a reply, Brigitte came up behind me as I sat at the table and put her hands on my shoulders. "Kip, I want to go home. I need to go back. Come home with me," she said, her voice soft and kind, and I knew she loved me as I loved her.

"No, Marie-Therese. I can't. Not now."

"Then maybe later."

"I can't see that far ahead right now."

"How will you live?" An idea lit her face. "The money. The money Diane had."

"No. Leave it. It's death money. Leave it with the dead." I nodded toward Brigitte and said to Dave. "Can you take her home?"

"Oh, Kip." Her voice was soft.

"I'm sorry. But I can't come with you."

Dave made a helpless kind of gesture and sighed. "Yeah. Sure."

I looked up at Dave. "If the police come...?"

"They could come any minute. If your friend can't get them out of here fast enough, the cops might be happy enough to decide these two killed each other. They probably won't care that Carbonne's got a bullet in him from a gun they can't find. Bad people, bad end. Everyone goes home happy." Dave wiped his brow and blew out a breath. "But your old man isn't going to be happy if I come home without you." He waited for me to change my mind. When I didn't, he said, "What are you going to do? You can't stay on the boat."

"I guess I'll go to Paris. I've got a couple of friends there." I looked at Brigitte. Or, rather, I looked at Marie-Therese and gave her a little shake of the head to let her know she shouldn't say anything about Mohamed and Hassan. I didn't want Dave coming back to track me down there, bring more trouble to our friends. "But I need to stay on the boat, just for a bit, until Dilip gets here and I can break it to him."

Dave muttered something about how maybe he should shoot me, too. Nevertheless, he pulled out his wallet and offered me a handful of euros.

"My father's?"

Dave shrugged. "I guess so, one way or the other."

I waved it away. "I've got enough to get me to Paris. There's a shawarma place where I can maybe get a job."

He frowned. "Are you really going to stay here?"

"I have to talk to a friend. He should be here soon."

I dreaded the talk with Dilip as I've never dreaded anything in my life, but I'd stopped running, and I had to accept my responsibility.

With a snort of disbelief, Dave looked at Brigitte. "You ready?" She nodded. He turned back to me. "I guess we gotta get going."

He held out his hand to pull me up from my chair.

I waved him away and stood up on my own.

24

A Haven in the Floating World

SO I NEVER WROTE the book exposing the sins of the father. I wrote this one instead.

I stayed with Mohamed and Hassan for a couple of weeks. There wasn't a job at the shawarma place, so I got work sweeping streets with Hassan. Afterwards, I continued to wander around Europe for a couple of months. It was strange to live without the certainty someone was after me. I'd been wrong about my father, about Luz, wrong about almost everything.

It had been hard to speak to Dilip, to tell him that, despite the purity of his love, despite the years of trying to keep her safe, she had finally, while he wasn't there, insisted on dying. And in her death, she had gotten rid of the man who had made her life not worth the living. I suppose she considered it a fair exchange. In doing it, though, she had left Dilip stranded.

I don't know what he did, finally. After we spoke, he said something about friends in Marseille. But I like to think that he made his way back to Sri Lanka, and on a fine, sunny morning, presented himself at the gates of the temple.

When I decided I'd wandered enough, when I'd thought it all through and understood where my heart lay, the decision wasn't hard. I knew where to go.

I've returned to the little room off the kitchen. After I help Jacques with the milking in the morning, they let me pass my afternoons scribbling away. Marie-Therese is a farm girl again. I, Wilfred, may yet make myself into a farm boy. And I am content in this small haven within the floating world.

Acknowledgements

As always, I owe my largest debt to my wife, Felicia, for her unending support. Also, thanks to my agent, Kimberley Cameron, for her hard work and kind advice. And a big shout-out to Kristy Makansi of Blank Slate Press and Lisa Miller of Amphorae Publishing for their support—and their patience. I want to also thank Marlin Goebel for a perceptive read of an earlier draft of this stsory and his very helpful suggestions on how to improve it.

About the Author

With his critically acclaimed novels, *Tangier* and *Madagascar*, and *Sri Lanka*, author Stephen Holgate's work has been compared to that of masters such as Graham Greene, John le Carré, and Alan Furst. *Tangier* gained the Independent Booksellers Silver Medal in fiction. *Madagascar* has gained similar acclaim, receiving a coveted starred review from *Publisher's Weekly* and being named as a finalist for the *Forward Reviews* Book of the Year in general fiction. Bookreader.com listed both *Tangier* and *Madagascar* among its top ten mystery/suspense books of the year. Characterized by intrigue, romance and danger, his books have quickly gained an appreciative audience among readers and critics alike. *To Live and Die in the Floating World* is his fourth novel.